Silas is the leader, Bob is the apprentice and Liz, Silas's mistress, is in between. In New York these con-artists do a 'business deal' worth millions. But back in London, Silas's plan to bilk an emergent African nation misfires. Then Bob takes over the running of the operation – and Liz. A Beirut bank is their target and each fascinating member of the brilliant trio gets what he or she deserves – each with a twist of lemon.

There is an ancient saying among the people of Mesopotamia, 'Four fingers stand between truth and lies', and if you hold your hand to your face you will find that measurement to be the distance between the eye and the ear.

LEN DEIGHTON

Only When I Larf

SPHERE BOOKS LIMITED

A SPHERE BOOK

Copyright © 1967 VICO Patentverwertungs-und
Vermögenverwaltungs-G.M.B.H. Lehargasse I,
Vienna, Austria

First published in Great Britain by Michael Joseph Ltd 1968
Published by Sphere Books 1968
Reprinted 1969, 1970, 1971, 1973, 1977, 1978 (twice),
1979, 1981, 1982, 1983, 1985, 1986, 1988, 1989

Printed and bound in Great Britain by
Collins, Glasgow

0 7221 2986 6

Sphere Books Ltd
A Division of
Macdonald & Co. (Publishers)Ltd
27 Wrights Lane
London W8 5TZ

A member of Maxwell Pergamon Publishing Corporation plc

ONLY WHEN I LARF

In 1925 a Czech nobleman writing on Ministère des Postes et Telegraphes notepaper invited bids from scrap metal merchants for 7000 tons of metal otherwise known as the Eiffel Tower. So successful was he that, having left Paris hurriedly, he returned one month later and sold it again.

As recently as 1966 the Colosseum changed hands. A West German leased it for 10 years at 20,000,000 lire per year (cash in advance) to an American tourist who wanted to adapt the top of it for a restaurant.

In 1949 a South African company purchased an airfield in England for 250,000 pounds sterling, giving a 10% deposit to a man in the uniform of an RAF Group Captain. In 1962 a Pole in Naples collected 90,000 dollars in deposits on U.S. Navy ships. In 1963 an Irishman from Kerry sold a Scandinavian fishing fleet to a consortium of English businessmen after flying them to Bergen to view the fleet at anchor.

In 1965 two English airline stewards took a 20,000 dollar deposit on a used Boeing airliner during a three day stop over in Tokyo.

To these men on land sea and air, this book is respectfully dedicated.

Chapter 1

BOB

We'd been eight and a half minutes earlier on the dress rehearsal. This time we were held up in a traffic jam at Lexington and Fiftieth Street. Midtown Manhattan on Friday afternoon is no place for tight schedules. I paid the cab driver with a couple of dollar bills, took fifty cents as change and gave him a two bit tip. Silas and Liz tumbled out and I heard Liz swearing softly and dabbing a spittle wet finger at the knee of her nylons.

Silas waited for no one; umbrella in one hand, travel bag in the other, he marched off into the shiny hall of the Continuum building. Liz, looking equally elegant, hurried after him. I scribbled $1.75 into my accounts notebook, stuffed it into my pocket and hurried after them. New York streets like a fairground; flashing lights, car horns, police whistles and all those organisation men with soft white shirts and hard pink faces hurrying so fast to nowhere that their grey flannel suits are going at the knees. It was late afternoon and there wasn't much action in the Continuum Building. The hall was shiny, and silent except for the tap of our shoes. On the left side of the foyer there was the Continuum Building Coffee and Do-nut shop, and a newspaper and tobacco kiosk. Neither seemed to be doing much business. The right of the lobby was a side entrance to the bank. That wasn't doing much business either, but we planned to do something about that.

I was wearing overalls and I put down the heavy bags for a moment while I unlocked the glass case, removed the 'For Rent' sign and clipped the white letters into place: '29th

Floor. Amalgamated Minerals.' Pop. I closed the case and looked around but no one seemed to care. I followed the others into the lift and Mick pressed the button for the twenty-ninth. Liz snatched a look at her ladder and Silas sniffed his carnation. Vroom went the lift.

'It'll be the twenty-ninth again,' said Mick.

'That's it,' I said, picking up his brogue without meaning to.

'You'll be seeing the big fight.'

'I will,' I said.

'That feller will never learn,' said Mick, shaking his head. Silas stared at me reprovingly.

'Have you had any more trouble from the O'Reilly twins?' I asked Mick.

'Not even a visit from the big feller,' said Mick. 'I knew me cousin Pat could fix the whole matter in a jiffy, but I didn't like to worry him with little domestic squabbles.' Silas looked at us both, then asked Mick, 'What action did your cousin Pat take?'

Mick looked at Silas suspiciously. It was the hard British accent that did it. The lift stopped. Mick leaned forward to Silas and lowered his voice, 'Bless you sir, he broke their legs.' He waited a moment before pushing the button. The doors opened with a burr. 'Their back legs,' added Mick. We got out. From my heavy bag I produced a card sign that said, 'Amalgamated Minerals Reception.' I hung it by the lift. As we walked along the corridor Silas switched on all the lights.

'Who the hell's that?' said Silas. He shivered.

'Mick, the liftman,'

'How do you know all about his friends and family?'

I said. 'I heard someone talking to him one day. So now I always say, "Had any more trouble from the O'Reilly twins Mick?" or "How are the O'Reilly twins," or. . . .' Silas grunted. As he walked along the corridor he closed the doors of the empty offices. Bonk, bonk, bonk.

I followed Silas and Liz into the offices the janitor had furnished for us. From behind the door's glass panel a voice said, 'I'm just about done.' The last of the putty fell onto a sheet of newspaper and the glass panel bearing the battered old words 'General Manager's Office' lowered gently to reveal the ugly face of the janitor. 'I've got rid of the cleaners and I've furnished both offices with the furniture you chose. It was heavy. . . .'

Almost without pausing in his stride, Silas placed a hundred dollars in tens between the man's teeth. That smile could have held another five grand.

Silas and Liz marched into the inner office. The janitor raised the new glass panel into place. On it was expensive gold-leaf lettering that read 'Amalgamated Minerals Inc. New York. Washington. Seattle. London. Stockholm. Office of Sir Stephen Latimer. President.'

You know how these New York executives start off in a bull pen. Then they get themselves promoted to a room without windows, window facing an air shaft and, if they really make the top, get an office with an outside view. This one was on a corner of the building: three windows. The janitor must have really raided the building; a fitted carpet, Knoll desk, squawk box, four phones. Mies van der Rohe chairs, and a tall Hepplewhite bookcase full of National Geographics. I went to the window; it had a view like an airline poster. On the roof of the Pan Am building a helicopter was warming up before flying to Kennedy Airport: Pockety, pockety, pockety. Clear blue air, skyscrapers and far below brightly coloured cars pulling into the kerb as fire engines wailed their way to Wall Street.

Silas coughed to attract my attention. Then he gave his roll brim hat, and umbrella to Liz as though he'd been arriving here to start work all his life. I had no overcoat, I took off my overalls. Silas got behind the teak desk and got the feel of the controls. Liz had got an electric drill out of the bag and plugged it into the wall socket. As I turned she gave it a test buzz and handed it to me. I began to drill holes through the thin partition wall. We had done it both ways on rehearsals. We'd taken sample hardboard and tested for the joists. We had used a mechanical saw and various drills. Twenty two holes with a three-quarter inch drill finishing with the saw had proved the quickest. Silas never begrudged money for research, it was an obsession with him.

Liz took framed photos from the bag and began to arrange them on the wall. They were all air photos of mine-heads or plant. Beautifully printed under each photo on the thick mounts it said things like 'Borke Sweden. Plant for Ore Processes. Amalgamated Mineral Svenska AB. Second Largest in Scandinavia.' Or it said, 'Mining Drill Manf. Co., Illinois, owned by Amalgamated Mineral Inc. New York.' Silas had researched each caption and the frames were light teak so that they would match the desk.

By the time I'd finished drilling and had broken a circular hole in the partition, Silas had arranged his personal photos on his desk. Photos of wife and families in front of a large country house, all featured a dopey man with a big moustache that Silas claimed was him a few years back. He helped me to fit the old fashioned wall-safe into the hole I'd made. I'd done it just right, so we didn't need any of the wooden wedges to hold it firmly into the partition wall. Silas fiddled with the combination, and opened and closed the safe door a few times. Zonk. It closed with a clang. Yeah, very convincing. After all, it was a real safe except that there was no back to it. Apart from a piece of black velvet to keep it dark, it was just a tube into the room next door.

'Two thirty three,' said Silas, looking at his watch. 'Stage One completed.' Twenty seven minutes to go before the bank closed.

'Stage one completed.' Liz said. She hung a picture over the door of the wall safe to hide it, like they do in films.

'Stage One completed.' I reported. 'But we are 25 cents miscalculated on the cab fare.' Silas nodded. He knew that I was trying to needle him, but he didn't react. What a stuffed shirt.

Liz was on the telephone talking to the bank downstairs in the foyer of the Building. She said, 'I'm Mrs. Amalgamin, and want to confirm our arrangement to collect close to three hundred thousand dollars in cash in just a few minutes. Well yes, I know I only have 557 dollars in my account right now, but we went all through that yesterday. The Funfunn Novelty Company owe us three hundred thousand dollars, and they have promised a cheque today. We need the cash right away.' There was a pause, and then Liz said, 'Well I don't see how there can be any difficulty. Funfunn Novelty Company are customers at your branch, and so are we. You promised to oblige us but if there's going to be any difficulty then I'll get on to head office right away. Well I should think so. Yes I told you, I've arranged that, Mr. Amalgamin – my husband, would never allow me to carry that amount of cash. The armoured car company will handle it and I shall just be there to pay in the Funfunn cheque and draw from our account.' She put down the phone. 'They had me worried for a moment. They don't have to do that you know.'

'Yeah,' I said. 'Well now all we have to worry about, is that bank clerk spotting one of our Funfunn jerks on his way through the foyer and getting into conversation with him.'

'Don't worry baby,' she mocked, 'Silas will keep it cool for you.'

'Get lost,' I said, and went to the next door office to check my equipment. There was a security guard uniform including white belt, holster and hat, and a cash box with chain and wrist lock. There was also a new pigskin document case, some documents and a fresh Nassau newspaper hot from Times Square where you can buy all the out of town dailies. I tried the hat on. It was a stupid hat. I wore it down over my eyes. My hair stuck out and I pulled a face in the mirror. Then I tipped it back at a rakish angle.

'You look sweet,' Liz said. I didn't know she was watching

13

and her voice made me jump. I said nothing. She came up behind me and we looked at each other in the mirror. She was a doll and I would have been grateful for a bit of hand to hand combat with her any time, but I didn't want a kiss on the ear in that condescending mummy-says-go-bye-byes way she has.

'Get lost' I said angrily, but she suddenly pulled my hat right down over my eyes and got out of the room before I could retaliate.

'You bitch,' I shouted, but I wasn't really angry. She laughed.

I looked at myself in a mirror. I'll tell you I looked pretty unconvincing as a security guard. My hair was too long and my skin was pale, the colour it always went in the winter if I didn't get a week in the sun somewhere. I was always a skinny little sod. Twenty six years old and as wiry and hard now as I had ever been, even in the nick. Liz and Silas were all right; it was a lucky day for me when I met them, but they never let me forget who was the junior partner. I mean, they really didn't.

Silas had been with Liz right from when I first met him. If I hadn't seen the score between them, I might have thought that Silas was queer. I'd had trouble with a queer while I was in the nick. Peter the bigamist they called him and it was nearly too late before I found out how he got the name. There was nothing queer about Silas but that doesn't mean that I knew what made him tick.

Things I didn't have; Silas had. Things I'll never have; Silas had, and let's face it, things I'll never want Silas had. He was urbane, you know what I mean? He could wear evening clothes like Fred Astaire wore them. He had a feeling of command. If I put on a white coat I was a house painter, if Silas put one on, he was a surgeon, you know the type? And of course women go for that bossy upper class manner, women were all crazy for Silas. Liz was, I just hoped I'd be able to pull birds like Liz when I got to be his age.

It was that war that did it. Before Silas was twenty two he was a major in the tank corps and had half a dozen medals. He was bossing a hundred people, and some of them were old enough to be his father. If they as much as answered back, I suppose they'd have been in front of a firing squad or something. And perhaps a few of them were! Well I mean, can you wonder he was bossy. I mean I like him, he had this sly sense of humour and we could kid each other along with neither of us giving even a flicker of a smile, and that was great, but when you got down to it, he was a cold fish. That was the war too, I suppose. I mean, you don't go around killing people for five years and come out the other end a warm-hearted philanthropist do you? I mean you don't.

He had this sort of computer brain, and to let emotion enter into his calculations would be like programming errors into the computer. He told me that. Several times he told me that. I don't know how Liz could stay in love with him so long. He was sort of in love with Liz, but he was a cold fish, and there would come one day when the computer would reject Liz's punch card, and I'm telling you he could turn away mid sentence and never come back. He was tough, and he had a terrifying temper that showed itself now and again. He had no friends whatsoever. They were all killed in the war Silas says. Yes, I said, and do you want me to guess who killed them? Liz got really angry when I said that, but I can tell you, he's been a rough bastard that Silas, so don't let that old school tie, and plumstone accent fool you.

He despises me. Silas despises me because I'm not educated properly and yet he pours cold sarcasm on every attempt I make to learn something. Every time he sees me reading a book he adds 'for little people' or 'simply explained for the under fives' to the title, to make me feel like a moron. I can see what he's trying to do. He would have liked me to stop educating myself. He was frightened that one day I would take over the leadership. He was frightened I'd take over Liz too. I could see the glint of that fear in his eyes at times. Liz

15

was much younger than Silas. Her family had known him for years apparently and Silas had started off keeping an eye on her and they had finished up living together. She says that Silas had asked her to marry him, but that she had refused. Years ago. Oh yeah. I doubted it; very much. Why would Silas have asked her that? The computer would have rejected that idea and sounded the buzzer. Silas had nothing to gain. And what Silas had nothing to gain from, Silas didn't do.

These operations didn't have any dash or real style – élan the French say – it was always Silas doing the big man and dangling his watch chain, while me and Liz were running around like a couple of coolies doing the real work. Now, if Silas had let me plan this operation things would be different. I'd have us posing as an aerobatics team that was selling its three planes to change over to jets. I'd told Silas that idea, but he wouldn't even listen properly. Or there was my other idea about us being a three person expedition on our way to find the lost treasures of Babylon. I could use my book on archaeology if we did that one. Then there was an idea I had, where I would be a very young financial genius who everyone wanted to be in with. A sort of secret power in the finance politics of Europe, toppling governments with a stroke of the pen. Scratch you chum.

Anything would be better than these capers in dreary offices. Imagine the old coot who sat here in this little hard-arse seat, every day from nine to five. Imagine beating that typewriter, answering the phone, yes sirring the boss until superannuation, and all for a hundred a week and all the pencils you can take home. Pow. Not me. Not me, man. I'm for the open road, the jet routes, Cannes, Nice, Monte; where the pickings are rich and the living is easy, the suckers are rising and the cabbage is high. I'd like to be there for the Grand Prix. I didn't look like a security guard, but a driver – a racing driver – that's what I looked like. He's coming into the casino turn, vroom vroom, and he's too fast, but no, he's controlling that skid, German corner won't kill this boy. Vroom, vroom, vroom. Up over the pavement. Both cars, their wheels missing by a millimetre, he's ahead of von Turpitz and down the hill and the duel begins. Vroom, vroom. It's unbelievable folks, they're setting a new fantastic lap record. Monte has never seen anything like this before and the crowd are going wild, wild, I tell you, wild.

'For God's sake stop making that noise,' said Liz putting her head around the door. 'They will be arriving soon.'

I pulled my security guard cap on more firmly.

'And don't dare smoke,' said Liz. 'You know how angry Silas gets. Have one of my toffees instead.' She put a toffee on the table.

'Vroom, I said. 'Vroom, vroom, vroom.' I gave her a sexy little hug but she pulled away from me. She went out and closed the door. I was dying for a cigarette but I didn't light one. Silas doesn't allow smoking on duty, unless the role calls for it, and I never upset him – really upset him I mean – when it's an operation. At other times I upset him quite a lot.

Chapter 2

LIZ

I wouldn't have called it an auspicious start, but Silas and Bob were bowing to each other, like a couple of Japanese Generals, and saying 'Stage One completed,' so I hung the framed photo over the dummy safe and phoned the bank to confirm that we'd be coming for the money. Then Bob went next door and I guessed he was trying on his security guard peaked cap and preening himself in the mirror. I hoped that he wouldn't have a cigarette because Silas would be sure to smell it and go into one of his tantrums. The two marks were expected at any minute. I debated whether to change my nylons; one of them had a tiny ladder, but the other had gone at the knee. Silas was scattering some land search papers across the desk. His face was taut and his lips pressed tight together with nerves. I wanted to go to him and put a hand on his arm, just so that he would look up and relax and smile for a moment, but before I could do so he said, 'Two thirty five. The driver should have them at the front hall soon. Take your position darling.' He looked perfect; black jacket, pinstripe trousers, gold watch chain and those strange half frame spectacles that he peered over abstractedly. I loved him. I smiled at him and he gave a brief smile back as though frightened to encourage me in case I wasted time embracing him.

We still needed a fake teleprinter message, so I hurried down the hall to the unoccupied teleprinter room. The janitor had pointed it out to me on the previous Saturday's visit. I switched it into local so that it would not transmit, and then typed a genuine Bahamas teleprinter number and Amalgamin as an answerback code. Under that I typed the phoney message from Nassau and then switched the machine back to normal working again. I left the torn-off sheet near Bob's uniform. There were a couple of genuine messages on the same sheet. I removed my earrings and necklace and tried to straighten my hair, but it was no use, it needed reshaping before it would ever look right again. Silas called to me, 'Get down to the lobby, caterpillar. I don't want those two idiots up here for at least five minutes, so stall them.'

'Just going darling,' I said. I put a pair of heavy, library-style spectacles around my neck on a neck string, and picked up my notebook. It was lucky I hurried, for the Lincoln hire-car that we had sent to collect the marks arrived just as I reached the lobby.

I greeted the marks and had a brief, confidential word with the driver. 'You are to pick up an Italian gentleman – Mr. Salvatore Lombardo – here outside this building at 3.06 precisely. O.K? Can you wait?'

'Maybe I can lady, maybe I can't,' said the driver. 'But if the fuzz starts crowding me, I'll roll around the block and pull into this same slot again. So, if I ain't here tell him to stay put. Italian guy huh?'

'White fedora, dark glasses and tan coat,' I said.

'Whadda say his name was, Al Capone?' said the driver, then laughed.

I leaned close to him and spoke softly, 'Try out a gag like that on Sal,' I growled, 'and you could wind up in the East River.' I hurried to catch up with the two marks who were waiting in the lobby. 'That's not the regular driver,' I said. 'We have so many drivers nowadays and they all forget their instructions.'

The marks nodded. There were two of them; Johnny Jones was about forty, over-weight, but attractive like a teddy bear in his soft overcoat. The other one – Karl Poster– was tall and distinguished looking, with grey eyes and a fine nose, down which he looked at me. He was the type they cast as unfaithful husbands in Italian films that get banned by the League of Decency.

'I was just going to get coffee for you,' I said. 'Our coffee machine upstairs is on the blink today.'

Karl looked me over slowly, like a comparison shopper in a slave market. 'Why don't we just take time out for a coffee here and now?' he said. He looked at his watch, 'We are five minutes early.'

'Fine,' I said turning back to the elevator.

'You have coffee too,' said Karl. He put his hand on my arm with just enough pressure to endorse the invitation, but not enough to make a girl look around for a cop.

We found a corner seat in the half empty coffee shop, and they insisted upon my having do-nuts too. Sugar coated do-nuts with chocolate chips inside.

'Sky's the limit,' explained Johnny the shorter one. 'Expense no object, it's our big day today. Is that right Karl?' Karl looked at him, and seemed annoyed at the ingenuous admission. 'Karl would never admit it. Eh Karl?' He slapped Karl's shoulder. 'But this is a big day for both of us. Let's have a smile, Karl.' Karl smiled reluctantly. Johnny turned to me, 'Have you worked for this company long?'

'Four years,' I said. 'Five next February.' I had it all pat. Marks often asked questions like that. How long have you been with this boss. What make was the company plane. Or there were trick questions to double check things that Silas had told them, like how long since your boss started wearing glasses or what kind of car does he drive.

I looked at them. I sometimes wondered why I didn't feel sorry for marks. Bob said he felt sorry for them sometimes, but I never felt really close to them. It's like reading about people dying in traffic accidents, if it isn't someone you know, it's almost impossible to care, isn't it? It's like feeling sorry for the dead angus when you are eating a really superb fillet with béarnaise. I mean, would it help the angus if I scraped the steak clean and just ate the béarnaise? Well, that's the way I felt about the marks; if I didn't eat them, someone else would, they were nature's casualties. That's the way I saw it.

'Do you like children?' asked Johnny the short one.

'My sister has three,' I offered. 'Twin boys, nearly five, and a three year old girl.'

'I've got a boy, nearly six,' said Johnny. He announced the age like it was a trump card, as though a son of seven would have been even better. 'Would you like to see a photo?'

'She doesn't want to see photos,' said Karl. Johnny looked offended. Karl amended his remark. 'Not your photos, nor mine,' he said. 'She's working, what would she want with them?' He ended the sentence on a note of apology.

'I'd like to see them. I really would,' I said. 'I love children.'

Johnny brought out his wallet. Under a transparent window in it there was a photo of a woman. The hair style was out of fashion, and the dark tones of the picture had faded. The woman had a strange fixed smile as though she knew she was going to be trapped inside a morocco leather wallet for six years. 'That's Ethel, my wife,' said the mark. 'She worked with us until the baby came. She was the brains behind the whole company, wasn't she Karl?' Karl nodded. 'She brought us out of the soft toy, and into the mechanicals and plastics. Ethel pushed us over the red line. She got our first contract with the big distributors here in the east. For a long time we were in Denver. Manhattan seemed big time to us when there were just the four of us working in Denver. Ethel helped me with the design work and Karl did the books and the advertisements. We worked around the clock.'

'She doesn't want to hear about Denver,' said Karl.

'Why not,' said the fat mark. 'It's quite a story you know,' he pulled photos from his wallet. 'It's quite a story,' he repeated quietly. 'We had only nine hundred dollars between us when we began.' He prodded the photos with his stubby fingers. 'That's my wife in the garden, Billy was three then, going on four.'

'And now?' I said. 'How big are you now?'

'Now we are big. We could get five million if we sold out today, if we bided our time we'd get six. That's the house, that's my wife, but she moved. The negative is sharp, but the print's not very good.'

'Five million is peanuts to a big company like this,' said Karl.

'A big firm like this; who owns it,' said Johnny. 'A company like ours; it's flesh and blood. It's most of your life, and most of mine. Am I right?' I nodded but Karl went on arguing.

'Ten million is peanuts. A company like this is world wide, their phone bill is probably more than a million a year.'

'You don't measure companies in dollars,' said Johnny, the fat one. 'You've got to reckon on it differently to that. You've got to reckon on it like it's a living thing; something that grows. We'd never sell out to just anyone.'

'No?' I said.

'Lord no,' he said. 'It would be like selling a dog. You'd need to know that it was going to a good home.'

'A company like this wouldn't need to know,' said Karl. 'A company like this works on a slide rule. Lawyers figure the profit and loss.'

The fat one smiled. 'Well perhaps they have to. After all they've got shareholders Karl.'

'They've got different sort of minds,' said Karl.

'I don't think we are like that,' I said.

'No,' said Karl coldly. 'Well you look like that.'

'Aw come on Karl,' said Johnny. 'Do you have any pics of your sister's kids?' He was anxious to assuage the effect of Karl's rudeness.

'No,' I said.

'What are their names?'

'The twins are Roger and Rodney and the girl is Rosalind,' I said.

Johnny beamed. 'Some folks do that don't they? They keep the same first letter for the names.'

'That's right,' I said. 'And there aren't too many girls names beginning with "r".'

'Rosemary,' said Karl. 'Rene.'

'Ruth,' said Johnny, 'and Rosalind.'

'They already used Rosalind,' said Karl.

'That's right they did,' said Johnny. 'Well there have to be more. Look, if I think of some really good ones, I'll send them to you here at the office. How would that be?'

'Thank you,' I said.

'Rodney,' mused Johnny. 'Say, you're English aren't you?'

'Yes,' I said. 'I was born in Gloucester.'

'We have a collection of English porcelain at home,' said Johnny. 'We have an English style of dog too, named Peter.'

'For Christ sake,' said Karl. Johnny smiled self-consciously. 'I'll just get some cigarettes,' he said. He walked across to the cigarette machine.

'He's nervous,' said Karl when he was out of earshot. 'This *is* a big moment for us. We've worked bare hand on that factory. Johnny's a bright guy, brighter than hell in fact. Don't underrate him because he's nervous. He doesn't do so much nowadays, but without his know-how on the mechanical side, we would never have got off the floor.'

'There are a lot of people passing through the President's office.' I said. 'Men on the threshold of making a fortune, and men due to be fired. I know all the signs of nerves, I've seen all of them.'

'No one was more edgy than I am today, I'll tell you.'

'You seem calm to me,' I said.

'Don't believe it. Johnny makes all the decisions about buying plant, staff, premises, but these exterior problems – the big finance decisions – he leaves to me. He does whatever I say.'

'That's fine,' I said.

'It's like not having a partner at all. If I make the wrong decision this morning I could ruin us. We both have wives and kids, and we are both too old to look around for employment.'

I said, 'You'd think you were in the foyer of the Federal Courthouse instead of on the verge of doing a deal with one of the biggest Corporations in America. I've never known this corporation back a loser. I think you are enjoying a little worry because you know that after this deal, you'll never look back.'

'What made you say Federal Courthouse?'

'No reason,' I said.

'I used to have the damndest nightmares about that building.'

'Tell me,' I looked quickly at my wrist watch.

'I've never told anyone before,' he said. 'But when I was a kid I used to help out in my father's shop on a Saturday. One day I stole three dollars from the till and took my kid brother to the movies. On the way back from the movies he kept threatening to tell my folks. He showed me a picture of the Federal Courthouse and he said that's where they took kids who stole money from their parents. He said they made the kids leap from the top of the building and that if they were innocent they just floated to the ground, but if they were guilty they fell and were killed. I was just terrified. I'd wake up in the middle of the night with the feeling that I was falling. You know that feeling?'

'They say your heart stops don't they? They say it's jumping like that, that starts it again.'

'I used to wake up with a start every night for weeks. I'd have this nightmare about falling off the Federal Court building. I used to sweat. I really suffered. I learned my lesson. I never stole again, not a dime.'

Johnny came back from the cigarette machine. 'Hadn't we better be getting upstairs?' he asked. He looked at both of us puzzled. 'What have you two been talking about?'

24

Karl said, 'I was just relating a dream I once had.'

'Never do that,' said Johnny. 'Never relate dreams, or the stories of films you saw, it bores everyone.'

Karl smiled at me. He didn't smile often, but when he did you could see it brewing up for quite a time. Now he opened his mouth and let it go. It was a big white smile and he held it between his teeth for a moment. It crinkled the corners of his bright eyes and he swung round to give me a profile shot. Wow, what a smile. I'll bet that had the girls of Denver running down the road with their skirts flying.

I took them upstairs to where Silas was waiting for us. 'Hello there Johnny, hello there Karl,' said Silas, striding across the room and pumping their hands. He waved them into armchairs and admired the view with them. Then he produced a silver flask and some glasses. 'Drink?' he said. Rule four; never drink on duty. If you must, make it a soft drink, say it's doctor's orders. So you can imagine I was surprised when Silas poured three large ones and began drinking with scarcely a pause to say cheers.

Silas was relaxing now as the operation got under way. They sipped at the Scotch, 'Special,' said Silas. 'One of the best whisky distilleries in Scotland just happens to be on an island that we own.' Both marks sipped the whisky and Johnny, the short one, said, 'Jumping Jehosofat, Stevie, that's smooth.'

'Bought it in 1959,' said Silas. 'Got five positive results on the mineral analysis, but so far we are not going ahead with any of them.' He looked at the whisky. 'Got to keep a sense of proportion, what?'

I interrupted their laughter. 'You've got our Stockholm Chemical Managing Director upstairs at three o'clock Sir Stephen,' I said.

'*Sir* Stephen?' yelled the sharp eyed one. '*Sir* Stephen? Are you a lord, Stevie?'

'Just a baronet,' Silas muttered. The sharp eyed mark

looked back at the door panel, nudged his partner and nodded towards it. The fat mark gave an almost imperceptible nod of acknowledgment. Silas had insisted that the gold lettered door panel would be worth the money.

Silas waved away their admiration. 'Give those away with packets of tea in England you know. All the chaps who were on Churchill's scientific advisory board during the war got a knighthood. Goodness knows why. Stop us writing our memoirs perhaps.'

'I don't follow you, Sir Latimer.'

'Sir Stephen we say. Well, you see, none of us people who were really close to Winnie, really close to him, felt it would be quite the thing to write our memoirs. When you are close to a man. . . .' He gave a shrug. 'Well anyway, none of us did. Left that for the Generals and the chaps who really did the fighting, what?'

The two marks smiled at each other. 'Anyway,' said Silas. 'I've got our chief man in Scandinavia coming through New York today. I've left his entertainment in the very capable hands of one of our vice presidents. A man with a little more stamina than I have.' Silas gave them a lecherous wink and the sharp eyed mark watched me out of the corner of his eye.

'But,' said Silas. 'In half an hour or so I'll have to go up to our penthouse suite and shake his hand.'

'We could let . . .' began the fat mark, sliding his bottom around in the chair.

'You are to stay right here,' said Silas firmly. 'That's why I received you in this office instead of one of the penthouse entertainment suites upstairs, in spite of the fact that I have no ice or soda here.'

'I've been in and out of this building a million times,' said Karl, 'and I've never seen no sign of a penthouse on the top floor. I thought the top floor was a radio station.'

'We bought that in '48,' said Silas. 'They were using too much space up there, so we spent a little money on the conver-

26

sion. Now the penthouses have the same entrance hall as the radio station reception.' Silas placed a finger along his nose. 'And, as you say, there is no sign. Discreet eh? You chaps must use it sometime. Perhaps a party next week? My Vice President in charge of entertainment has some remarkable resources,' he paused, 'or perhaps I'm just a little old fashioned.'

I could see Silas was getting carried away so I went next door and buzzed him on the intercom.

'It's Mr. Glover Junior, Sir Stephen, he's flown in from Nassau on the company plane. He says it's urgent.'

'Get him,' said Silas.

Bob was waiting outside. Silas's vicuna overcoat was a little too large for him, but he wore it draped around his shoulders. He was shaved and his hair neatly parted, I'd pressed his suit to perfection and with his gold cufflinks and quiet tie he looked tough and adult and rather dishy. I hadn't noticed that before.

'Don't try the stutter,' I warned. 'You know what happens; you forget to do it halfway through.'

'Out of my way, princess,' said Bob, and gave me a familiar nudge. One day Silas would catch him doing that and say that I've encouraged it. I've never encouraged it. There's only one man in my life; Silas. I have to have the best, but Bob was rather dishy.

He opened the office door with a crash.

'Yes?' said Silas, not simulating his irritation.

'Mr. G. . . .' Bob began, overplaying his stutter very considerably. 'Graham King sent me.' Bob finished. Silas nodded, 'This is Otis Glover, from the Nassau office,' he said to the marks. 'What is it?' he said to Bob.

'Mr. King is worried about the nomin . . .'

'Nominees,' supplied Silas.

Bob nodded. 'No need to worry about them,' said Silas beaming with goodwill. 'Here they are,' he made an extravagant gesture toward the marks as though he had just

27

manufactured them.

'King is worried about them,' said Bob. 'He says that we don't know them.'

'We?'

'Amalgamated Minerals B . . . Bahamas Ltd.' said Bob. He was overdoing the stutter.

Silas introduced the marks to Bob. I find it difficult to remember them. There were so many faces that they become one composite face; credulous, boggle eyed, greedy. Silas always remembered them. Every little detail; their native towns and companies they owned, their ailments, cars and fetishes, and even their wife's and kids first names.

'Now you do know them,' said Silas. 'So that problem is disposed of.'

'N . . . n . . . n . . . no sir,' said Bob. 'We'll need more than that if they are going to be allowed to bid with two million dollars of Corporation money.'

Silas took off his half-frame glasses and motioned Bob into a chair. 'Look Glover, these gentlemen will be with you on the company jet this afternoon. . . .'

Bob interrupted him, 'But I've been sent here to say that if the nominees invest on their own behalf there must be certain conditions.'

'Conditions?' said Silas. 'These gentlemen are friends of mine. They must be allowed something for their trouble.'

'They are getting something,' said Bob. 'The villa in Rock Sound is being prepared. . . .'

'Rock Sound is beautiful,' said Silas to the marks, 'that's the finest of all the V.I.P. villas. Fishing, swimming, sun bathing; my word, how I envy you.'

Bob continued doggedly, 'The yacht is under sailing orders and the servants have been told to prepare for two couples.'

'But there's only two of us,' interrupted Johnny.

'The night is young,' said Silas. 'This evening there'll be a party in your honour, music, dancing, fine food, drink and with lots of beautiful girls.'

'Oh,' said the mark, and stole a self conscious glance at me. I didn't react.

Bob said, 'All they have to do is to sign a couple of papers and pin our cheque to them. These nominee bids are very simple. We usually use one of our Bay Street friends.'

'That's for you to decide when it's a local deal, but when New York is involved, then I choose the nominees,' said Silas.

'I'm just a messenger,' said Bob. 'Mr. Graham King will be telexing you about it.'

'Miss Grimdyke. Go and see if there's anything on the telex from Nassau.'

I went and collected the fake message that I had typed with the machine set at local. When I brought it back Silas and Bob had finished the small quarrel that they had rehearsed. I looked around at them, pretending not to comprehend the strained silence. Silas grabbed the telex from me.

```
AMALGAMATED MINERALS NYC
AMALGAMIN NASSAU BAHAMAS

TO SIR STEPHEN LATIMER
FROM GRAHAM KING

MY FELLOW DIRECTORS ALL OPPOSE ANY PLAN
TO USE OUTSIDE MONEY BUT I WILL AGREE IN
SPITE OF THAT IF YOU WILL CONFIRM THAT YOUR
ACCOUNT ALREADY HOLDS THE NOMINEES
PARTICIPATION STOP   GLOVER IS ON THE
COMPANY JET AND WILL BE WITH YOU AT ANY
MOMENT STOP   VILLAS READY ARE WE TO ARRANGE
SUPER FACIL PARTY TONIGHT?   I WILL STAY NEAR
THIS TELEPRINTER IF THERE IS ANY DIFFICULTY
GLOVER WILL SPEAK ON MY BEHALF.
GRAHAM + + +

AMALGAMATED MINERALS NYC
```

Silas let the wire drift from his hands into those of the

marks. Bob pretended to search for cigarettes and dropped a copy of a Nassau morning newspaper on the desk.

'What I don't understand,' said Bob. 'Is why we need outside money at all. Why can't our stockholders supply the money? After all, the report said that we could expect a 78 per cent return on the investment.'

'Ha, ha, ha,' said Silas. The marks laughed too, although they seemed just as keen as Bob to hear the answer. Johnny, the short mark, took the Nassau newspaper and put it into his pocket.

'A simple question, from a simple mind,' said Silas. 'So I'll try to make it a simple answer.'

Johnny laughed again, but softly, so as not to miss the reply. Silas said, 'I appreciate your loyalty to the company Glover, to say nothing of your loyalty to the shareholders, but the story leaking out would tip our hand about the new harbour site immediately. Why, I've never even sent a memo to our Vice-Presidents. Yesterday, you had never heard of it Glover, am I right?'

'Y . . . y . . . y . . . y . . . you're right.'

'This is secret; top damned cosmic secret as we used to say in the war.'

'Can I ask you something?' said Johnny the mark.

'Shoot,' said Silas.

'After the deal goes through, and the land that Amalgamated Minerals doesn't need, is resold, from where will we be repaid?'

'I know what you are thinking,' laughed Silas. 'Sure, take your 78 per cent profit and tuck it away in good old tax-free Bahamas. No one will know. You will have paid Amalgamated Minerals New York City some money, and then got the same amount back again as far as the US tax people are concerned. Sure, buy a small hotel with your profits and you'll be earning steady money right there in the sun.'

'That would be great,' said Johnny.

'Big companies do it all the time,' said Silas. 'Why

shouldn't a couple of young men like you have a break once in a while.'

The marks – who no one but Silas would have had the nerve to describe as young men – nodded their agreement. Silas poured another whisky for all of them and sipped gently. Then he excused himself for a moment and left the room.

Bob offered his cigarettes around and as he lit one for Johnny he said, 'When did you pay in your cheque for the extra bid?'

The marks exchanged glances.

'W . . . what's going on here?' asked Bob plaintively.

'We haven't paid it yet,' said Johnny.

Silas returned. 'They haven't paid the money,' complained Bob to Silas, 'and it's too late now, the bank will be shut in a few minutes.'

'That's all right,' said Silas.

'I'm v . . . v . . . v . . . very sorry sir,' said Bob, 'but my orders are to confirm that Amalgamin hold the extra money.'

'It will be all right.'

'No,' said Bob. 'It's not all right.'

'Is it dignified Glover,' asked Silas, 'to argue the matter in front of my guests?'

'No,' said Bob, 'but nor is it dignified to ask me to r . . . r . . . r . . . risk my job to help your friends make a lot of money. The telex put it clearly. If I confirm that you hold the money in your account when it's not true, it will be more than my job's worth.'

Silas pursed his lips. 'Perhaps you are right my boy.' Bob pursued the thought, 'So these gentlemen won't be coming back with me to Nassau?'

'There must be some way of getting over it,' said Silas. 'Look Glover,' he said, being suddenly warm and reasonable, 'suppose we see their cheque for a quarter of a million dollars, isn't that as good as holding it?'

'It isn't sir.'

'Be reasonable Glover. These are serious businessmen, they aren't going to let us down.'

The marks made noises like men who wouldn't let anyone down.

'All right,' said Bob.

'Bravo,' said Silas and the marks looked pleased. 'Well that's what we will do,' said Silas.

Bob produced his small black notebook.

'Another quarter million,' repeated Silas. Bob wrote that down.

'And the name of the nominee company that will bid?' asked Bob.

'The Funfunn Novelty Company,' said Silas.

'F . . . funfunn Novelty Company,' said Bob. He sat down and laughed heartily. 'Are you feeling O.K. sir? Why don't you sit down for a moment and take two of your tablets.'

'That's enough of that Glover. Theirs is a large and prosperous concern. I'm very happy for us to be associated with them.'

'So am I,' said Bob still laughing, 'but perhaps we can now . . . er. . . .' He made a motion with his hand.

'Make out the cheque for this rather rude young man,' Silas directed the marks as though he was *their* managing director. 'And then you can put it right back into your pocket again. Just show him that the cheque exists.'

The marks didn't hesitate. Karl produced his cheque book and the other fumbled for a pen. Silas did nothing to help them. He didn't even offer them Winston Churchill's pen.

'Damned red tape,' Silas said angrily, 'that's what this is. Over his shoulder he said to the marks, 'Don't put Inc., it may be paid into the Amalgamin Ltd. Bahamas company. Leave it Amalgamin, just Amalgamin. Pure red tape, no need for this cheque to be made out at all.'

I watched the marks: Jones and Poster. Sign in your best handwriting. Down went the nib. Kyrie. Three thousand voices split the darkness like a shaft of golden sunlight.

Valkyrie; echo of hunting horns and tall flames of the pyre. The Vienna State Orchestra and Chorus responded to the stroke of Poster's pen. Gods of Valhalla assemble in the red night sky as the cheque slid smoothly into Silas's slim hand.

'That looks bad,' said Silas.

'What does?' said the marks, who hadn't expected their life savings to be received with such bad grace.

'That will mean Amalgamated Minerals bidding two million, two hundred and *sixty* thousand dollars,' explained Silas. 'It's not a good sign that. I mean . . .' he smiled, 'it looks as though our company is scraping the very bottom of its financial resources to have an odd 10,000 on it like that.'

'I'll rewrite it,' said Karl. 'We scraped together every available dollar. That's the whole mortgage.'

'You can rewrite it some other time,' said Silas. 'Just let him see it and then put it back in your pocket.' The mark passed it across to Bob who gave it the most perfunctory of glances and slid it back across the desk. Karl opened his wallet and was about to slide it inside when Bob said, 'Wait a moment sir. My orders say it must be paid into the Amalgamated Minerals account. I appreciate your complete trust in your friends' intentions, but a man holding his own cheque is no collateral by any standard of measurement, and you can't deny it.'

'You are a pedant Glover. That's why you will never reach the highest echelons of international commerce, as these gentlemen already have done. But if it will satisfy you. . . .' Silas got up with a loud sigh and walked across to the dummy safe. He swung the picture aside. 'The cheque can go into the safe now.' Silas rapped the safe front with his knuckle. 'I will send off the message saying that we hold the money. After the message has been transmitted I'll open the safe and return the cheque to my friends. Will that satisfy you Glover? Silas brought a key from his waistcoat and opened the ancient little safe.

The marks were not consulted. They watched Bob

anxiously. Bob bit his lip, but finally said, 'I don't like it.'

'I don't care what you like,' said Silas. 'No one can possibly dispute the fairness of that.' He turned to the marks and smiled graciously. 'Not even the Funfunn Novelty Company. They can stand guard over the safe for the five minutes it will take Miss Grimsdyke to get the message on the wire.' Silas reached for his message pad and spoke as he wrote on it. It was all so clear and inevitable that it would have taken a strong man to change the tide of events. He passed me the pad, 'Read that aloud Miss Grimsdyke. I read, 'Arrange best super-facil party ever, stop, I hold over quarter million additional participation by nominees, stop. They arrive on company jet about five, signed Latimer.'

'Fine,' said Silas. 'Now Miss Grimsdyke, if you will let me have the Amalgamated Minerals cheque for our two million dollars we can rest them both in the safe until these gentlemen leave this afternoon for Nassau.'

I opened the buff coloured folder and handed him the magnificent cheque that we had prepared. It depicted a buxom woman holding a cornucopia with Amalgamated Minerals written on it. She was scattering wheat, fruit and flowers all over our address. He took his pen off the desk. 'See that pen,' said Silas. 'Winnie gave it to me, it signed the Atlantic Charter. The only souvenir dear old Winnie ever gave me. Bless him.' He took the pen and signed the cheque with a flourish. 'The other necessary signatures are already there,' he said. He picked up the Funfunn cheque and our grand looking fake and gave them both to Karl. It was artistry the way Silas handled them. One was a lifetime of effort and savings and the other piece of paper quite worthless, it was artistry the way Silas reversed their values.

'Put them both in the safe,' he said. He gave Karl the key to the safe and turned away, and so did Bob. I was the only person who saw the marks open the safe and plonk the cheques into it. There was a half second of indecision, but Silas turning away took care of that. It was the exact moment of balance, like a crystal clear soprano or a mountain top at dawn. This was the moment you came back for again and again.

'Now don't leave the room,' Silas told the marks. 'Is the safe door firmly closed? The key turns twice.'

Karl nodded. I was still standing by the desk smelling the heady perfume that pervades a room in which a large cheque has been signed.

'Go ahead, Miss Grimsdyke,' prompted Silas, who knew my weakness for such moments. 'Get along to the telex.'

'Rona,' said the short one – Johnny. 'Have you got Rona?'

'No,' I said. 'Rona is good.'

'I'll think of more,' said Johnny.

I nodded my thanks and made for the door. Silas was screwing up his face, trying to understand why the mark had suddenly said Rona like that.

'I'll go with you,' said Bob. 'I'll send the confirmatory telex to Mr. King.'

'Good chap,' said Silas. When I got outside I closed the door behind me and heaved a sigh of relief. Once in the next office, Bob took off Silas's vicuna coat and threw it across the chair. I picked it up and folded it neatly. Bob changed into the Security Guard coat. Through the wooden partition, I heard Silas laugh loudly. I walked quietly across the room to the false end of the safe. I flipped back the black velvet curtain and removed the two cheques. I looked at my watch, we were exactly on schedule. I slipped a plain gold wedding ring onto my finger.

Bob donned the Security Guard cap and gun belt, and I tucked his surplus hair up under the hatband. He snapped the wrist lock on to his arm and then tested it and the case locks too. His notebook was on the table and he pointed to each listed action as he did them. False documents cleared away, no clothing on chairs etc., wrist lock oiled working and in place. Case locks, oiled working and in place. Security uniform buttoned correctly and clean and brushed. Gunbelt on, and a correctly placed strap over right shoulder. Shoes shined. I nodded approval to Bob.

The last line read, 'leave office floor at two fifty eight.' As the sweep-second hand came up, I went in the hall. Bob followed.

While closing the office door I heard a voice through the partition wall, 'But wasn't it the craziest coincidence that we both bank downstairs in the same branch of the same bank?'

'Well of course,' said Silas. 'We didn't bank there until we heard that you did.' They all laughed. We took the freight elevator to avoid Mick. Bob looked just great in his uniform, but he had a sudden attack of stage fright in the lift. 'Supposing the bank won't pass across that amount of cash? It's a hell of a lot.'

'Stop worrying Bob,' I said. 'How many times have we rehearsed it? Four times. Each time they have let us have it, and each time the cheque has gone through. They are well softened up by now. This morning I called them and said I was Funfunn's cashier and I was issuing the cheque. We've done everything. They think I have some illegal racket going, but they don't care about that, as long as the cheque goes through.'

'But we're going to ask them for a quarter million in cash.'

'For some people,' I said, 'that's not a lot of money. All I have to do is look like one of those people.'

'You're right,' Bob said. He dried his hands on his handkerchief.

The bank was a big plate-glass place with black leather and stainless steel and bright eyed little clerks who tried to pick me up. Today they were running around watching the clock, anxious to close the doors and clear up early for the weekend.

'You only just made it,' the clerk said.

'I'm sorry,' I said. 'But I told you on the 'phone that we'd only just make it. The traffic is very heavy today.'

'There you go,' said the bank clerk. 'And I was just telling Jerry that traffic was running light this afternoon.'

'Not the cross-town,' I said. 'That's where you get trouble.'

The clerks nodded. 'I'm Mrs. Amalgamin,' I said. 'This guard is taking Mr. Amalgamin a quarter of a million dollars in cash.'

'He's going to have a big weekend,' said the clerk.

'Nah,' said Bob. 'He ran out of cigarettes is all. You don't know how these guys in exurbia live.' I glared at him, but smiled at the clerk.

The clerk reached for the cash. 'Hundreds?'

He had a bundle of brand new hundreds in his hand. I didn't want them. 'Tens. It's for the plant,' I said.

'That's a funny name,' said the clerk. 'Amalgamin I mean, why have they written it with a gap in the middle of the name?'

'The next time you see the cashier of Funfunn Novelty Company you'll just have to ask him,' I said. 'Because frankly it's not a firm we want to do business with again.'

'It's not the cashier,' said the clerk. 'It's two partners. Both partners sign.'

'Um,' I said. I finished writing a cheque for $260,000. I slid it across the counter. I calculated that would leave $557.49 less bank charges in the account we had opened in the name of Mr. and Mrs. Amalgamin.

'Is it Greek?' said the clerk.

'What?' I said.

'The name. Is it a Greek name, Amalgamin?'

'Estonian,' I said. 'It's a common Estonian name. There's whole blocks full of Amalgamins, in the Bronx.'

'No fooling,' said the clerk. 'It's a nice name.'

'We're not complaining,' I said.

'That case won't hold them,' said the clerk.

'It will,' I said. 'The same thing happened last Easter. That size cash case will hold the notes. Then we can fill up with packs of coin.'

He shrugged. 'One thing I'll tell you,' said the clerk. 'If I'm stuck out in Jersey for the weekend, with just a quarter million dollars between me and boredom; I'll have you deliver it, not him.' He stabbed a finger at Bob.

I smiled and acted embarrassed, and then they started. One nice, soft, crumpled, used ten-dollar bill fell into that case and they kept falling like green snowflakes.

'I know Mr. Karl Poster of Funfunn Novelties,' said the clerk. 'I know them both in fact, but Mr. Poster I know best. I like him.' He went on packing the dollar bills into the case. 'Never too busy to pass the time of day.' He broke one bundle of notes so that he could get half of them down the side of the case. 'Plays squash at lunchtimes. He's good, really good, beats me every time. Pro class, I'd say.'

Bob was watching me out of the corner of his eye. The clerk said, 'So you don't like him, well I think he's a nice guy.'

'We've got a dispute with his company,' I said. 'They're slow to pay. Karl Poster is another thing again. I like Karl Poster.' The funny thing was, I did like him, Karl Poster was my type.

'He's a nice guy,' said the clerk. He closed the case and held it while Bob locked it and snapped the chain and bracelet to his wrist. 'That should do you now. Get heisted with that, and they take you too.' The clerk gave a little salute. 'Take it away colonel,' he said. 'Happy weekend.'

Chapter 3

SILAS

Bob and Liz departed exactly on schedule. I turned to the two marks. Jones the short, red-faced one polished his shoes with a Kleenex tissue. He saw me looking at him and tucked the tissue out of sight.

'I'll run through the project again,' I said. 'I want you to be quite sure of what's happening. You can still back out of this anytime and no bad feeling.'

Johnny Jones, the shorter of the two, adjusted his mono-grammed pocket handkerchief and stretched his hand out in a gesture of friendly negation that revealed a heavy gold wristwatch. He said, 'You needn't explain the scheme, Sir Stephen. . . .'

'Not my way of working,' I said fiercely. I had them now. People talk of confidence *tricks* only if they know nothing about them. There is no set trick, no set plan. You get the marks into a state of trance, motivated entirely by their own avarice. Paranoia in reverse I call it, a desire to trust or depend upon. These two fellows were already touring their VIP harem in the Bahamas, or somewhere downtown spending their 78 per cent profit. They hardly heard the words I spoke except in the way that a subject hears the soft assurances of a hypnotist.

I flipped the switch of the squawk-box. 'Get me Graham in Nassau,' I said into the dead instrument. 'Book a call for 5.30.' I turned to the marks. 'Unless you are completely au fait with the procedures and the safeguards for your investment then *I* wouldn't go ahead.' I chuckled, 'I really wouldn't. Do you know, the year before last, in Rome, I pulled out of a twenty-two million dollar deal, because my old friend the late Alfred Krupp said it was too technical for him to understand it. You see, I want you to test and mistrust me, because I have to test and mistrust the people I deal with.'

Johnny Jones, the short mark, giggled. 'But you are the most honest man I ever met. Why, the way you followed me out of the Club and gave me back a five dollar bill when I didn't even remember dropping it. And the way you gave me the key of your apartment when you had only known me for an hour. You are the most trusting guy I ever did meet.'

I looked him straight in the eye and nodded gravely. I said, 'It's nothing of which to be proud. The President of a company shouldn't be too trusting, no matter what his personal feelings. Young Glover is right. When you are running a giant corporation, you've no business to trust anyone. He's right, one of these days I'll trust the wrong man and God knows what might happen.' I bit my lip and let them think I'd been a little embarrassed by the argument with Bob.

'Come on Sir Stevie,' said Karl. He was the quieter of the two. He was tall and conservatively dressed in a shiny synthetic suit. I thought at first he was going to be trouble, but now I could see that I had them both. I really had them. I could get them dancing naked on the desk top, or throwing themselves out of the window. I was drunk with the power of it and terribly tempted to see how far I could take them. I almost suggested that all of us went out to the airport. I began weaving a fantasy story for them around that idea, imagining Bob's face and Liz's fright if I arrived on the airport concourse with these two and had them wave us off on the London flight. Wheeeee . . .

'That's it,' said the fat one. 'Let yourself go. A little bit of that son of a gun we met at the Playboy Club the other night.' I realised that I had Wheeed aloud.

I sat down in the swivel chair, switched on the desk light

and put my head under it, pretending that it was a cold shower. Ug. 'You must forgive me gentlemen,' I said slowly. 'But you'll find that I live two lives. One life is my own and personal, but in the other one I take responsibility for a multi billion dollar corporation with over six hundred thousand employees of all nationalities. Just one foolish error could put all those people out of a job.'

'And put you out of a job too,' said Karl. We laughed. According to schedule Bob and Liz would be downstairs and presenting the cheque now. NOW. The fat one said, 'Work and play are like Scotch and water. Keep them well apart, hey?' I poured more drinks.

I laughed politely. There was a silence. Johnny, the fat one, reached for a comb and ran it quickly through his thinning hair. I said, 'You've probably heard the story of the English explorers who were attacked by African natives. This tall English chap is struck by a spear and then another, until there are so many spears in him that he looks like a pin cushion. Another member of the expedition looks at him and says, "My goodness, Roger, you are terribly, terribly cut about, you poor feller. Does it hurt?" and the fellow with the spears in him says, "No, by jove, Sydney. Only when I laugh".'

The marks laughed heartily and so did I. By now those bills should be packing tight into that case. I laughed without hurrying. The fat mark brought out a silk handkerchief and dried his merry eyes. I flipped up the squawk box switch and then switched it off.

I said, 'That's a secret signal to me that I should go upstairs for a moment. If you gentlemen would give me fifteen minutes to say goodbye to our Stockholm chief and another ten to arrange an extra security guard for this floor over the weekend, I'll be right back,' I paused at the door. 'What's more gentlemen, I think this will give you a few minutes to have a private discussion about your investment, without having me here. We're not bugged here, at least if we are, they haven't told me.' We laughed. 'Remember, there's no need for a final decision until Monday morning when the bids go in. Tell my secretary and Otis Glover that I will be back in time to take that call to Nassau. Meanwhile look after the key of the safe, there's a Pentagon Contract in there.' I turned when I was at the door. 'Goodness, and my pen from Winnie. No matter, I'll be back in a moment.' Karl put the key into his pocket and nodded to me.

I left my roll brim hat ($30), umbrella ($46.50), some leather framed pictures and my old two dollar fountain pen (total $78.50), on the desk.

I went next door. Everything was there waiting for me. I retied my necktie in a loose knot, then I pinned the collar with a large gold pin. A jewelled stickpin went into the front of the tie and onto my fingers I slipped four flashy rings.

I took off my braces and loosened my belt one notch. Then I walked across the room to let my trousers settle on my hips. It changes one's style of walking quite considerably, or at least it did mine.

I removed the watch chain from my waistcoat and fixed it to my trousers like a key chain. I emptied a small flask of heavily scented oil into my palm and put it on my hair. I rubbed it in, and parted my hair nearer to the middle. I dabbed lotion on my chin and followed it with talc. I climbed into my vicuna coat that Bob had worn earlier. I tied the belt, turned up my collar and put on a white fedora and dark glasses. Sal Lombardo. The whole process took less than sixty seconds.

I hit the button for the express lift. Mick was in it. I saw his nose wrinkle as my perfumes wafted over to him.

'Going to the big fight?'

'Ya,' I said hoarsely, 'I sure am buddy.'

'That Zapello will get a beating I'm thinking.'

'Beating smeeting. The champ's going into da tank. Don't waste your money on dat bum.'

'Is that right? Do you know him?'

'Know him? I own both dose bambinos.'

'Is that right,' said Mick respectfully. We travelled on in silence. On the street level I got out. Mick said, 'Goodbye mister.'

'Ciao,' I shouted. 'Ciao baby, ciao.' I hurried across the lobby. The Lincoln hire car was waiting outside. 'I'm Sal Lombardo,' I told him. 'The Pan Am Building and make it snappy.'

'Sure thing,' said the driver.

The Pan Am building was just a couple of minutes away, from its roof the scheduled helicopter was about to leave. I didn't hurry, my seat was booked and young Bob and Liz were already seated. In separate seats of course. I looked at my watch. The whole operation had been timed and costed out to perfection, apart from a small matter of 25 cents on the cab bill because of a traffic jam. That was entirely Bob's responsibility and I decided to make him pay it out of his own pocket. From Kennedy there was the connecting jet for London, everything was exactly on schedule.

My God I was tired. My dark glasses blacked out the world, and I was appreciative of that. I'd had enough of the world for a few hours. From a few rows behind me I could hear Bob's voice. He was teaching the stewardess a trick with two dice, and they were both giggling. They were annoying all the other passengers, as well as being far too conspicuous for my taste. My God, Bob was carrying all the money in that case of his. You'd think that just for once he would have been content to be quiet. I wish I had let him bring that damn book about archaeology with him, but it would have looked suspicious, a security guard in uniform carrying 'Our Civilisation Begins – an illustrated encyclopedia for little folk.'

I tipped the white fedora over my eyes. I had tired of being Sal Lombardo. I wished that I had remained Sir Stephen Latimer for the plane journey to London. I'd have got better service as Latimer, especially on a British airline.

Each of us was travelling alone. God I was tired. I'm always tired when it's over. It's the responsibility, the planning, the tension and judgment. Sometimes a last minute decision can throw the whole strategy into reverse. It was no use looking to the others for help or guidance. Bob was a child. At best he was a waif with the moral judgment of a five year old, at worst a young felon. Liz was older and more responsible and I loved her, but she was still in her twenties, and still a young, silly impressionable girl, behind the thin veneer of sophistication that I had supplied. I loved Liz and I was fond of Bob but sometimes I wondered what I was doing with them. Tonight I would have given everything I owned for an evening's conversation. I missed that, more than anything. Sometimes I'd try to remember old conversations I'd had many years ago, arguments in the mess, long long discussions sitting in a tank in the middle of the desert. They were all gone now, the replacements were never the same as the men you had trained with.

That's true of life too, the friends you make after you are twenty-five are not like your old friends. My old friends are gone. Still in the desert. They all went the same night, at least nearly all of them did. Liz's father died that night. The Regiment lost twenty officers, and the regiment never truly recovered. Neither did I.

'Wake up Silas,' said Captain Leadbetter. I hadn't fully recovered from the explosion and fire. I opened my eyes, Leadbetter looked quite a mess. His face was covered with grey dust, his chin unshaven, hair messed up, and the front of his shirt was caked with dark brown blotches. He saw me staring at it. 'Not mine,' he said. 'My gunner's.' He spoke in that anxious, top-speed way, that children bring home news from school.

'Colonel Mason, Dusty, Perce, Major Graham, Major Little, Sergeant Hughes and Chichester in the first five minutes. Bloody eighty eight of course. Should see them.

44

Turrets just fly off and land twenty yards away. Bertie led C Squadron in then, but it took him a few minutes to form up, so they had ranged him in. I got out riding on the back of Frogmorton's tank. Bloody hot, I'll tell you, with those 88's chucking it over. Froggie didn't know I was there for half a mile, what a lark. We've lost eighteen tanks destroyed and another three damaged and abandoned. Jerry will have them repaired and in action again tomorrow, you see. They'll be shooting at us.'

I got to my feet. Leadbetter started to talk again, but I silenced him. 'We've lost the colonel?'

'That's what I'm telling you; the Colonel, Dusty, Perce, Graham and Major Little, and Sergeant Pearce, Sergeant Brophy, Staff Foreman.'

'You mean their tanks, didn't they get out?'

'You haven't seen these 88's Silas. There's no getting out, they just blow you apart, bits fly like feathers from a pheasant hit fair and square. They laid down H.E. after they'd clobbered us, and then they put infantry in. We won't see any of them again Silas.'

'Get a drink, and that's an order,' I'd seen it before; the high-pitched voice, and fluent talk, just an inch away from hysteria. He'd break in an hour or so.

'O.K. chief,' he said happily. 'You are the C.O. now that Mason, Bertie, and Dusty Miller and Little have copped it.'

'Yes,' I said. 'That makes me the senior officer.'

Leadbetter stared out through the tent flap for a long time, then he spoke again. 'Old Mason must have guessed what we were heading into. I wondered why he left you here at HQ Squadron yesterday. The C.O. was a good old stick wasn't he?' I'd been reprimanded by the colonel only a few hours before, I could almost see him standing where Leadbetter now stood.

'Yes,' I said. 'He was.'

Funny to think of Colonel Mason as the father of Liz. I wondered what he would have thought of both of us today.

What would any of our fathers think of any of us? I wished my father had lived longer. I was only a child when he died, and I had never had a real chance to become his friend. He was a wise man, everyone agreed about that, and everyone had gone to him for advice. If only he had given me more. A reserved man, for no one knew how sick he was until it was too late; no one knew, not even my mother. I remembered being angry that he would not carry me home the day before he died. Poor father.

I was fond of Liz and Bob but I couldn't really talk with them. If only there was someone to whom I could talk. Sometimes, truth to tell, I felt more at home in the homes and offices of the men we swindled, than in the clubs, bars, restaurants and international hotels where we spent our ill-gotten gains. It was merely a trick of fate that I was not, in reality, the President of Amalgamated Minerals or some similar concern in the world of international commerce. Or was it. Perhaps I was just fooling myself, as I was expert at fooling others. Perhaps I was just a criminal as my mother had once told me I was. 'A hit and run driver,' she had called me, banging into people's lives and causing them pain and distress. She had been referring to the divorce and to the swindle in Frankfurt 1946. I came almost unscathed out of both, but as a prediction it was not too wide of the mark. I was a disappointment to her, after my dashing career in the army nothing was beyond my power, and precious little beyond my ambition.

Karl Poster, the tall thin mark. I had a feeling he wasn't completely convinced at the very end. As I went out through the office door I had looked at him, and he had doubt written right across his face. I'd been worried that he'd follow me out of the building. What could we get. It's hard to say, but if the city put up a really astute attorney there could be a dozen or more charges. Using that building as a site for a fraud was probably an offence, and then our fancy cheque was a forgery. Can you imagine ten years in prison. I'd never live through it your honour. Very well, says the judge, just do as much as you can of it. Very funny. Ten years, fifteen perhaps. Would an American prison be better than a British prison. I'd often thought of that. Central heating, running water, better food but more violence. Greater chance of being hurt by the other prisoners. Still I'd survived the war. I'd done a bloody sight more than survived it; I'd thrived on it. That's why I'd never stopped fighting it. This was my war, and Liz and Bob were my army. Not much of an army, but then a commander has to adapt to his resources. That was the secret of command in battle; flexibility and full utilisation of resources. Terrain, men, weapons, skills and surprise. Now I was talking to myself as though I was a mark. This was a war all right, but I wanted to sign a separate peace. I'd taken all the combat I could handle. Ten years in prison; that was the sort of wound from which I would no longer recover. Each time I seemed to make more mistakes. I covered them, but they were mistakes. In the old days I made none. Liz had stalled them in the lobby, very well, but I should have made sure that that damned hire car arrived exactly on time, not five minutes early. Bob's stutter, why didn't I think of that, I might have guessed he'd try to use it. It was the most unconvincing stutter I had ever heard. The stupid little fool. Well, I'd make sure he never tried that again.

One more operation. I must have a very small drink. I reached the flask from my inside pocket. I must have a very small drink. The old crone in the next seat is looking at me in a disapproving way. Where does she think she is, the Royal Enclosure? It's a bloody aeroplane madam and I'm having a drink. Your health. Look at her face. She heard that last bit. Damn her. Damn them all in fact. I'm the victor laureate, and that's a two hundred and sixty thousand gun salute in that black case. I won. So why don't I stop worrying, I won and I'll go on winning. A man doesn't burn himself out, that's bosh. Liz loves me, adores me. I'm the

47

leader and she's the kind of girl who stays with the leader. Bob will never be a leader. She knows that. She's told me so a million times. He's pathetic, that's what Bob is, a cipher, a psychological archetype orphan, brave as only the brainless can be. I've seen regiments of Bobs under fire, without enough imagination to be scared. I've got too much imagination, that's my trouble, if I have any trouble, which I don't for one moment admit. Perhaps I had less imagination when I was young, perhaps that's why I was so brave. As you get older, you get wiser and less brave, that's why the higher you go in command the farther from the fighting line they put you, until the man who really controls the battle is not even in artillery range. Ten years. My God; ten years. Would Liz wait. Would any woman. Why should they.

Check the stewardess call-button, adjust the air supply, tighten the lap strap. Chocks away. The aeroplane drones on and all I can see below me is endless white cloud. Richthofen's Flying Circus would be over the lines this morning. Fancy sending half-trained kids against them in crates like these.

Across the grey German sky, dawn slashed bright red weals. Tackatackatacka. Kick the rudder bar, there goes young Bob; a black feather dipped in red flame. The wind screams in the wires as I turn, tighter than the Red Baron. Tackatacka . . . tackatacka. Mercilessly the twin Vickers guns stitch the bright fabric. Inches below my fuselage the thin wirelike tracers curve and fall away. Roger Wilco. Left, left, steady. A small shed, the intelligence officer said, in it enough heavy water to put the Nazis months ahead in the race for the atomic bomb. Steady, steady. Another fierce cannonade all around us, followed by the ominous rattle of shrapnel against the engine nacelle. Losing height. The others were stealing sidelong glances at me. My jaw stiffened. Losing height rapidly now. Steady, bombs gone: Down they go. Down, down, down until they are the merest specks against the green of the airfield. Crash, an indescribable explosion. It's as much as I can hold the control column. Intelligence were right. Enough heavy water to destroy the whole of southern England. Lower now. We are done for. This is it boys, too low to use the brollys I'm afraid. Hold on to your hats fellows, down we go. What a landing skipper, who'd believe that three engines are feathered and the whole fuselage shot to shreds. I just smile back. What's our best chance? Split up chaps, it's no *O flag* for me, it's cross-country, and living on the land, travel by night, lie up by day, and avoid the villages where the dogs bark. It's the compass in the button, and silk scarf map of the Rhineland that have been with me for fifty-five missions. Oh well, this is it chaps. See you all in blighty.

'Please fasten your seat belts we are about to descend for London airport,' said the stewardess. I'd need warmer clothes than this in Britain. I could use a cup of coffee. Damned uncomfortable things aeroplanes.

Chapter 4

BOB

I'd walked straight out of the bank carrying a bag full of folding money, and feeling as conspicuous as hell dressed up with blue and white uniform, badges, artillery and all, but not a passer-by gave me so much as a glance. I separated from Liz and walked into the men's toilet of the Continuum Building. The brown paper bundle of clothes was where I had left it in the towel disposal bin. I locked myself in a cubicle. I pulled out the cloth zipper bag that was sewn into the lid lining of the cash case. I put the uniform and toy pistol into it, closed it, locked it and dumped it. I removed the Security Company metal plate from the case and it became an ordinary leather document case. The chain I unclipped and dropped into the toilet cistern. They only check them every twenty years. I went into the washroom, put a dime into the electric shaver and shaved off my moustache. Vroom vroom. I'd had it for two years and I was sorry to see it go. It was a real Pedro Armandariz. I trimmed it back to a Doug Fairbanks and finally a thin Errol Flynn before demolishing it altogether. Easy come, easy go. I put a little talc across the white upper lip and I was a new man. I'd been frightened that one of the bank clerks would come into the men's room while I was killing my face-fungus, but I needn't have worried. They have their own toilet right there in the bank.

Liz was waiting. She'd reversed her coat and put on a hairpiece which hung loose at the back. She looked no more than nineteen with that little-girl hairdo. She looked great, great! I know that she was angry at me for staring at her, but it would have been more suspicious not to have stared. She looked *sensationnelle*. Oh boy, she did. She'd reversed her coat to become an ocelot.

That helicopter trip is a futuristic freak-out. It's like throwing yourself off a skyscraper in slow motion. Can you imagine that big jet copter inching off the edge of the Pan Am building, then suddenly 57 floors below, Park Avenue full of yellow cabs slides under us. Almost near enough to touch is the Chrysler spike. I looked for the Continuum building where those two little toy men were guarding the front of that false safe; crunch. I opened the envelope that had my air ticket and expenses in it. (Silas would be angry if I spent any of the operation money en route). There it was, a neat type-written slip with plane times and a bar in London where I should leave a message if there was an emergency. Just like a military operation. Silas sat up the front and never looked out of the window. Liz was just looking at her nails and looking at the men who were looking at her, which gave her quite a lot of action. At Kennedy I changed on to the big jet plane. For hour after hour it hummed on across the Atlantic with the stewards trying to sell cheap lighters and artificial silk scarfs, and serving little plastic dinners. Any police message would say travelling together, so why make things easy; first class to London direct for Liz, first class via Shannon for Silas, and a tourist flight to Manchester for me with a train ride down to London. But there would be no police messages; certainly not today, not tomorrow either, nor Monday. Well, Monday maybe. Police messages. Imagine getting off this aeroplane and have a couple of smiling law men waiting to put the irons across you.

Charlie was a smiling law man. Charlie was the most vicious screw on the block. A big fat smiling type with a balding head and a gold tooth. It was like he realised that he looked like a nasty piece of work and finally let art follow nature. He caught me with the two ounces of snout right in my hand, grabbed me by the hair and swung me round in the exercise yard until my feet slid from under me; then he

51

let go. Slam against the wall.

Peter the bigamist saved me from being kicked bloody. He had nerves of steel Peter did. He stood up to Charlie without a word and Charlie backed down.

Charlie was going to get me for that. I mean, could anyone doubt it. He'd backed down in front of a yard full of hard cases and that was a dangerous thing for a screw to do. So Charlie would put the boot into me. It was just a matter of time.

'It's just a matter of time sonny,' Charlie said. He didn't believe in discipline except by knocking people around.

'He'll get you,' Peter the bigamist warned me. 'And when he has a go at you, kick the shit out of him, it's your only chance.'

'Yeah O.K.' I said, and I looked at Charlie who was a giant and wondered which bit of him I'd kick first when he started to have a go at me. It's no good worrying, I always say. But I always worry.

*　　*　　*

The next time I shaved was Monday morning. We were in our London flat eating breakfast. It was a pretty little place. The windows were poky and my room was no bigger than a cupboard, but it was cozy and warm. The mews outside was cobbled and our neighbours were starlets and young stockbrokers, as well as chauffeurs who lived near their cars and washed them and polished them and could be heard banging garage doors at three o'clock in the morning. The flat was so small – a 'mews cottage' the agent's list said – that it didn't need much furniture to make it 'fully furnished.' My bed was the kind you have to have if something goes wrong with your backbone, and the refrigerator would only hold three bottles of champagne and a tin of caviar. Silas said we would have to get another one if we wanted to keep milk and butter cool too. There was one thing that I liked; an electric toaster. I plugged it in near the table so that I could make toast without going into the kitchen. I bought lots of wrapped bread, and I posted them into that machine as fast as I could spread butter and jam on them. I like toast very much, and with this machine you could select it to be dark, light or medium. Dark, I liked best.

Silas was dressed up in a silk dressing gown and paisley scarf and Liz was in a fluffy sort of coat with an ostrich feather collar. Right, but I didn't see any reason to come to the table like the first act of an English play, so I was taking a little toast and coffee and shaving at the same time.

Silas said, 'You look like a survivor from a particularly harrowing sea disaster.' I pulled my dressing gown tighter and folded the collar more neatly.

Silas said, 'Why aren't you up at dawn doing Royal Canadian Air Force exercises?'

'I haven't even got an aeroplane,' I said.

'Must you use that terrible machine at the breakfast table?' I switched the razor off.

'I've thought of a good thing to do with this,' I said.

'Have you?' said Silas.

I said, 'Shave a round piece from the top of your head like you are going bald, see?'

Silas grunted.

'Start selling hair restorer, and you can prove your hair is really growing back. Because it would be, on account of you've shaved it. Got me? They'd come running for that one, I tell you.'

'Pass me the butter,' said Silas. He turned his newspaper inside out while I took some more coffee. 'And don't rest your elbows on the meal table.'

'They're not my elbows,' I said, 'they're my knees,' Liz giggled and so did I.

'I wish you wouldn't do that,' said Silas.

Well, I hadn't even noticed that I'd belched, but I know it's one of those things that he's very funny about. 'It's

53

considered very polite to do that in China,' I said.

'Really,' said Silas. 'I'll remember that when we enter that vast and ever growing area of operations.'

Liz said, '300,000 suckers born every minute.'

Silas gave his remember-they-are-only-young-people, type of smile and I called the cat. The cat went with the flat. Its name was Santa Claus. Or, I suppose that might have been claws, as a joke. I called the cat and offered it a bit of buttered toast, but it didn't respond. I put a little apricot jam on it and called the cat again. It ran toward me but kept on going and jumped up onto Silas's knee. Silas stroked it without even noticing it, and the cat stared up at him as Liz did sometimes. Some men are like that, without doing anything, cats and women just adore them. I finished shaving and went on reading my book.

'What's everyone doing this morning?' said Silas. 'After we leave the bank I mean.'

'Are we going to the bank first?' said Liz.

'Of course we are,' said Silas. 'What do you want to do, leave all that money lying around under the bed? Certainly, that's the first thing to do; get that stuff into a good strong vault.'

'Are we going to buy a car?' Liz said.

'I've arranged all that,' said Silas. He pushed the cat off his knee.

'I want a car of my own,' I said. 'I'm fed up with having to ask you every time I want to go anywhere.'

'Just as you wish,' said Silas. 'If you want to undertake all the trouble and expense, then do.'

'I want a red car.'

'Very well,' said Silas putting down his newspaper. 'Have any car you wish. I shall of course deduct expenses and set aside our "projects fund" for the next operation, but after that there will still remain a sizeable payment for each of you.' I said, 'Can I buy two cars? A Mini Cooper as well as a Rolls.'

'No,' said Silas. 'I bought two cars when I was a young man.'

I was going to say something corny like "did they have cars then?" but I didn't want to spoil his good mood. Silas went on, 'I had them both delivered simultaneously and they were outside the door shining like an RSM's boots. The neighbours were discussing them, and my younger brother stood near them just to get a bit of the glory. I went out and looked at each of them, as though making sure they were what I ordered, and then I got into the front one and started it up. The motor caught first time, and I pumped the accelerator and made the devil of a din. I made sure the gear lever was fully in, because I didn't want the gears to crash, and then I let in the clutch. Too quickly of course, I wasn't a very skilled driver. But I had the gear in reverse and bang I went back into the other car and smashed both of them severely. I can remember the neighbours trying not to laugh. My God the humiliation. I never owned two cars again. Never, no matter how much money I made on an operation, I never bought two cars.'

'A yellow car would be gorgeous,' Liz said. 'Yellow like mustard.'

'It's not a bad job this one,' said Silas. 'You'll have enough for a mink or a diamond.'

'I just want you,' said Liz and she kissed Silas. He was embarrassed but he needn't have been. He should have been proud.

'We will have a really good time. A happy time I mean,' Silas said. Perhaps he was thinking about smashing up those cars when he was a kid, because he gave one of his rare loud laughs. It was disconcerting when he did that, because it was awfully easy to get the feeling that the joke was on you.

I said, 'I'm going to study.'

'Are you going to take lessons in animal magnetism?' said Liz. She ruffled my hair.

'Leave him alone,' said Silas. 'That might be a good idea

55

old son. Study what?'

I said, 'A foreign language, or history, or learn to fly a plane. Perhaps I'll study archaeology seriously, I think I could get really interested in that. Archaeology perhaps, that would be great.'

'Archaeology tomorrow,' said Silas. 'Today we're spending.' He tipped his coffee cup up to show that he wanted more.

Liz went into the kitchen to make some more coffee. I looked up from my book, 'I might learn gardening. Market gardening that could be very interesting.'

'What book are you reading?' asked Silas.

'Careers for boys,' I said.

'Careers for boys,' Silas screamed like it was the funniest thing he'd ever heard.

'Archaeology or flying a plane,' I said. 'They are my short list.'

Silas went to the kitchen door and shouted to Liz, 'You know what wonder boy is going to do?' Liz shouted, 'no.' Silas shouted, 'Learn to fly a plane. Brrrr.'

Silas started making a noise like a heavy aeroplane. It was typical that he didn't whistle like a jet plane. He went brar-rar-rar-rar, like he says the Nazi bombers went during the war, when he won all his medals. I didn't look up from my book. He went rar-rar-rar, with his hands held out like wings, banking as he came around the sofa. 'This is X. Xray to tower. X.Xray to tower, how are you receiving me? Over,' He said it in his stage American voice, running around the room.

I didn't want to get involved with the silly old twit, so without looking up from my book, I said, 'Receiving you loud and clear X.Xray, over.' He came low over the coffee table to buzz me, then he said, 'X.Xray to tower. My bomb load is jammed in the bomb bay. Request permission to land on runway 180. Over.'

'Permission refused X.Xray,' I told him. 'Go up to 20,000

56

feet. Set your compass due south toward the channel and bale out. Do you hear me, bale out. Over.' I turned to watch him for a moment.

Silas was still buzzing around the room with his arms out and now he went up to 20,000 running backwards and forwards along the silk sofa shouting 'X.Xray to tower. What, and risk this crate crashing on some women and kids somewhere in Surrey? No sirree. Over.' I read my book pretending that I didn't know he was jumping up and down on the sofa. I said, 'Tower to X.Xray. This is your Commanding Officer speaking. Now listen Butch. You're to set that ship on a course to the channel and bail out and that's an order. Do you hear me, that's an order goddammit. Over.'

'X.Xray to tower. There seems to be something wrong with my radio equipment. I'm coming in to try a landing. Let me have every light you've got.' Silas came swooping across the carpet at waist level going rar-rar-rar and imitating a spluttering motor while I tipped over the light and switched it on. Silas was making a terrific noise now, and getting lower and lower. He was being terrific, but I went on half reading. He did another circuit, still losing height, dropping a wing and correcting like the ace he was. He brought her in cool and steady right down the flight path over the rug and went into the fireplace among the tongs and brushes with a crunch like the end of the world.

'Errrh . . .' I started being the crash wagon.

'What the hell are you doing in the fireplace Silas?' Liz said from the doorway. Poor old Silas lay there, his broken body arched, where the airframe had snapped and one wing pointing drunkenly at the sky.

Women have no imagination. Silas was a simple case of arrested development. He had a mental age of about sixteen. That's why he'd been captain of his school and won medals in the war. And that's the reason he was such a natural at this confidence trick lark. But if Liz had tried to understand him better, and not put him down every time he was being a little childish, he might have developed into a human being instead of a clapped-out old tyrant.

'Silas just won the medal of honour,' I snapped at Liz. 'That's what he's doing in the fireplace.'

Chapter 5

LIZ

And my mother says wouldn't I like to have children. What I'd like is one adult man. I can't even go and make a jug of coffee without finding mentally retarded delinquents rolling around in the fireplace, playing aeroplanes. Silas got to his feet slowly and began fiddling with one of his gold cufflinks to persuade me that he'd been searching for it in the hearth. I poured out the coffee in silence. Bob pretended to read his book, then slowly he looked up at me and winked. It was difficult to remain angry.

Bob called to the cat again. It stared at him insolently and then went and brushed itself against Silas's leg. Silas stroked it perfunctorily but it wouldn't leave him.

'My car should be ready today. But first I must buy some clothes. I want shirts and two good English suits, and I'm thinking of buying a black leather overcoat.'

'Down to the ankle?' asked Bob. Silas nodded. Bob said, 'And a trilby hat turned down at the back, and little steel-rimmed spectacles.' Bob clicked his heels, 'So, Lieber madchen,' he said. 'May I present Oberbannfuhrer Schmidt of the Gestapo. Ach, he has a vay mit der madchen, hein? Nicht wahr?'

'Why don't you get dressed?' I said. He was still wearing his moth-eaten dressing gown, and this morning had dropped egg yolk and jam down the collar. His hair was uncombed and his chin only partly shaved. In his mouth there was a cigarette end that had shed ash on the table cloth to make large grey shapes where he had unsuccessfully attempted to brush it away. Silas on the other hand, in spite of his air disaster, was uncrumpled in silk dressing gown, and immaculate paisley scarf pinned into place in his open neck silk shirt. They were as different as two people could be.

Silas wore his Sal Lombardo outfit for our shopping spree in Bond Street. His hands were heavy with rings and gold identity bracelet, and his wrinkled, rugged face was masked by large sunglasses. He wore the vicuna coat, its belt tied in a rough knot and completed the effect with a white silk tie and black shirt with pinned collar. He kept saying 'Izzat so buddy?' and 'dwanna get kilt?' and as we left the flat he shot Bob with an imaginary sub machine gun.

He was smoking a large cigar as he led the way into Wighens – one of the most expensive of London's discreet gentlemen's outfitters.

'Sir?'

'I wanna suit,' said Silas.

'Yes, sir,' said the white-faced, stoop-shouldered shop assistant. 'What sort of suit did you have in mind?'

'One of these Limey dude outfits, tight trousers, nipped-in waist . . . you know; one of those dopey roundtop hats, whadya call em, Derbys?'

'Bowlers sir,' said the man, making no attempt to conceal his distaste.

'And stripe pants, old fashioned kind of jacket; ready-made, black. Stiff white collar, striped shirt. The whole bit, got me, the whole faggy bit. It knocks me out.'

'I think sir,' said the assistant, 'that there's a shop quite nearby that would be more suitable. I'll find out the exact address . . .'

'Listen boo-boo,' said Silas, 'dwanna get kilt mac?' 'You think I ain't good enough for your crummy clothes. Is that it?' He poked his finger inside his pocket.

'Not at all sir,' said the man, in a state of magnificently restrained panic.

'Then get the glad-rags handsome, make it snappy.'

'Sure thing,' said the assistant in a high voice. 'Very well sir, of course, sir, right away.' He waved Silas through a curtained doorway.

I could hear their voices in the fitting room. 'That's the trousers sir, the pants I mean.' There was a brief silence.

'Great threads,' said Silas.

'And the jacket looks well sir.'

'Not so dusty,' said Silas. A lot of the hoarseness was disappearing as he got into his native costume. 'In fact, rather good.'

'Indeed sir,' said the assistant. 'Perhaps . . . just a moment . . . there sir; a perfect fit.'

Silas came striding out of the fitting room, with the shop assistant dancing around him, tugging and patting, and nodding enthusiastically. He removed his jewellery and reached toward a tie rack – marked 'school and regimental'. He spanned it, grabbed one, and threw it around his neck, knotting it in one of those tiny English neurotic knots.

'That's an Old Harrovian,' said the assistant, some of his old hostility returning.

'That's right,' nodded Silas. 'I was school captain before the war.' Silas removed his sun glasses and put them into his top pocket.

'I like a chap who's not ashamed of his background, give me Peterhouse, Tanks and an M.C.C. while you're there.'

'Yes sir,' said the assistant. He gently took the sunglasses from Silas's top pocket, folded a white lawn 'kerchief to make two points and tucked it into the pocket. He leaned back to admire his handiwork and then smoothed the pocket.

Silas stepped over to the umbrella rack and began examining them with the concentration of a duellist choosing a rapier.

'Pigskin gloves?' said the assistant.

'Top hole,' said Silas. 'And a bowler; size seven, long fitting if you have it.'

'Right away sir,' said the assistant. By now Silas was speaking in a British accent that you could cut with a knife. His back was ramrod straight and he paced up and down, doing curious little turnabouts, and running the ferrule of his umbrella along the shelves of merchandise, and swinging it around and catching it.

The manager came hurrying from his office. I thought he was bringing something for Silas but he ran right by him to the door. He peered and said, 'There's two of them.' The shop assistant handed Silas his parcels with a preoccupied air. He said to the manager. 'There are two Rolls Royces outside.'

'They will be for us,' said Silas calmly from the rear of the shop, without even turning round to see the effect of his words. 'One black one for me, and a red one for my young friend here.'

'You fool, Silas,' I said. 'Are they hired?'

'Hired?' said Silas disdainfully. 'Certainly not.'

'You fool,' said Bob in admiration.

'Send your account there,' said Silas, handing the bowing manager a card. He walked out to receive the salutes of two grey uniformed men from the car showroom.

'And these sir?' asked the assistant following him onto the pavement and holding a box containing the Sal Lombardo outfit.

'Put it on the back seat,' said Silas. 'I like being him sometimes.'

Our shopping spree ended with the two Rolls Royces. Bob didn't even wait long enough to get himself a change of clothes. He was still in his roll-neck sweater and blue jeans.

What a magnificent car Silas had ordered. He had more foresight than Bob and I would ever have. Silas had ordered our black Rolls months before, when it was a matter of pure optimism that he would be able to pay for it.

It was a sleek black convertible and catered to a neurotic desire for privacy that was typical of Silas. The rear window was dark blue glass and the windows of the passenger compartment – including the driver's partition – had opaque blinds that blacked it out completely at the touch of a switch.

Instead of a bench seat at the rear, there were two luxury reclining aircraft seats which revolved electrically. There were no jump seats, instead there was a built-in cocktail cabinet and a miniature wardrobe complete with a tiny sink and a tall mirror. As Bob said when Silas was showing it off, we'd never be without living accommodation while we had a car like that. Silas made me sit in the reclining seat and tip it back while the stereo tape recorder played, and the shades went up and down, and the wardrobe doors were flipping open. When each of us had tried every seat and inspected all the gadgets, Bob said we should have a trip into the countryside.

Bob's gorgeous red Rolls was easy to spot in the busy Piccadilly traffic, and Silas kept on his tail. We whirled around Piccadilly Circus and up to Marble Arch, then on to High Wycombe. The Chiltern Hills darkened in a sudden squall, the rain beating hard against the gleaming coach-work. Then, just as quickly, it was bright again. I had forgotten how beautiful the English countryside could be. There were still thatched cottages and village greens where ducks splashed into the pond at the sound of our approach. Whether Bob knew his way I don't know, but he turned into narrow country lanes and inched slowly through a herd of self possessed Jerseys. He sailed over hump backed bridges and followed finger posts that, ignoring the large towns, directed us to smaller and smaller hamlets with detours through farm yards and tractor paths.

We went down a country road, and Bob, taking a corner too sharply, got one wheel stuck in a muddy ditch. The wheels spun uselessly. Silas crept up alongside in our open Rolls. He leaned across me.

'Ahoy, are y' heeving a wee bit of difficulty young mister Macallister?' called Silas.

'It's nothing ye ken, Andrew,' Bob replied leaning across to his window. 'It's just one o' the pistons on the bonny wee steam engine I invented last week.'

'Steam may be braw for crossing the Clyde laddie, but it will never take y' across the Atlantic,' yelled Silas.

'Mine's a fine ship Andrew. A fast bonny ship, and we'll be taking a wee deoch and dorris in Sauchiehall Street days before you dock.'

'Steam' yelled Silas, 'It's fit for toys laddie.' Bob revved the engine of the Rolls, and swore softly when the car failed to move. Silas smiled mockingly. Bob said, 'One day Andrew in the not far distant future – ships powered by steam will be crossing the Atlantic as regularly as ye tak y' morning porritch.'

There was a distant roll of thunder. Silas said, 'It's blowing up a mighty braw storm laddie. Would ye not be wiser to be taken in tow the noo? Coal may be a fine new way of propulsion, but whatever goes awa' wi' my ship, she'll never want for wind, ye ken.' Silas had our roof down and I felt a dab of rain. Silas looked up apprehensively at the clouds.

'You'll never want for wind yoursel', Andrew,' shouted Bob. 'Your fine ship's a wee bit open atween decks. I thinks she's making water.'

'Don't be disgusting, young mister Macallister,' shouted Silas. 'Don't be disgusting.' He pressed a button and the roof closed. Our Rolls moved forward leaving Bob still unable to move, as I turned back to watch he tried again very very slowly, and on the second attempt the car climbed back onto the tarmac. He came racing after us and hooted loudly. Soon the rain stopped and the sun came out again.

We sped confidently along waving and laughing, euphoric in our riches and bovine with success like three proud parents just delivered of a bouncing quarter million dollars. I stroked the soft leather of the seat. I loved those cars. I loved them in the morning; cold, gleaming and spotless, and I loved them at midday, mud-splattered and warm. At twilight their huge yellow lights blinked lazily as we turned into the long driveway of a country hotel. It had been a long day and we all went straight upstairs. Silas and I took separate rooms. We always did. Silas always said that then he knew I was joining him from choice and not necessity. I used my room to bath and dress, and gave Silas a tap on my way downstairs. He had a couple of phone calls to make and said he'd be down later.

I looked into Bob's room. He hadn't spent a lot of time dressing. His shirt was frayed and his tie was greasy because he insisted that it was a waste of time reknotting ties, and always slipped it over his head like a halter. His shoes were scuffed. Suede shoes, he said, were sensible; which meant that he never cleaned his. He was reading.

'It's fantastic,' he said. 'Mohenjo-daro; a sort of lost city of the ancient world. Destroyed by some mysterious army in about 1,500 BC (the exact date is hard to determine. . . .)'

'Are you reading archaeology books again?' I said.

'Modern scholars – remembering that the Aryan war god Indra is also known as *puramdara* – feel they might be able to offer a clue.'

'I'm going down to the bar,' I told him. 'Silas is phoning London.'

'*Puramdara* means fort destroyer of course.'

'Of course,' I said.

'Want to see the pictures? There they are. Their necks still adorned with beads and bracelets of faience, terracotta, etched carnelian agate and gold.' I shuddered. 'I'm going down for a drink,' I said, but I didn't move. He put an arm around me, without looking up from his book.

'The Indus Valley, that's where I'm going. I might unearth the mystery of its origin; still the most sought-after secret of the ancient world.'

'Yes,' I said. He turned around and looked up at me, 'I wish we lived in some remote little village somewhere in the country like this,' he said. 'Don't you?'

'Silas wouldn't like it,' I said.

'I wasn't thinking of Silas.'

'I know exactly what you were thinking,' I said. He

pushed his hair back from his eyes and was a little embarrassed. He was a handsome little brute, and I found myself looking at him in a way that I shouldn't have done. For a moment the atmosphere was charged.

'Come down to the bar when you're ready,' I said. 'I'm waiting there for Silas,' I patted his head and disengaged myself from his embrace.

It was a terribly pretty hotel; acres and acres of ground with a vast lake, smooth lawn and lots of trees. Behind the hotel was a river stretch famous for its fishing and outside I could hear a group of anglers talking.

It was just getting dark. The rainstorms had left the clouds swollen and red eyed. The trees were silhouetted against them, and under the trees rested our Rolls Royce motor cars.

The lounge was full of that very comfortable, beaten-up old furniture that only the English have. There was a large log fire smoking gently behind a selection of highly polished fire irons. In front of the fire there were a few ancient English people, making their afternoon tea last until supper time by calling for endless jugs of hot water. The barman was giving the glasses an extra polish.

I sat at the bar so that I could get at the peanuts. I ordered a Bloody Mary, but as I opened my bag to pay, a thin white hand gave the barman a pound note.

'Make it another one, the same,' said the man's voice.

It was Guthrie Grey, a young man with wavy hair and extra teeth that I had seen around Chelsea. I remember the mad party where I'd first noticed him. He'd plucked a tulip from a cut-glass vase and bitten the bright flower off at the neck. He chewed it and swallowed it, throwing the stalk across the room. A servant girl had watched him in eye popping dismay, and brushed past me to place herself between the vase and Geegee.

'Those tulips cost two and sixpence each,' said the maid.

'Delicious,' said Geegee. 'Here's five bob. I'll have another.' And he reached beyond her for another prize bloom and devoured it before she could catch her breath.

'Delicious,' he had repeated and offered to buy me one, but I had declined, and the maid, with two half crowns clamped in her tiny red hands, had hurried tearfully away. He'd begun to talk to me. He was a solicitor and, working against the stiff competition that London's legal scene provides, had proved to be one of the most incompetent solicitors in living memory. Twice, only the complex amenities of the law and the brotherly love of lawyers had saved him from being sued for negligence. Luckily Grey – or Geegee as he was known – had not allowed that to influence his good humour, and he was still able to treat his work with the same careless bonhomie with which he attended countless noisy parties. Geegee, looking not a day over 40, was nearly 28.

'What are you doing here old darling?' he said. He tugged at the knees of his brown suit and perched himself precariously alongside me on a bar stool.

'I have a new car,' I said. 'I just came out for a breath of air. What are you doing?'

'Working. I'm moving away from the legal profession actually. Nowadays I do a lot of public relations work. It's much more entertaining, this P.R. stuff.' The drinks came along.

'Cheers, Geegee,' I said. 'Here's to entertainment.'

'Entertainment,' said Geegee, 'is half my life.'

'Oh,' I said, laughingly. 'And what's the other half?'

'Ritual,' said Geegee unctuously. 'The sinful ritual of hard commerce.' He bared his teeth in a silent ritual laugh.

'Is that what you are doing here?' I asked him.

'Yes,' he said. 'We handle Magazaria.'

'Do you eat it or rub it on your spots?'

'It's what they call an emergent African nation darling,' he said. 'I'm taking their War Minister down to see some brass-hat chums of mine. Won't be any use though. That's

67

why I'm lushing him up a bit *en route*. Let him down by easy stages, what?' he smiled again.

'What won't be of any use?'

'He wants to buy guns, bombs and tanks for his army, but the Ministry of Defence won't play ball.'

'That's too bad.'

'Too right, old girl. My firm could lose the whole account if those blighters upset him. They say -- on the quiet - that he's planning a *coup d'etat* and they don't want to be involved. You know how the Ministry of Defence are, darling, if they can find a way of saying no. Still I suppose you don't know how the Ministry of Defence are.' He laughed.

'As a matter of fact,' I said, 'I do know. My uncle Dudley is one of the senior people there. I don't know exactly what he does, but he's in charge of the Weapons and Equipment Department. Would that be surplus and obsolescent equipment?'

'My darling girl, it would indeed be exactly that, but one man's surplus my sweet is another man's treasure.' He finished his drink and had another. 'Could you have a word with nunkie?'

'Well if you are taking him down there today to get a decision, I doubt if I could get it reversed.'

'Look my love. If you are going to pull some strings, I'll head him away from that fatal meeting.'

'I'll need the names of the people so far involved,' I said. 'Uncle won't do a thing until he's studied the office politics.'

'Understood old girl,' he wrote the names of his contacts on a piece of paper. I selected one of the names, Major General Maurice Symonds-Forstenholme. 'I know him,' I said. 'Why don't I talk to him instead?'

'Old Forstenholme?'

'If it's the man I'm thinking of, he's rather taken with me.'

'Good God, old Forstenholme? Who'd have thought it?'

'I'll phone him now if you like,' I said.

'What a splendid idea,' said Geegee. 'Do you know the number?'

'No,' I said.

'I'll get the directories to find it. He lives in Surrey some-where. We'll take the call upstairs eh?'

'Don't get ideas Geegee.'

'Oh, I say, no.'

He raised his hands and crossed his heart, but he needn't have done. I know a harmless boob when I see one. I took a red silk square from my bag, and tied it to the strap.

Directory enquiries found the phone number of this General. He was in Surrey as Geegee had said. 'You're not putting me on?' said Geegee. 'You do really know him?'

'To tell you a secret,' I said, 'we once had a tête-a-tête dinner at the Savoy. I know him rather well.' Geegee asked the hotel telephonist to get the General. Five minutes later the phone rang. 'General Forstenholme?' said Geegee. 'Just one moment General.' Geegee gave me the phone. I said. 'You'll never guess . . . it's Liz Smallwood. You know Admiral Smallwood's daughter. My uncle is Sir Dudley Cavendish at the Ministry. Ha ha ha. Well, I wasn't sure you would remember, it's some time ago. Oh, you are an old flatterer. Terribly well. Yes, he's well too. Well, I've been doing all the yawny usuals; Monte, Perthshire and St. Moritz. Well look, Forsty . . . ah yes, I did remember. Look Forsty, they tell me you are the absolute top level man on this meeting with the African politicians. . . . Yes Magazaria, it's the funniest name I ever heard of. Well, I think you ought to let them have whatever they want Forsty, I've known them all for years and they are terribly nice, terribly reliable . . . but, Forsty, they are so terribly pro-British and you know how unusual that is nowadays. Yes, pro-British, terribly pro-British. Well, perhaps that's just their way of talking. I mean it can be frightfully embarrassing *telling* someone how much you adore them, you must find that. . . . Well that's the same for them,' then I said, 'Just a moment Forsty, I can't hear you properly, I must turn the radio down.' I capped the phone and said to Geegee, 'That's torn it, he wants to know what my Uncle Dudley, in the Ministry, thinks of Magazaria and the War Minister.'

'He's all for it,' said Geegee. 'Tell him, he's all for it, loves it. Just crazy for it.' I shushed Geegee, and uncapped the phone.

'Uncle Dudley is madly for it. He thinks he's really reliable, he thinks. . . .'

Geegee hissed, 'Mr. Ibo Awawa.'

'Mr. Ibo Awawa is the kindest and most reliable man in Africa . . . yes, well apart from white people, I suppose he meant.'

Geegee was getting anxious.

'Lowther?' I said, 'and he is the man who can say yes or no . . . and the committee will just accept his recommendation like that? Did I meet him? . . . Well, there were so many people there, and such a lot of champagne. . . . Yes, yes, I'll write it down, I'm just getting a pencil, wait a moment.'

Geegee had a pencil to hand so fast that he tore the stitching on his waistcoat pocket. I wrote the name down carefully. 'Brigadier S. Lowther, D.S.O., M.C. I wrote, being unable to think of another name with the initials S.L.

Silas Lowther is Silas's real name. At least I think it is. Whatever alias he used, it had to have the initials S.L. because Silas had so many shirts, hair brushes, suitcases, studs and handkerchiefs bearing that monogram.

To the phone I said, 'Well, couldn't I have his private address? I don't want to phone the Ministry. They keep you waiting hours at the switchboard. 25 Baker Place Mews East, London, W.1. No phone, well, that's all right, I'll get the phone number from directories, that's how I got your number, Forsty darling. No, now it's written down in my address book. Of course I will, how can you say such a thing? Well, I don't call that old, not old in your *ways*. In your *ways* you are very, very, young. Oh. Of course and so must you.

Goodbye Forsty, you've been a darling. Goodbye.' I hung up, just as General Forstenholme had done after the first few incomprehensible sentences. A hoaxer, he'd called me.

'And this chap is the fellow, eh?' said Geegee.

'He's your man,' I said, giving Geegee the slip of paper with our mews flat address. 'What he decides goes?'

'That's it,' I said. 'So now you can buy me a large meal. I want to meet Mr. Ibo Awawa, the War Minister, and hear everything I can about Magazaria.'

'You'll hear that,' said Geegee. 'But it's pretty dull stuff.'

'Not to me it isn't,' I said.

We had dinner in the main dining room; Geegee, Awawa and myself. A strange trio: Geegee, tall, thin and awkward and, like so many Englishmen of his type, perpetually embarrassed in the presence of a woman. Awawa on the other hand, in spite of his peasant origins, or maybe because of them, completely at ease from the moment he appeared. He was a gay old buffer. A big bull of a man, thick set shoulders and large muscular hands all of which made him pretty sexually attractive as far as I was concerned, although perhaps I'd be reluctant to admit it to Silas. His skin was as black as coal, looking even darker because of his grey moustache. He had a large mouth and he smiled often.

I'd have thought Geegee would have acted the part of the host, ordering the wines and that sort of thing, but not at all. Awawa wasn't a man who let others make decisions, if he could help it. 'Don't have the sole,' Awawa told me. 'I had it for lunch. It's frozen, and the Mornay sauce is floury.'

'What shall I have then?'

'You are offended.'

'Not in the least, what shall I have?'

'First; the lobster. I saw the crates marked, "Live Lobsters" so they will be fresh, not frozen. After that take a steak, the waiter told me that it's local meat, and they hang it for a week. It will be superb.'

'I can't bear the idea of live lobsters being crammed up

inside those crates,' I said. 'It gives me the creeps. I'd sooner have a frozen lobster than a tortured one.

'You must not be squeamish, said Awawa. 'In my country they do worse things than that to men.

'Why don't you stop them?' I said.

'Perhaps one day I shall,' said Awawa. Out of the corner of my eye I saw Geegee's face twitch. Or was it the smallest possible shake of the head.

'You can't blame us any longer, Mr. Awawa,' I said. 'You are running your own country now aren't you?'

'Running it,' said Awawa and for a moment he did not answer. 'If we had our own natural resources and were financially solvent, then we would be running it, but that I'm afraid, is not the case.

'My people are ignorant. They want education, but also they want consumer goods of the sort they see in Hollywood films. They want refrigerators and motor cars and large houses. It's difficult to explain to them that it is better – at this stage – to be poor but educated.'

'Is it better?'

'It is,' said Awawa. 'But, I made my money out of selling worldly goods, so I am rather suspect when I tell my people to not covet them.' He smiled as though that closed the subject. The waiter arrived. Awawa and Geegee ordered lobster and steak, and I ordered foie gras and steak. 'And don't say foie gras isn't cruel,' said Awawa.

'Is it?' I said. Men always love to explain things, so I give them every chance I can.

'I'd better not tell you,' said Awawa, 'until after the meal.'

'Very well. Tell me about your worldly goods.' He hesitated at first, but it was not difficult to get him talking.

'There is not much to tell. My parents were the very poorest peasants it's possible to imagine. When I was thirteen I went to Port Bovi. We were a big family and my father was happy to have one less to feed – or rather not feed. My first job was sweeping the floor in a workshop. British soldiers and civilians worked there repairing telephones, typewriters and that sort of thing. It was the thirties, and the British thought that they would be running my country for ever. So did I.

'It was a good job, as jobs for thirteen year old negro children in Port Bovi went in the thirties. Some of the Englishmen there were kind and pleasant men. Some of them were victims of the depression that had provided the British Army with a generous supply of manpower. I swept up carefully, for I didn't want to lose that job. When I saw a piece of metal shining among the dust I picked it out and returned it to the workbench.

'The next vital stage of my life came when I realised that certain shaped pieces of metal were needed on the bench where the telephones were repaired, and other shapes of metal were needed on the typewriter bench. Not long after that we got a new sweeper, and I was promoted to being a general dogsbody; getting the tea and carrying the crates and occasionally – happy day – handling a screwdriver, and handling a typewriter.

'I well remember the first day of the war; September the third, nineteen thirty-nine. How we all cheered. The British cheered too, and were happy that we were cheering, but they didn't know why we were cheering. We hoped that the British would go away to the war and leave us in peace. At first we were disappointed, for even more soldiers came. More civil servants came too. The Americans came and rebuilt the port, so that huge ships could now stop there. All the time more and more ships, more and more men, more and more aeroplanes, more and more offices and forms to fill out, reports to complete and things to order.'

'More and more typewriters,' I said.

'Exactly. And by now I was developing a talent for mending typewriters.'

'And when the war ended?'

'You think that there were less typewriters then? No Miss

73

Smallwood, armies sometimes suffer casualties but civil services only expand. By 1947 there were so many typewriters in the country that the British Administration invited tenders for a company to take over the servicing of them. I was a skilled typewriter repairman by that time. I had some headed notepaper printed and, using what was perhaps the best typewriter in the country, I applied for the contract. It was a fine looking letter that I typed. I signed it, Head of Contract Dept. The only other companies applying for the contract were in Britain, my bid was far below theirs. What's more I offered to buy condemned typewriters, which although no good by European standards, were repairable given the hours I put in on them.'

'Were the British angry when they found they had given a contract to one of their lowly workers?'

'Let us say apprehensive, but by that time I spoke good English. I had always got along very well with the people in the workshops, none of whom wanted to set up a typewriter business themselves, so it was all quite acceptable. By the time the British withdrew I was rich. My name was put forward as a possible member of the new government. I'd never had anything to do with politics before, so everyone thought I was on their side; I was accepted. Simple.'

'So you say,' I said.

'Well I have omitted some of the miserable bits,' he smiled.

'What sort of miserable bits?'

'When rich white soldiers without women live among starving families, tragedies occur. Such things have scarred the memories and still they cripple the reason of our men.'

'These guns you want, are they a part of the miserable bit?'

'Yes. They are.'

'Shooting people will make things better?'

'I doubt it, but then I don't want to shoot anyone. The guns are merely a token, a weight upon one side of a scales that are already unfairly laden the other way.'

74

'Who has his thumb on the scale pan right now?' I asked.

'Ah here comes the lobster. It's cruel to keep it in a crate, you say. Well, you may be right, but I shall enjoy every mouthful. If one of these days I suffer the same fate, I only hope that someone enjoys every mouthful of me. Mayonnaise. Thank you, yes. Mayonnaise will complete the pleasure.' He smiled suddenly. 'Cheer up, Miss Smallwood. A beautiful girl like you should not look so concerned. Leave the worrying for ugly old men like me. And ugly young men like Mr. Grey, eh, Grey?' He laughed and slapped Geegee's arm.

'Goodness,' said Geegee. 'Yes indeed.'

'You haven't answered my question,' I told Awawa.

'What was the question?' he said.

'Guns mean war,' I said. 'Why must men have wars?'

'The voice of womanhood, and reason raised accusingly against the senseless violence of the male,' said Awawa. 'Well we've heard that one before Miss Smallwood, but women are less able to cooperate with each other, than men are. Women are less tolerant than men, and women in business more ruthless than men.'

'That's just a generalisation,' I told him. 'Give me an example.'

'I can prove my point only in negative terms,' said Awawa. 'Isn't it enough that there is not one company you can think of, that is run entirely by women? When people tell me that I am prejudiced against women, I ask them if they know a woman who had a woman lawyer or a woman architect. At one time I employed both. No, if you want to know who is most intolerant of women's emancipation, it is women.'

'You are evading the question again,' I said. 'That's just like a politician, isn't it Geegee?'

'Don't bring me into this old darling,' said Geegee. 'I've got a vested interest in keeping Mr. Awawa on the winning side of his arguments.'

'Why does there have to be a *winning* side?' I asked.

'Why can't one argue without being competitive?'

'My dear girl,' said Awawa. 'We live in a competitive society. It's the very crux of our system. Capitalism produces the best cars and refrigerators. . . .'

'. . . and typewriters.'

'Yes and typewriters, and guns too. Each man competes with his fellow man. You say to a man, "buy this motor car because it goes faster, and will therefore make you more powerful, more important, more virile, more desirable, than the man next door." And then you also say to him, "But don't go fast in your car, and if you see the man next door, don't overtake him to prove that you are more powerful than he is." Well of course the world becomes neurotic. Two different commands, random punishments for each; that's how they give monkeys ulcers.'

'What has that to do with guns?' I asked him.

'The logical end-product of competition is physical competition.' He smiled. 'For the individual the two purest forms of free enterprise are prostitution (passive form), and robbery with violence (active form).' He turned to Geegee. 'What do you say to that, Grey?' he asked.

'What me sir? Prostitution every time sir, if you ask me. Sin every time,' Geegee wasn't the idiot that he liked to be thought. He'd been listening to Awawa very closely but was determined to be the buffoon.

'And so Miss Smallwood,' said Awawa. 'The apparent outcome of world-wide free enterprise is technology. The obvious outcome of world-wide competition is warfare; *ipso facto*: technological warfare.'

'You are a cynical man Mr. Awawa,' I said. 'So that's your opinion: war will destroy us?'

'Perhaps man will reach some sort of political compromise that will modify the undisciplined competitive urges, that at present we are allowing to run riot. Already in Europe there is an attempt to form supra national bodies, the U.N. is not without some brilliant successes. In Africa I look forward to broader and broader political thinking.'

'Oh come along,' I protested. 'Hardly a week goes by, without some new subdivisions in Africa. I see no sign of federation there.'

'Divide and rule is the philosophy of all the great nations, Miss Smallwood, and their power and influence is immense. None of them would welcome a Federated States of Africa to the political arena.'

'But you are going to do something about that?'

'Philosophy, Miss Smallwood, like charity, should begin at home.'

'Even the philosophy of guns?'

'Sometimes, Miss Smallwood, although I can see you don't agree.'

'I don't agree. I don't disagree, luckily I don't have to make a decision, but it won't influence my introduction to my Uncle's friends if that's what you mean.'

Awawa bowed politely. 'Your steak is getting cold Miss Smallwood," said Awawa. 'Béarnaise?' He helped me to a portion. 'On the steak?'

'Yes,' I said. 'On the steak.' It was too late to help the angus.

Chapter 6

SILAS

I was settling down in my room for half an hour with a drink and the business pages of *The Times*, when Bob came running in to tell me that Liz had displayed the fully operational marker.

'She's tied the red scarf on her bag. Do you think she's on to something?' he asked.

'It's hard to say,' I told him. 'She's been wrong before, more than once, but if you have a signal system, then the other members of the expedition must stick to the procedure.' I pulled my shoes on.

'So we're leaving the hotel?'

'Yes,' I said, 'but wait a few minutes. We mustn't walk through the bar while she's there. Being seen, even fleetingly, by a mark has spoiled more operations than any other factor.'

'How do you know? I mean, I'm sure you're right, but how do you know?' asked Bob.

'Research,' I said. I put on my jacket and adjusted the handkerchief in my top pocket. I poured myself a small drink of red wine. I offered a glass to Bob, but he didn't want any. After a short pause we went outside. I decided to leave Bob's Rolls for Liz, and I left a message to that effect with the manager. It was a dark night with just a scrap of moon. It would be a long drive back. I debated whether to ask the kitchen for sandwiches and take the opened bottle of wine with us. Bob jingled the car keys in his hand, 'Shall I drive?' he said. He rubbed the windscreen with his handkerchief.

'No I'll drive,' I told him. He looked at me wondering if I'd been drinking.

'Whatever you say,' he said.

No other mess drank like ours. That long gleaming oak table. It must have been twenty feet long and shining so bright that every face in the mess was reflected upside down amongst the cutlery and glasses. Or am I misremembering. Was that some other evening in a peacetime mess in England, commanding officers glowering down on us from oak panelled walls, mess silver ranged down the table, and a silver trolley that bore the port along the gleaming tabletop.

Colonel Mason sat watching the slow ritual of the evening meal. The junior officers were nervous of him. Bertie, the adjutant, had drunk a lot and so had I. Now and again some officer, feeling uncomfortable in the strained silence, would remark upon the enemy build-up to the north of us. Bertie had some story about Rommel fitting high velocity guns to his Mark 4 tanks, but Bertie was too drunk to remember the details properly. Old Colonel Mason said something about his officers not talking shop. 'It's coming,' said Bertie, turning on the Colonel and speaking very loudly. 'And you mark my words. A big tank battle. It's the only thing that can stop Rommel now, and even if our casualties are double his, G.H.Q. Cairo will consider that cheap.'

Colonel Mason stood up, his face taut with anger. He wore breeches and highly polished riding boots; for a cavalry man these damn tanks were nothing but a passing phase. He was a peacetime soldier. After-dinner talk was horses, not battles; and Generals were prescient, just, and impeccably right. He walked slowly the length of the mess tent.

'If my mess can't hold its drink, we'll have water on the table,' he said. 'You should take a leaf from Captain Lowther's book.' He looked at me. 'I'll say this for you, Lowther, you hold your drink better than any man in the mess.' He turned and opened the tent flap noisily.

I waited until the Colonel had left the mess and then I got

unsteadily to my feet. I was quite drunk, the chianti had been circulating for hours in the heady, almost silent, meal over which Mason liked to preside. I took one last swig of wine. It was a damn sight more to my taste than the usual Stella beer.

Bertie said softly, 'He's going sand-happy. He'd be happier in the Afrika Korps if you ask me.'

'*Ma'alesh*,' I said. That meant I couldn't care less, and it was our favourite word at the time.

I left the mess tent. It was dark out here in the desert miles away from any town. I saw the blur of a cigarette end as my troop sergeant threw it down and doused it under his foot.

'Hello Brian,' I said. 'I'm the best drinking man in the mess.' There was no point in not remarking on it. From there he must have heard every word that was said in the tent.

'That's it sir,' he said. The taste of the captured Italian wine was still in my mouth. It was as still as only a desert night can be. Everyone was in night-leaguer and except for a few flashes on the horizon there was not a movement anywhere. Drinking had made me feel hot and I longed for a breath of wind.

'It's a long drive,' Brian warned, 'a lot of it on sand.'

'I'll drive,' I said. 'Where's the gharry?' He looked at me carefully before handing me the keys of the loaded Bedford lorry. He was a conscript, a young Londoner full of energy and personally loyal to me as well as being a first class tank man and best damned troop sergeant in the Regiment. I liked young Brian. He climbed into the lorry with me and wiped the windscreen with a dirty handkerchief. 'Whatever you say,' Bob said.

It was 1.48 a.m. When Liz arrived back at the mews flat having driven through the night from Dorset. She was excited, breathless and slightly tipsy. She kicked her shoes across the lounge and dropped into a soft chair. 'This is it,' she pronounced. 'And that red Rolls really did it right for an Admiral's daughter.' Perhaps it was some trick of the light or the way she held her head but she looked like a little girl just home from school.

'Do the report properly,' I told her.

'You want a written report tonight, darling?'

'No, the morning will do for that, but sort out the facts now in a businesslike way.'

'My contact is Guthrie Grey (known as Geegee), solicitor, but now working for a public relations company. That company is the P.R. for a new African nation named Magazaria.'

Bob said, 'Never heard of it.'

'Why should you have?' said Liz. 'It's not much bigger than Regent's Park, but it's loaded with copper and tin.' Bob said, 'We could use Amalgamated Minerals again. Use the same notepaper and cables. . . .'

'No,' said Liz. 'This is much better than that.'

I had a feeling right then that this was going to be a good operation. A very good operation.

'Report the men,' I told Liz, getting out my notebook. 'Carry on with Grey.'

Liz said, 'Guthrie Grey "Geegee." White. Male. 28. Heterosexual, British born, British citizen. Balliol College, Oxford, then became a solicitor. Earnings: approx two and a half thousand a year, plus small private income. Politically conservative but uncommitted. Religion: Christian, with intermittent church attendances. Unathletic, but average build (about 12 stone). Five feet ten. Not very attractive physically but quite presentable. Shy with strangers but becomes talkative. Rational in argument, not very emotional. Probably would like to be married, with children. Not highly sexed. Expensive suit, two or three years old. Leisure: parties, theatre going, badminton and squash, but usually as a spectator. Sailing in the summer. Drinks: a bit above average, but not above a PR man's average. Has a flat in London and often visits his parents house in Hampshire. His father is a prosperous country solicitor.'

'Well done,' I said. 'And the other one?'

81

'Ibo Awawa. Negro. Male, 48 or thereabouts, hetero-sexual. Magazarian born, Magazarian citizen. Salary four thousand sterling, plus about three in corruption. (Both these figures are from Geegee.) Politics: Pan African but to some extent motivated by self-interest. Moslem religion, virtually non-practising except for being teetotal. His election image is religious. Unathletic, fairly heavy build (perhaps 15 stone). Somewhat attractive physically, has a commanding presence. Talkative, very emotional. Not very rational in argument. Is married with two wives and at least eleven children. (Geegee's figures again.) Highly sexed and probably very attractive to certain women. Expensive, London bought clothes. Leisure: well, as I say, highly sexed. Apart from that, his time is entirely devoted to furthering his political am-bition. He's determined to go places. Doesn't drink. No money in the family. Parents were peasants. They are both dead.'

I finished writing in my notebook. I smiled appreciatively at Liz. 'An excellent report,' I said.

Liz told us about the dinner and the story of Awawa's type-writer business and career.

'And now?' I asked.

'He's the War Minister. He's a sharp fellow. He's seen these African revolutions before and noticed that the man with the army behind him sits in the driving seat. He wants to buy guns for his soldiers.'

'To stage a coup?' I asked.

'Hard to say, but from what Geegee dropped, the War Office think he wants to stage a coup. That's why Geegee has been told, unofficially, that Awawa won't get arms from Britain.'

'Why would they tell Geegee?' Bob asked.

'It's a good way to handle it,' I said. 'Let the PR man break it gently. He's got most to lose if Awawa is upset.'

Liz said, 'Awawa wants guns . . .'

'Any sort of guns?' I asked. I was writing her replies

in shorthand.

Liz shook her head, 'Anti-tank guns primarily. And ammunition. Bazookas.'

'Bazookas. Right. Anything else?'

'That's what he wants most, but he'd also buy machine pistols, and hand grenades. Mind you I'd say he'd buy almost anything, except steel helmets, uniforms, rifles and rifle ammunition. The British left him loads of those.'

'What did you tell him?' I asked Liz.

Liz explained her false phone call to General Forstenholme. She had cast me in the role of Brigadier Lowther. Single. Small private income. Excellent social connections. Good war record. Important job at the Defence Ministry. Living alone in this mews flat. A few girl friends (among which Liz was not cast) and lots of ambition. Well, that shouldn't be too difficult.

It was clear that Liz and Bob must move out before morning. It would compromise the whole operation if the marks saw either of them around here. 'I'll get you each a suite at the Chester,' I said. 'We'll go now and finish this council of war over there.'

Bob and Liz scooped their possessions up in their arms and bundled them into the back seat of Bob's Rolls. I put on my overcoat and reached for the new bowler hat. No, I decided I wouldn't wear the bowler. I had been having a little trouble with my head lately. Sometimes it was so swollen that I couldn't get my hat on. At other times my skull had contracted in a frightening way. I hoped that it was only a temporary ailment, but if it didn't cure itself soon I would have to consult a quack. It was no good looking to Liz or Bob for sympathy. I put the bowler hat aside regretfully.

We all went to the Chester Hotel, which was only 10 minutes drive. By the time we got there it was 2.15 a.m. They mustered every man jack of the staff to carry that stuff up to the two suites I rented. I hadn't realised how much stuff the two of them had purchased in our short stay in London.

There was about three dozen dresses, hundreds of shoes, two miniature TV sets, Bob's fur coat, Santa Claus the cat, a rocking chair that I feared belonged to the mews cottage, a folding motor cycle, more LP records than I could count, and a huge stereo player. Bob had a complete set of the *Encyclopædia Britannica* and bundles of archaeology books tied up with string, a portable typewriter and a stainless steel spade. The endless chain of uniformed staff were marching through the hotel like the bearers of a particularly lavish safari. When all the stuff was in the right suites, and Bob's car parked nearby, we slumped down in Bob's suite and rang for room service.

A short thick-set waiter knocked on the door and entered.

'Yes sir?' he said.

'We could do with a little refreshment,' said Bob. 'A jug of chocolate, some biscuits and a bottle of brandy, soda and ice.'

'Right sir,' said the waiter.

'You're Spider Cohen, aren't you?' said Bob. The waiter grinned shyly like a girl. He nodded and retired. 'It's a feller I know,' Bob explained to us.

'I don't doubt it,' I said. 'You seem to know all the un-influential people in London.'

'That's it,' agreed Bob cheerfully. 'I have a lot of friends that I only see every couple of years or so. I have a sort of superficial relationship with all my friends.'

'Now that I've seen one of them, I can see the wisdom of that,' I said.

Liz said, 'When you persuade Ibo Awawa that you can approve the arms sale from the British Defence Ministry; he'll pay. And he'd pay in used oncers, no cheques or money transfers. He's prepared to pay cash. He said so.'

I said, 'Did you imply that I could be sweetened?'

'No,' said Liz. 'I didn't know how you'd want to play it.'

'Right,' I said.

Bob said, 'Couldn't we have him deposit a case full of

money at an office in the Defence Ministry? I could be a staff officer waiting in the entrance.'

'No,' I said. 'No. No. No.' I leaned forward and explained quietly. 'A con man is a judo fighter. There's no mark that would fall for a trick if he saw the script and read his dialogue first. The mark must be in a state of hypnosis, he has to be entranced, but frantic. It's his own speed that makes him tumble. And that speed and momentum must be avarice. A man who isn't greedy can never fall prey to a con trick. So greed must be built into the proposition. The second factor is illegality. To prevent the mark bouncing back at us and going to the police, our proposition must have a suggestion of illicit dealing without, if possible, doing illegal things ourselves.' Bob and Liz sat there with pained expressions on their faces to show me that they had heard that lecture one hundred times before, but I affected not to notice. Perhaps I would say it many more hundred times before we were through. I ran a tight unit, and if that meant repeating my lecture every week, then I'd do that, whatever kind of look they wore. I leaned back and closed my eyes in concentration.

Bob interrupted my thoughts, 'That man in Paris wasn't motivated by his own greed,' he said. 'He thought he was giving his money to Oxfam.'

'Sometimes there are exceptions,' I explained 'Sometimes there are operational emergencies.'

'You mean sometimes we are broke,' said Bob.

'I mean exactly that,' I said.

'I told this man Awawa that you had enough authority to agree to the sale,' Liz said, getting that conversation back to the matter at hand.

'I'll make it better than that,' I said. 'I'm going to be the officer who condemns equipment. Got it?'

'No,' said Bob.

I explained, 'We tell him that I will – for a price – condemn some anti-tank guns. They will then be sold as scrap metal, but actually they will be in excellent condition. Now, what we really do is buy, and then deliver to him scrap metal from the War Ministry, London. It will be packed in the right sort of cases marked 'scrap metal' and complete with War Ministry consignment notes, manifests and the whole damn paper work. Not a thing for us to forge; it will be genuine. He pays us about one hundred times the real price ánd bribes me to boot. It's beautiful.'

'It sounds good,' said Liz. She was a sensible girl. She saw immediately that my plan was sound operationally. I said, 'We'll have the stuff shipped to the docks by the railway company. The crates will be available in the railway yards. I'll get hold of a couple of real weapons, even if we have to have them made by a film prop manufacturer. If this Geegee fellow and Ibo Awawa want to look inside, we'll open one case – our special case – and show them the goods.'

'They'll find out eventually,' said Bob, who always whines about my plans, but never offers better alternative ones.

'Yes they will,' I said. 'And inside the cases they'll find scrap metal, just like it says on the shipping documents. So what's the complaint, and who does he complain to?'

'He complains to you,' said Bob.

'Right,' I said. 'Except I won't be around here.'

'The only one that will be around here,' said Liz. 'Is my friend Geegee.'

'Exactly,' I said. 'Yet one more chance to practise his public relations.'

Chapter 7

BOB

Silas taught me everything I know. O.K. But why is he always the earl who's selling his pictures, or the chairman of the board, or the millionaire who doesn't quite understand these documents he has? And why am I always the chauffeur, or the file clerk who will get the papers from the files? Or the butler, or the man who owns the land Silas is buying, but I don't know how it's just swamped with oil. This is what I was thinking struggling back to the Chester with the two army uniforms.

I sank down exhausted, ready for a zizz, when there was a light tap at the door. Silas came in wearing a bowler hat rakishly set to one side of his head. He had to do that with the small one, the large one slipped down on his ears. I'd bought two more bowlers from that shop where Silas had bought his outfit. One was a quarter inch bigger than Silas's size, the other was a quarter inch smaller. I'd been substituting the three of them, wow, had I got Silas worried. He'd been stroking his forehead a lot, and peering at himself closely in the mirror. The previous day I'd caught him with a tape measure.

Silas put the small size bowler aside and inspected the uniforms. I put mine on. I thought I looked all right but Silas said, 'and old Paddy gave you that?' My gear was rough like sandpaper and as stiff as a plank with great baggy trousers and an awful hat. Silas's uniform was a smooth barathea, properly waisted and slim legged. On the chest there were a couple of rows of medals and on the collar red tabs. The peaked cap was soft and stylish, and garnished with gold leaves. Silas put it on. He strode up and down saluting himself in the mirror as he passed it, while I stood near the fireplace looking like an old sandbag. Silas stopped saluting and said, 'Carry on colonel,' to himself in the mirror. Then he turned around to look at me carefully. For a little while he said nothing. Then he said again, 'And so old Paddy gave you that?'

'Yes,' I said.

'He must be losing his grip,' Silas said.

'What's wrong with it?' I asked.

Silas walked across the room and then looked up, as though just catching sight of me. 'Look at yourself laddie,' he said in a Brigadier style voice. I looked at myself – a lance corporal in the Transport Corps – and shrugged. Silas changed into my lance corporal's blouse. Once he got it on he kept shouting 'company halt' and jumping up and down to land with a terrific crash of the heels. 'Belt tightened, suck your stomach in,' he chanted in a funny contralto voice. 'Thumbs in line with the seam of the trousers and feet at forty-five degrees. Head up, chin in. Eyes straight ahead and alert to orders.'

I put Silas's Brigadier's coat on. 'That's frightfully good,' I said. 'I'd never realised it before, but you are a natural born corporal my dear chap.' I paraded up and down imitating Silas's Brigadier turn.

'You're like a debutante at a coming out ball. You horrible little thing,' Silas said, putting his face close to mine and bellowing loudly. 'Don't you have any idea of how to look like a soldier? Atten-shun,' he roared and I slammed my feet down hard to obey.

'Don't you know how to be a soldier?'

'Of course I don't. I've never been a soldier, have I?' He tut-tutted and put his big-wheel uniform on again. 'That's the trouble with all you kids,' said Silas. 'Worse thing they ever did in Britain stopping National Service. That's what's wrong with the country if you ask me.'

'Well I'm not going to ask you,' I promised. 'The Army is the biggest con trick of all time and I'm not keen to be taken in by it.'

'A con trick?' said Silas. 'What do you mean?'

'It's obvious isn't it? The fellers with the high ranks, high wages, chauffeurs and chateaux live miles from the fighting, and tell the marks who get five bob a day where to go and get shot at; it's the classic con trick the army is.'

'Is it?' said Silas choking on his anger. 'Well it's a pity you don't find it easy to act like a mark for five minutes,' I said.

'If you think I'm not convincing enough as a lousy lance corporal in the Transport Corps, then I'll be the Tank Brigadier, because it seems to me that I'd find that role a lot easier to perform.'

'Easier to perform,' Silas spat the words back at me in hysterical distaste. 'Easier one to perform,' he smiled grimly. 'So that's what you think is it; you long haired, slack shouldered, whining beatnik. You wretched piece of flotsam from the class war. When I found you you didn't have two halfpennies for a penny. A lot of help you've been to me since. Perhaps I could have expected a little gratitude or appreciation, respect even. But you don't even have a desire to learn. You don't get any better at this job, you take no interest in what I'm trying to teach you, you don't even have a desire to understand what I tell you. It's all come too easy to you. Easier to perform. Well I was a Brigadier – a real one – when you were dribbling down your bib. See that,' Silas tapped his cane on one of the medals. 'Alamein, first wave of tanks. We lost so many tanks in that show, that I never again met anyone with whom I had done my training.' Silas looked sad now. He seldom mentioned the war, but whenever he did he looked sad.

'You're a rebel, aren't you,' he said. 'And you think you're the world's first rebel. I know the feeling, because at your age we are all rebels, but in the thirties we had something to rebel against. Hitler was ranting and raving and so was Mussolini, and plenty of my friends were listening to the ravings and telling me they made sense. I was a rebel laddie, like you I thought I'd discovered rebellion as an art form. I was an accountant with a merchant bank in the city. My God it was difficult to get that job. I was being groomed for stardom. I had special duties, and two days a week, a course in advanced banking. I would have been an important international banker by now, but I could see that the war had to come, so I chucked the whole thing in and got a commission in the tanks. War was declared and I was sitting on top of the world. Straightaway they made me an acting captain. Well that was my rebellion. From merchant bank to acting temporary unpaid captain.'

I said, 'I don't mind you always talking to me as if I am an idiot, but don't expect to break my heart about the interruption of your education, because the interruption to my education came when I was fifteen. My Mum needed the money.'

'Well, that was your fault,' said Silas. 'There are scholarships and grants and that sort of thing. Everyone has equal opportunities nowadays.'

'Get stuffed,' I said. 'Sure. If they want to learn the history of the British Empire, simple addition and a few words of French, and become a foreman or a salesman. But the fellows who run things, are still sitting in the Athenaeum and putting their son's names down for Eton. They are still taking the cream and running the country, but proles like me are supposed to be grateful for a chance to learn elementary algebra.'

'You are behind the times. There has been a social revolution in this country since then.'

'A few cockney photographers and a Lancashire pop group makes a lot of cash and get their pictures in the paper, and that's the revolution, but it doesn't fool me. It's all a big, big con trick, bigger and more ruthless than we could ever dream of. Things haven't changed a bit and there's no sign that they ever will.'

'Well I'll give you your chance at an education,' said Silas. 'I'm going to give you a crash course in being a soldier. I'm going to make you the best lance corporal, the most knowledgable NCO, in the Queen's army. So forget about Nebuchadnezzar and the road to Babylon for a couple of days and learn a few things of more immediate importance.' He opened some of his books. One was called King's Regulations and another showed army badges, and another had photos of different kinds of guns and tanks. 'By the time we go down to collect that scout car from old Kaplan you are going to be a soldier. Do you hear me; a soldier. And the first thing we start with, is cutting off the long greasy hair.'

'That bloody barber's murdered your hair kiddoo.' Peter the bigamist could talk out of the side of his mouth so that you couldn't see his lips move. I didn't say anything.

'Charlie would never touch you if I was looking after you.'

I still said nothing, 'If you change your mind,' said Peter the bigamist, 'let me know. Want a smoke?'

'No thanks,' I said.

'Charlie's going to duff you up on Friday morning kiddoo,' he said. His whole attitude had changed now. He was just as spiteful as Charlie but twice as clever. I tell you clever geezers can be a menace in the nick, somehow it's like they blame the other prisoners that they are inside. I didn't ask him how he knew it would be Friday, but he was going to tell me all right. Finally he said, 'Big Charlie's been transferred.'

'When's he go?' I asked. Peter smiled and I was mad at myself for asking.

'He's been transferred to some prison up north. He goes on Friday, the ten a.m. lorry. He's arranged to open up on your landing and that's when he'll do you. Watch out for the bastard kiddoo.'

'I'll kill the sod,' I said.

Peter the bigamist gave a sour little smile. 'That's the stuff.'

He swept the dust into a ridge and bent down to drag it on to a piece of cardboard. When he had it nicely balanced he flipped a thin home-made cigarette so it fell at my feet.

'Compliments of the management,' said Peter.

'No, ta,' I said. 'I'm giving it up.' I walked away.

'O.K. Keep in touch,' he called.

*   *   *

It was an impressive looking vehicle. In some ways I liked it better than the Rolls. A Ferret Mark 2, Silas called it. A crazy thing, quite small, with angular armoured plating and very thick, rubber tyres that were probably almost bullet proof. There were metal gadgets stuck all over it. Silas insisted that I learned what they all were. The hatches could be closed right down, until there was only a tiny slit for the driver to see through. The driving mirrors were quite large and under them there were smoke dischargers. There were two headlights and slots for the Bren gun, or the Browning 0.30 inch. It had a Rolls Royce B.60 petrol engine, six cylinders in line, 4,265 ccs, developing ninety-six brake horse power and 3,300 revs. It had fluid coupling and four wheel drive. I don't know what it did to the gallon but we seemed to be drinking juice like a roomful of Irish navvies.

Of course we couldn't take it into a civvy filling station so Silas had filled up a dozen jerricans and stored them inside, which made it even more cramped than before. It was only intended to hold a crew of two anyway; commander and driver; and I don't have to tell you who was the commander.

Old Kaplan at the metal yard had painted the scout car, and had cannibalised fire extinguishers and head lamps from other cars so that ours was in great condition. The Ferret armoured car was in the far corner of the dump, and on the first day we went down there Silas told me that I must be able to jump in and out of the vehicle with 'an easy familiarity.' That meant that I was breaking my shins and bruising my arms on all the projections, while Silas was barking orders at me like a maniac drill sergeant that I remembered from a film on television. In that film the drill sergeant had ended up by strangling his wife. By afternoon I learned to drive the car. It had a five speed pre-selector, power steering and brakes. I'd never handled anything like it before, but within an hour and a half even Silas had to admit I was throwing it around the yard like an expert.

The following day we returned to the yard, collected the scout car and began the real operation. I would have felt better if we had changed into the uniforms nearer to our destination, but not Silas. We drove out of the junk yard all dressed up in our uniforms. We had dirtied them a shade and put overalls over them. We looked like a couple of battle scarred heroes. So much so, that when we stopped at the roadside for a smoke I made rude signs to an artillery convoy that went past and the soldiers yelled back at me. After it had gone I felt nervous. I realised that it would only need one of those military police outriders to ask us who we were, to start off a disastrous chain of events. You couldn't tell that to Silas, of course. He always had some glib military dictum ready, but never any sensible answer. I wiped my sweaty hands on my uniform.

'Don't get nervous,' Silas said. I didn't answer him. Silas doesn't get nervous, he just gets into a bad temper. It's all right for him being in a bad temper, because he always plays the role of the general or millionaire or something, but just ask yourself if they'd smell a rat if it was the butler, or the office boy, or the lance corporal driver throwing tantrums. 'I told you not to get nervous,' Silas repeated.

'I'm not *getting* flipping nervou₄' I said. 'I was nervous already.'

'Follow that convoy,' said Silas.

I climbed back into the car. 'What if they stop us and ask for a driving licence?' I said.

'We got the vehicle legally,' said Silas. 'Your ordinary civil driving licence covers you for driving this. Chelsea yobbos buy them for their country estates. We hired the uniforms to play a prank on an old school chum. So what do we get; a tenner fine?'

'I suppose so,' I said. I started up the car and dashed after the tail of the convoy. We got to the Royal Armoured Corps tank exercise grounds in Dorset well before lunch.

It was a fine sunny day with just a few white clouds to make the sky seem bluer. For miles in every direction the ground was churned up by the Centurion and Chieftain tanks. Some curious formation of the soil caused each curving track mark to reveal different colours. Great scars of white and red and grey were painted across the landscape like gigantic brush marks of a Nash or Piper painting.

'Stop,' shouted Silas. I slammed on the anchors and we slid into the verge, with a cloud of dust and a smell of rubber. Silas was really living his role. 'For Christ sake driver. Take a little more care with this vehicle will you. It has to be signed over in good condition at eight o'clock tonight.'

I gave him a salute. 'Twenty hundred hours we Army chappies say,' I told him. 'Well, don't worry. Old Kaplan isn't going to put you on a charge if you're five minutes late, or get a scratch on the paintwork. He's got two fields full of them and he only wants sixty quid apiece for them, even if you write it off.' Silas turned on me furiously, 'Haven't I told you ten thousand times to keep in character when we are fully operational.'

'O.K.' I said. I got out of the car and walked away from him. I avoid him when he gets in a rage and he's always dead touchy when we are just going into a job. Now, it doesn't affect me like that. I never get all het-up like he does. I just get sweaty hands. I tore a twig off the hedgerow. Silas came over to me and looked at the training ground through his field glasses. 'Six Centurion Mark fives on that hillock,' he mused aloud. 'The Vigilant launcher is there where the little group of soldiers are standing. No tell a lie, one of them is a Mark Two with the old seventeen pounder gun. I didn't know there were any of those around any more. Wouldn't be surprised if that was the target tank. Yes it's painted with a white cross.'

'How did you find out that they were demonstrating the Vigilant missile today?' I asked him.

'Simple. I phoned up the Press Officer and asked. The Government sell this hardware you know. They aren't keeping it secret. They've sold more Centurion Mark Fives to foreign armies than you've had hot dinners.'

'So it's just Ibo's bad luck that they won't sell him his stuff?'

'Look at it,' said Silas. 'More as our good luck. Three hundred thousand pounds worth of good luck.'

The tanks started up with a roar that you could hear clearly, even from as far away as we were. 'Thar they go,' I said, in my Bonanza voice.

Silas said, 'They are moving out westwards. Three hundred thousand head of cabbage on the hoof to Pecos.'

I held a twig by the end and smacked myself hard with my fist. 'I think they got me, old timer', I gasped. 'Trumpeter sound recall.' I held the shaft and groaned.

'Injuns,' said Silas. He spat into the ditch. 'Hold still lootenant,' He pulled the twig out and looked at it. 'Waal, I don't know what they taught you at that gol-darned fancy pants West Point Academy, but that's no huntin' arrow.'

I said, 'Gee whiz, ol' timer, if they have war parties as far north as this, what about those wimmin 'n kids left unprotected back in Fort Dexter?'

'Geronimo,' shouted Silas, so loud that I feared his voice might carry as far as the soldiers around the guns on the far hillock. Then we both ran to the scout car. I was there first. The motor was still running and I let in the clutch, just as Silas vaulted into the top. He clasped his hands across his peaked cap and sank low into his seat.

'Yahooo,' he shouted. 'Wagons Roll. Let's go see how the west was won.'

We were due to meet the marks at a horse brassy little Inn near to the tank grounds. I was frightened that there'd be a lot of army people in there, and that they would suss us, but Silas said that they would almost all be in the mess at lunchtime, and that any others would keep their distance when they saw his red staff tabs. Before we went inside I gave Silas a brand new pound note from the centre of a run of ten in my wallet. It was a trick we'd done many times and although nowadays we didn't need the money, we still did it just for fun. You'll see how it works – if you don't already guess – as my story goes on. Silas went up to the bar and said, 'One large whisky, with soda and ice for me, and a pint of bitter for my driver.'

'Yes sir,' said the barman, so used to soldiers that he hardly looked up. He took the new pound note and gave Silas the change. We stood at the bar with Silas attempting to bridge our social differences by topics like football, pre-selector gearboxes and the leave roster. Silas said, 'Did you go home at Easter?' and I said, 'No, I stayed on camp to save money. I've got ten days to come next month, I'll go home then.'

Silas nodded and said some stuff about the weather and I played the reluctant private. Then Silas asked the barman if there was somewhere he could get a wash and get out of his overalls. The barman said he could go upstairs and use the bathroom in the hotel. I suppose that was because Silas was an officer, because when I asked him the same thing he sent me to the outside lavatory, where there was a gale blowing through the door and only cold water in the sink. I came back into the bar drying my hands on my trousers.

There were about twelve people drinking there by that time, mostly civilians from the tank depot. There was no sign of Silas. I decided to do the second half of my pound note trick. I ordered a pint of bitter and gave him a clean ten shilling note. When he gave me the change I said, 'Excuse me, but that was a pound I gave you.' He said no it wasn't, and I said yes it was. Then I said, 'Well, if you'll be good enough to look in your till, you'll have to admit that I'm right.' I spread the brand new pound notes across the counter and there was one of the numbered sequence missing. 'And that's the one you'll find in your till.' There were a couple of civvies watching the barman. He looked in his till and found the note of course. He went very quiet and gave me the extra ten bob. I've never trusted those ones that go quiet, and I shouldn't have trusted this bastard.

I'd only been drinking my bitter for a couple of minutes and there was still no sign of Silas when the barman went out and came back and said very quietly and politely. 'Excuse me sir, there are a couple of gentlemen asking for you in the hotel foyer. That's through that door there.' I thought the marks must have arrived early, so I pushed my beer aside and went to meet them. Was I surprised to find two dirty great military policemen standing there. They were motor cycle MPs, complete with breeches, blancoed webbing and white crash helmets.

'What's all this pound note stuff, squaddie?' said one of them.

'It's simple,' I said. 'Just like I told the barman. It was a pound note. He found it in his cash drawer.'

'Did he now?' said the redcap. They looked at each other. They were a tough looking couple. One of them must have been pushing fifty with a nasty scar that was only partly concealed by a large moustache. His chest was smothered in campaign ribbons. 'Let's see your wallet, sonny. Think we haven't seen that one before? I was doing that trick in bars in Cairo when you were just a twinkle in your father's eyeball.

One of your mates passed that first quid over, then you pass across a ten bob note and come the innocent.' He did a squeaky voice, 'Just look in your cash register barman sir. Well this barman's seen that trick before and so have we. So you're coming along with us, and don't think you won't be charged with a civvie offence too.'

'That would be damned inconvenient, corporal.' Silas came down the hotel staircase tapping his hand with his swagger stick. The two redcaps were at rigid attention and saluting.

Silas walked up very close to me. His nose was very close to mine, 'What the bloody blue blazes have you been doing Cartwright?'

'I passed a ten bob note sir, said it was a quid. I'm sorry sir. Could have been a mistake.'

'You artful little horror,' said Silas. 'You crafty little soldier. You horrible, horrible man. What are you?'

'I'm a horrible man sir,' I said.

'That's right,' said Silas slowly. 'A slimy, horrible, good for nothing wretch.'

'Working with someone else sir,' said the MP, 'one of those civvies probably.'

'What have I told you about drinking and consorting with civvies,' said Silas. 'I hate civvies. Got me. I hate civvies, and if I ever see you near a civvie again I'll castrate you. Got me?'

'You mean apart from birds sir?' I said. I didn't have to *act* terrified, those MPs were just about to ask for my papers and if Silas didn't stop overdoing it, they would ask for his any minute. I thought he was going to strike me with his little cane. He was waving it around as though he was taking the London Philharmonic through the 1812 overture.

'If I didn't need you over the next ten days, I'd let them take you away and burn you. Do you know that?'

'Yes sir.' I said. I could see that the older of the two

military coppers was determined to take me in. He turned to Silas, 'I'm afraid sir, it's a serious charge. It's a civvie offence too sir.'

'Don't talk to me about civvies,' Silas said, showing more annoyance than he had with me. I almost thought he was going to tell the copper that he was not acting his part properly, but he didn't. The copper flinched. 'I hate civvies,' said Silas. 'And no civvie court is going to have one of my boys . . . is that the India General Service medal?'

'Yes sir,' said the elder cop. 'And the North West Frontier Bar.'

'Good show,' said Silas. 'What would that be, nineteen thirty-eight?'

'That's it sir, thirty-eight. I was a boy soldier.'

'You must have gone through the depot at about the same time as I did. Do you remember the name of the adjutant there?'

'No sir,' said the copper. 'It's a long time ago now.' Silas smiled. 'Lowther was his name,' said Silas. 'He was my father.'

'Really sir?' said the military cop trying to be as pleased about it as Silas obviously was. What a chancer Silas was, his old man had never even been in the army. Silas's father was a doctor.

'This calls for a drink,' said Silas. 'And you can leave this little turd to me. Cartwright?'

'Yes sir,' I said.

'Get out to that vehicle. Get cold water and the leather. I want it spotless. I want it shining. I'm going to look inside and if there's a speck of dust anywhere, Cartwright, you are for the high jump. I want it clean on the top and clean under the mudguards. I want it so clean that it disappears. And if it isn't, you'll disappear; into the glass house for three months. Got me?'

I didn't answer for a minute. It was freezing cold outside, and I knew that he'd have to back-down, if I said I'd sooner be taken away by the two MPs. On the other hand, Silas gets out of touch with reality, on these operations. I mean, I could quite believe that he'd get so lost in his part, that he'd let them take me away.

'Yes sir,' I finally said.

'And give this corporal the barman's ten shillings.' I gave it to him, 'It was a mistake,' I said.

'It certainly was,' said Silas sarcastically, and as all three of them turned away to go into the bar, I heard Silas say, 'It would have been hard to make it stick, I realised that, when he started to plead that it was a mistake. Hard to disprove things like that.'

I went outside and the barman gave me a bucket of water. Iced water it probably was, by the temperature of it. My knuckles were blue with the cold as I began to wash the scout car. If old Kaplan could have seen me he would have giggled; cleaning that damned car, cleaner than it had ever been, before returning it to his dirty old dump yard.

The marks arrived at 1.30 p.m. They were in a Lincoln Continental. A uniformed chauffeur was driving and in the back seat there were two spades in bank manager suits and a white-faced fancy dan with watch chain and flower; Geegee Grey.

'Brigadier Lowther?' says the ofay.

'I'll get him,' I said. I dashed into the bar. Silas and the two military cops were well away, chatting about the war.

'The African delegation is here,' I said saluting carefully.

'These are the chaps,' said Silas. 'I'd better pretend you two are with me officially, otherwise there might be questions asked about us drinking together. These Foreign Office blighters can be as tricky as anything.' The two redcaps came out with Silas. Silas saluted all of them, even Geegee, and then said to the MPs, 'Thank you for all the work you've put in. I don't think we will need an escort back to London. It's just an informal trip.'

The MPs both threw Silas a great salute and then kicked up their bikes and roared away. 'I thought we'd better keep it unofficial,' said Silas.

'It's the wish of my government, that this whole matter is kept as discreet as possible,' said the War Minister.

'Right,' said Silas. 'I'll lead the way in my vehicle. Tell your driver to follow. Our best view is from the road, unless you want to go over to the other delegation.'

'No,' said the War Minister.

We got into the scout car. I drove down the road slowly, 'We'll have to discard that number pound note trick,' I said.

'Yes,' said Silas. He was angry.

'Lucky your recognising that medal.'

'No luck about it,' said Silas. 'Research. If I've told you once, I've told you a thousand times. This profession isn't for slackers or idiots, or people who want money for nothing. You've got to work, study, concentrate. I have spent the last three days working; Army Regulations, memoirs, medal recognition, tank recognition. I know more about the army than most of the officers on this camp. Give me ten minutes with any of them and I'll convince them that *they* are imposters.'

'Silas you are a stupid old sod,' I said.

Silas smiled. We drove in silence for a bit, then Silas said, 'You want to get down to some serious study of your profession, and forget this frivolous archaeology rubbish. That will never get you anywhere,' and of course he was right, in a way.

I slowed down as we neared the place we had selected. Silas said, 'If this fellow is planning a putsch, he'll need anti-infantry, anti-personnel stuff as well as anti-tank. Make sure you tell him this Vigilant is great against infantry. I've invented an infra red device for it. You know your dialogue?'

Yes,' I said.

We stopped at the same place as before. The Lincoln stopped too. Silas went back and tapped his peak with his cane. He gave his smoothest smile.

'We are over there on the hillock,' Silas said. 'The weapon is called Vigilant. It's the first, one-man, anti-tank guided missile that is completely portable.' Instead of getting enthusiastic, Silas reeled off the data as though he had become bored with repeating it so often. 'From cover, one man can control batteries of six missiles. After half a day's training we expect any infantry man to achieve nine out of ten hits. . . .'

'Training like this?' said Ibo Awawa. 'With a real tank? That would be expensive.' He poured Silas a glass of wine and handed it to him. For himself he poured water.

'No, in simulators,' said Silas. 'We'll probably get you one of those too. At 1,500 yards we expect solely turret hits. Built-in to the missile there is a stabilising device which gives immediate response to the operator's aim, rather than a curving in toward the desired direction. This makes obtaining hits considerably more simple than with other similar wire-guided missiles. It is, without doubt, the most remarkable anti-tank weapon ever invented. Here is a simple diagram and some data. I'm afraid that it's only typewritten and roneoed, but that's our standard instruction sheet. The infantry man walking is carrying a box containing the missile. The box is also a launcher. It takes two seconds to set-up and – including the launcher – the missile weighs only 51 pounds. They are suitable for mounting on vehicles – such as the Ferret I'm using – and on helicopters.' As he was saying this, there was a roar of motor cycles and the two MP bikes came roaring down the road from the direction of the main camp. They slowed up as they got to us, but only in order to wave to Silas who held his wine glass aloft to them as they went past, all smiles and exhaust smoke. Silas hardly paused in his explanation.

'The operator guides it by means of that sight he's holding.'

'That changes the ailerons or something?' asked Geegee, anxious to sound intelligent.

'Solid fuel propulsion,' rattled off Silas. 'Trailing edge wing flaps and the gyro-stabilised autopilot are both actuated by gas bled from the rocket motor. Exact dimensions are printed on the sheet you have there, but roughly speaking the missile measures three and a half feet long and less than one foot across. I can tell you gentlemen, it's a killer; of tanks, soft vehicles, infantry, or anything it comes across.'

Mr. Ibo Awawa nodded enthusiastically. 'It's a cold wind,' he said. 'Get into the car.' Silas got into the Lincoln, he went on talking, but I couldn't hear what was said after that. I saw the chauffeur produce another large box. He took more wine, cold chicken, pate and salad, and arranged it on a neat folding table that had been built into the coachwork of the Lincoln. I decided to build one into my red Rolls. I could see Silas rabbiting away and stuffing canapes and drink into his face. Eventually, they remembered me, sitting in the freezing cold armoured scout car. They sent me a leg of chicken and a glass of coca-cola. Geegee brought it. He said, 'The Brigadier tells me that you are not allowed alcohol while on duty.'

'Oh yes,' I said. Geegee climbed up onto the turret. He was a tall bloke, wearing an Austin Reed ready-made suit and a drip-dry shirt, through which his string vest was visible. He watched me eat the chicken. When I'd finished it he offered me a cigar. 'I don't mind,' I said taking one. He took it back from me and trimmed it with his gold cutter. Then he gave it to me again and lit it. 'Known your Brigadier long?'

'*Don't* know him,' I said.

'*Don't* know him?' said Geegee.

'How would *I* get to know a Brigadier?'

'I've put it badly,' said Geegee. 'How long have you been with him?'

'Been with him, on and off, two years,' I said. 'But I've known him as an officer on the unit for four.'

'A long time,' pronounced Geegee.

'It flipping well is,' I said. 'Too flippin' long, but this is a cushy number.'

I puffed at the cigar, watching the gun and tanks. One of the tanks started its motor and went lumbering off over the rim of the nearest ridge. It came up into position again, hull well up. I stole a glance at the other car. Silas was leaning forward pointing and the War Minister had the field glasses to his eyes listening to Silas's commentary. The War Minister must have said something to his aide, for he opened the car door, got out and came walking across to me and Geegee in the scout car.

'Hello Charles,' said Geegee.

Charles was a very dark negro dressed in an expensive tweed suit and tweed hat. His brogue shoes were polished like glass and he touched the armoured sides of the vehicle as though it might have been sprayed with deadly virus. When he spoke, it was in a frail Oxford accent with some of the pronunciations so absurd that I could hardly understand him.

'Hello Geegee dear chap,' said Charles.

'Feel like a spot of air?' asked Geegee.

'His nibs thought it would be good for me,' Geegee said, to me. 'Your Brigadier seems to be getting on well with the old man.'

'He's a smashing bloke,' I said. 'He gets on well with everyone. He's a smashing officer that Brigadier Lowther. He's strict, but always dead fair, and so fussy about the equipment, you'd never believe. He comes down the lines inspecting the guns – course he's the officer that condemns the artillery and anti-tank guns. . . .'

'Yes we did know that,' drawled Charles.

I continued, 'Sometimes he'll say, "don't no one bother with that one no more. Stop cleaning that one right now, lads. I can see right now as how I'll be condemning of it. If Staff says anything about it being dirty, say as how I said it's condemned." Another time he was deciding about equipment going for re-use. He says to the lads as how we've got to remember that guns that is resold to foreign armies is going to be used by soldiers just like us, but foreign. "So look after your guns," he says. "You wouldn't want no breech block blowing back and crippling some poor pongo, no matter what country he's in. They are our colleagues," he says.'

'Well I'd never thought about it like that before. It's funny flipping way of putting it, but I can see exactly what he means. Another time there are guns for resale. He takes a quick butchers at the recoil mechanism and he says "scrap, scrap, scrap," all the way down the whole flipping line of forty-five guns. Well there's hardly a mark on 'em, they are practically brand new. So course we all look at him, don't we? He says, "Resold guns is going to be used by some poor pongo somewhere. A lot of these guns look nice now, but I've been through the records of these guns. I looked at the history of those breech blocks and I can tell you metal fatigue has taken its toll. I won't see no pongos endangered by dodgy gear," he said. Well, actually he said, "I won't see no soldiers endangered by faulty equipment," but you get the drift of it. "They are brothers in arms," he said. Brothers in arms. Yeah, I can tell you gents, he's a right funny geezer, that Brigadier Lowther.'

I took a deep drag at my cigar while Geegee and Charles exchanged glances. They were now sure that Silas was one of the biggest fiddlers wearing khaki. There was a rapping sound from the window of the Lincoln. Silas was pointing across the exercise ground. The tank was moving again. On the other hillock the Vigilant fired. The little missile took off, trailing a wire and altering direction as the soldier controlled it with his aiming device. It seemed to pause as it neared the target tank then there was a big bang. The Centurion shuddered and stopped. Two more shots went in through the front armour and then there was a low roar as she started to flame.

'She's brewing up,' I said.

'That's three shots,' said Charles.

'Through the front armour,' I said. 'That stuff is 152 mm. thick in some places. If he'd been hull-up, the first shot would have knocked him out.' The roaring got louder, as the radio controlled tank disappeared in a sheet of flame.

Silas and the War Minister got out of the Lincoln. Silas was smiling. 'What did you think of it, Cartwright?' he called to me.

'That Vigilant's a super weapon, sir. I was just telling these gents. If she'd been hull-up, the first one would have brewed her up. And of course at night we could do the same thing with the I.R. lock on device. . . .'

Silas held his cane to his lips.

The War Minister said, 'What is the I.R. lock on device?'

Silas said, 'It's not really for publication, but it will be early next year, so it can't hurt to tell you. Might even be able to get you a few, but they'll be damned pricey. It's an infra red device that locks onto any warm target and follows it. Just press the button. That tank could have been destroyed at night without the tank crew ever seeing the missile.'

'Heat?' said the War Minister. 'It would be effective against infantry?'

'The heat of the human body will do it,' said Silas. 'It's an expensive way of doing it but against a column of infantry those anti-tank missiles will do more damage than shrapnel.'

'Will they?' said the War Minister thoughtfully. 'That's frightful, isn't it?'

'Yes,' said Silas. 'But it's as an anti-tank missile that your army will be employing it, isn't that right?'

'Who can say?' said the War Minister.

'Exactly,' said Silas.

Chapter 8

LIZ

I had got back to our mews flat tipsy that night, after having dinner with Mr. Ibo Awawa and Geegee, Silas was attentive and businesslike. He wrote down everything in his little notebook. It looked good to all of us, but Silas was right, it wouldn't do for Bob and me to remain in the mews flat. We moved the cars first, then packed our bags and took adjoining suites at the Chester Hotel.

They argued a bit at the desk about Santa Claus, but I knew that Silas wouldn't remember to feed it. Neither of us felt sleepy when we got there at 3.30 a.m. We sent for cocoa and brandy and sat there talking about the new job. Bob was still in his dirty roll-neck sweater and jeans. He kept complaining about his *picaresque* roles and swearing that he wouldn't be Silas's army driver for this next operation, but we all knew that when it came to the crunch, Bob would do as Silas directed.

Silas had found Bob – adopted him one might almost say – three or four years ago, when Bob was doing small time swindles.

'A regular gas meter bandit I was when old Silas met me. I was doing little mail order fiddles.'

'You were selling by mail order?'

'Advertising, "superb steel engraving of HM the Queen originally commissioned by the British Government for only 10/6" and sending them a threepenny stamp? No, I wasn't bright enough to do that. I was sending to mail order companies for eight quid watches, and cheap binoculars and car accessories. I'd send the first payment to each of ten adverts simultaneously, then, when they sent me the stuff I'd move on and flog it from door to door. No company will pursue someone for a debt under ten pounds; it's not worth it. They'd spend more than that chasing you.'

'It sounds dangerous,' I said. I could not imagine him doing it. He looked so frail that going to prison would kill him. 'Drink your cocoa,' I said.

'No, it's not dangerous. Silas told me that mail order debts have only a 33 per cent recovery success. Ordinary debts are recovered about 75 per cent of the time. Silas said I'd hit upon a good safe swindle, but he made me realise that firstly, I was a really small-time crook, and secondly that it was inevitable that I'd get caught. Inevitable.'

'What happened?'

'I was doing my door-to-door in Leeds. I got into a punch-up with another salesman, when along comes the law. Six months porridge. Horrible it was. Never again. I got in touch with Silas on the day I came out of nick.'

'I love Silas,' I said.

Bob stared at me.

'Well he's got it,' said Bob. 'I suppose everyone loves him. Have you watched a mark falling in love with him? Those two charlies in New York were a good example; both of them falling over themselves just for a kind word, just for a handshake, a smile or a glance from Silas. That's love, and Silas knows it, he struts and postures and bathes in it.'

'That's right,' I said. 'It's love all right. And like a lover, he keeps pushing the relationship to the brink of dissolution.'

'Disillusion,' corrected Bob.

'Yes,' I said. 'And it's not just with the marks he does that.'

'You mean he does it with us?' asked Bob.

'Well you *know* he does. He sneers or makes sour jokes and never ceases to criticise until I'm ready to scream or hit him, but he watches things so carefully that just before the breaking point he'll switch on the charm and sweet-talk so hard that I am throwing my arms around him and swearing everlasting love.'

'Yeah. I've watched you,' Bob agreed.

'I know,' I said. 'And I despise myself, do you know that?'

'Yes,' said Bob. 'I know.' He poured a little cream into his saucer and put it on the floor. Santa Claus looked at it for a long time. Finally it walked across and lapped a little of it.

'Do you think he's going to marry you?' said Bob.

'I don't know,' I said. 'He asked me once, a long time ago.'

'He's selfish,' said Bob. 'And self-centred. He'll never marry again. Never marry anyone.'

'I've not thought about it,' I said.

'Don't give me that,' said Bob. 'You've never thought about it? We may be living a pretty emancipated life, but don't tell me you've never thought about it. Don't give me that.'

'You mind your own business,' I said. 'Keep your mouth shut and do your job and carry out your instructions just as Silas says, and I'll do the same thing and we'll make money and we'll be all right.'

'I didn't mean to make you cry,' said Bob.

'All I'm interested in is the money,' I said. 'There will be three hundred thousand pounds to share next week. I'll not be crying for Silas. I'll not be crying for any man.'

'I didn't mean crying,' said Bob. 'I don't know why I said crying, must have been a slip of the tongue.' He put his arm round me and offered me his large grimy handkerchief.

*　　*　　*

Silas once calculated that 90 per cent of the detected conmen are caught through carelessness. From his analysis of twenty-eight cases he concluded that over 75 per cent were caught because they had been seen together while pretending to be strangers. Silas was quite fanatical about keeping us separate during an operation, which meant that I spent a lot of time alone. Some people enjoy being alone. Bob was delighted to be left with a large pile of books about ancient civilisations being dug up in the sand, but I need to be with people. It isn't human to be alone for long periods. I did a couple of tasks for the operation. I went along to the Defence Ministry and pretended that I was writing an article about the army for a children's magazine. I found out all the facts and figures of the anti-tank gun demonstrations. Silas became very excited when I told him and organised at very short notice an army surplus vehicle and uniforms for him and Bob.

I was worried about them going all that way impersonating soldiers but all Bob could think of, is that he wanted to be a sergeant instead of a private soldier. 'Why don't you let him be a sergeant?' I said to Silas. Silas said, 'I'll have enough trouble passing him off as a human.'

I know what Silas meant, because even with his hair cut and his uniform dirtied up to look well-used, Bob still looked as unsoldierlike as it's possible to be. Silas on the other hand, delighted in his uniform. I wondered how significant it was that he chose to recreate his old one complete to the last medal and badge. The war must have been the high water mark of Silas's life. The glamour and saluting, the risks, the orders and obedience were all part of Silas's daily creed. Indeed they were part of his almost daily lectures to Bob and me. But I fear Bob and I were poor material for Silas's army.

It all went well at Bovington. In fact it all went magnificently. They watched the firing on schedule and after a lunch of cold chicken, served in the back of the Magazarian Embassy car, Mr. Ibo Awawa gave Silas a signed contract for the anti-tank weapons, and added more for some fictitious infra red device that Silas had talked him into.

Awawa told Silas to arrange the transit of the stuff through a little company that Geegee had. They had used it before, he said, for 'discreet transactions'. Silas was delighted. He quite understood, he told Mr. Ibo Awawa, but as he was only a poor army officer he would need money to buy the guns, because even if they were to be described as scrap metal, the price was still way outside his wage bracket. Without another word Awawa wrote him out a personal cheque for fifteen thousand pounds. 'That's just for immediate expenses,' he said. 'Mr. Grey will pay you for the "scrap" after you have bid for it.'

'They don't auction scrap metal,' said Silas. 'The dealer's ring would make a fortune by conspiring to keep the price down. They sell scrap metal at set prices, according to whether it's pure metal or whether there are other materials affixed to make recovery difficult.' As Silas explained, he didn't want them thinking there would be an auction, or the next thing you knew they would be coming along to watch the bids and finding out how much it really cost.

Mr. Ibo Awawa was a dream to deal with. All the documents were soon completed. Silas signed the counterfoils and kept this huge piece of parchment that begins, 'The Realm of Magazaria by order in council,' and is full of 'whereofs' and 'parties of the first part' Silas said it was as good as gold, and read it aloud to us twice. I was pleased, but Bob kept complaining about Silas making him clean the car, and seemed to not notice this document that guaranteed us three hundred thousand pounds. Silas said that Bob nearly messed up the whole thing by pulling the sequence bank-note trick and getting caught. If it hadn't been for Silas, Bob would have been in prison that night, but Silas didn't mention it in front of him, and Bob said it was partly Silas's fault. Bob kept telling me about the daily life of the Hittites or what the Babylonians ate for breakfast. My mother said that a man's life went in periods of eight years. The first eight years, she said, they got German measles and whooping cough and diphtheria, the second eight years they discovered girls and fell off bicycles. Then, pimples, sports cars and stiff collars until at the age of 24 according to my mother's theory, they 'settled down'. Bob must have been settling down.

It was very tedious for the people around him, and I hoped like hell that he wasn't going to be like this for the next eight years, until he reached what my mother called the 'dentures and unfaithfulness stage.'

I had a sudden attack of domesticity. I cleaned the mews cottage from top to toe. I sorted the linen closets and ranged the glasses and china in brightly polished ranks. I bought ashtrays, napkins and vases and filled the rooms with fresh flowers.

Bob noticed the way I had changed the place and remarked on it. I could have hugged him, for Silas never so much as grunted a word of appreciation. I found myself always tensed-up and worried when Silas was around me. It wasn't that he complained or argued, but I had the feeling that he no longer needed my help or opinion or love. Silas had withdrawn into his shell and he'd go for hours without speaking. I wished he'd do some damn thing that I could understand, even if he'd hit me it would have been better than what was happening to us now.

We all had to be exceptionally careful when using the mews cottage because it would only need Geegee to see the three of us all together for him to suss the whole scene. So when we went round there we were careful, making sure there was no one sitting around in parked cars taking more interest than was normal in a newspaper held upside down.

The evening before going to stencil the crates at Southampton we spent the evening at home in the cottage. I loved being there, cooking for the two men and sweeping the floor and watching TV. Silas never wanted to watch the same programmes that Bob and I wanted. How he could watch those quiz games and variety shows I'll never understand. He had been restless all through the play, but Bob and I had both wanted to see it, so he was forced to watch it too.

'Well, I wouldn't have carried him across that damn jungle,' said Silas.

'What else could they do?' I said.

'Dump him,' said Silas. 'The pilot was running the show. He had to think of the good of all of them.'

Bob said, 'You couldn't leave him for the killer ants.'

'Killer ants,' snorted Silas. 'Well, that's all rubbish. There are no killer ants, they just invented that stuff about killer ants.'

'He was injured,' I said. 'They had to carry him with them.'

'How could they dump him?' asked Bob.

Silas said, 'Explain to the old architect that carrying him could mean the death of all of them. If they hadn't carried the old architect, then the wireless operator wouldn't have collapsed just as they had the radio going again. The pilot was in command, he should have dumped him.'

I said, 'I thought the old architect was lovely. I liked him best of all. I could never have dumped him.'

'You said you liked the pilot,' said Silas.

'I did like the pilot, but I liked the old architect best.'

'How could they dump him?' said Bob.

'Don't keep saying, how could they dump him,' said Silas. 'If you'd been in the war you'd know. You merely explain to him that it's in the interests of the others that he is dumped. Or perhaps you say your arm aches; you can't carry him any farther.'

'Your arm aches?' I said.

'He'd take the hint,' said Silas. 'You say your arm aches, and the man who's slowing you up would take the hint.'

'My arm aches,' repeated Bob. 'I'll have to remember that next time I want to dump someone in the jungle. Just say my arm aches and leave him for the killer ants.'

'There are no killer ants,' said Silas. 'I told you.'

The TV news came on and Silas shushed us. There was a picture of some tatty palm trees and some machine guns firing, then there was a narrow street with negro soldiers walking down it. 'Soldiers of the 15th Regiment of the Republic of Magazaria were mopping up today after a mutiny by the Magazarian Security forces. A statement by the Magazarian Minister of Interior said that Port Bovi was quiet today after a night of spasmodic resistance by the mutineers.' On the screen there were some soldiers shooting along an empty street and that same phoney old sound track that the TV news uses every time there's some silent war film. The news commentator went on; "Five Senior Officers of the Magazarian Army were executed by firing squad in the main square of Port Bovi late last night before a crowd of four thousand onlookers. The sentenced officers were brought to Freedom Square by Magazarian Air Force helicopters. They were sentenced for their part in an attempted coup two days ago."

'It's begun,' said Silas.

'It's horrible,' I said. 'I wish we weren't mixed up with it. I hate the idea of helping people to kill each other.'

'We're not helping them,' explained Silas. 'From us they just get scrap metal.'

'I wish we weren't mixed up with it,' I said.

The news reader said, 'And here's some remarkable film from New York. For over an hour today firemen and emergency squads stood by while a man deliberated over throwing himself off the top of a building near Wall Street. Keeping in contact by means of walkie-talkies, two teams of rescue workers climbed across the roof to the place where the man was preparing to throw himself from the Federal Court building.'

The camera shook as it followed the men climbing over the roof of the great temple-like building. Searchlights picked out the figure of a man holding tight to gods and horses as he moved slowly across the face of the pediment. On the steps below him a group of firemen holding a canvas blanket were stumbling over the steps trying to keep it under him. The camera zoomed in to the man as he inched among the stone figures all of which were slightly bigger than life size, like people in a nightmare. Suddenly he turned and leaped in a great dive that took him well away from the firemen beneath and hit the steps like a bundle of dirty laundry. The announcer said, 'New York traffic was held up today for one hour but the rescue workers were too late. The man – Karl Poster – a wealthy New York toy manufacturer – had recently suffered heavy financial losses. Pictures by telstar satellite. Sport. Burnley today inflicted a four goal defeat. . . .'

Silas switched the TV to another channel. A man with a funny hat and false nose was saying, '. . . I'm hurrying to the doctor. I don't like the look of my mother in law . . .' I eased my shoes on and got up. I put on my coat. Silas watched me. 'Look here,' he said, 'I'll tell you what we'll do. . . .'

'Leave me alone Silas,' I said. 'I want to go back to the hotel.'

Silas grabbed my arms. I thought he was going to shake me, but we stood there looking at each other for a moment and then he released me, 'We'll talk about it in the morning.'

'That would be best,' I agreed.

'I'm going back to the hotel too,' said Bob.

Silas dropped into his armchair and switched up the sound on the TV '. . . I'll come with you said the policeman. I can't stand the sight of mine. . . .' The canned applause went wild.

'Goodnight Silas,' I said, but Silas was guffawing loudly. As I went down the steep staircase to the front door Bob was just behind me. It was moonlight in the mews, everything was shiny and blue. I hurried noisily along the cobbled mews but Bob came after me.

'I'll walk with you,' said Bob. He took my arm.

'You don't have to look after me, I'll be all right on my own.'

'It's no trouble,' said Bob. 'If you really slow me up, I'll just tell you my arm aches.'

'Yes,' I said. 'Anytime I'm too much trouble, just tell me

your arm aches.' He pulled me close to him and kissed me gently on the cheek.

The following week Silas bid for the scrap metal; one hundred and ninety cases of it. Silas asked them to pack it in a certain size of packing case, and this cost extra and took three days more. The cases had to be long enough to hold the Vigilant missiles. Finally the cases were sent down to a railway yard, where stuff waited until it was transferred to the docks. Silas and Bob had to go down there to look at it, and since there was no way in which the Magazarians or Geegee could know it was there, Silas decided that it would be safe to take me along. It was freezing, freezing cold. Silas wouldn't allow me to take my mink. He said it would attract attention, although I said that railway men wouldn't be able to distinguish between ermine and coney. I ended up wearing Silas's sheepskin jacket and my tailored green slacks and high boots. I was glad I did. That yard was like an ante room for the arctic. Here and there, little groups of men in old army overcoats huddled around fires made from broken packing cases. The wind came down the railway tracks like an express train and we had to go stepping over the rails and trying to avoid the puddles that wore thin crusts of grey ice and snapped like dinner plates under foot.

Our one hundred and ninety cases were ranged up on the far side of the yard. We had brought one case with us on a hired lorry and Silas gave the railwaymen a pound apiece to move it with their fork lift truck and put it in an accessible position near the railway bank. Inside the case we had brought, Silas had packed six Vigilant missiles. He had got them from a place which hires guns to film companies and he'd paid a high price to have them repainted and greased. Silas marked this crate with a small red mark so that when they came into the yard with Ibo Awawa and Geegee he'd know which one to reluctantly open.

Silas and Bob got out stencils and marked all the cases 'B.H.C. and Co. Import, Port Bovi, Magazarian Republic.'

which was the company that Geegee and Awawa used for 'discreet transactions'. Then for good measure they stencilled each case 'Ordnance, with care,' and then crossed that out. The stencilling took them nearly two hours and the lorry didn't have a heater. I would have helped them but they said I would attract too much attention.

Bob did most of the work. Silas spent most of his time telling Bob he had the stencil upside down or pointing out crates he had missed. Both of them were tired by the time the work was finished. Now they really looked like manual labourers; their faces grimy and their leather jackets paint-splashed and dusty. We all squeezed into the front seat of the lorry and Bob said he was hungry and wanted to pull up at every greasy spoon we passed. Eventually Silas agreed. Although he put on a great show of distaste when we entered the café, he bit into his sausage sandwiches as hungrily as any of us.

Chapter 9

BOB

It was a long time since I had been in a 'good pull-up for car men,' complete with pin tables, slabs of bread pudding and a communal spoon. Silas was in a good mood too. In the truck he was making little humming sounds that were not unmusical. Almost in our hand was the largest amount of money any of us had ever seen. Until then I had practically decided to take up archaeology and leave this con-trick business. I felt out of place with them. I was always alone. Silas was a difficult man to talk to; when you confided in him he usually told you to be a man or pull yourself together or stop reading your useless books. And I couldn't really talk to Liz either, because although I was crazy about her, there was always the risk that she would tell me I was being disloyal and then repeat what I'd said right back to Silas.

So I kept myself to myself. I'd tried to explain about civilisation to both of them, but neither would listen to me. It was quite clear to me from the books I'd read that the first men to wander upon the earth had hunted and fought and cared only for their own family. Later in communities such as the Tigris Euphrates valley, the Nile and the Yellow River, which flooded periodically, men had to work together to protect their crops against the flooding and form communities of common interest and common good. That's what progress really is, and we should learn from that. Being a con man was anti-social. I told them again, over the banger sandwiches, but Liz just giggled. For some reason she found this worker's café funny. I told her not to be a snob. I told Silas too. Silas said, 'These river communities that formed;

were there not wise men or witch doctors or medicine men who advised the community, predicted the seasons and warned them of impending flood?'

'I suppose so,' I said.

'They based their predictions upon the condition of the moon?'

'Probably,' I said.

'Of course they did,' said Silas. 'Well they didn't go around telling everyone about the moon. They were clever, they invented spells, dances and rituals. Their knowledge and observation of the ways of the world had put them into a position of wealth and power, and they held onto it. That's right?' He pushed his half full mug of tea away.

'Don't you want that?' I asked. He shook his head. I drank it while thinking about what he said.

Professor von Schreider's book *Mesopotamia; Melting Pot of Peoples* hadn't put it like that, but Silas could screw any set of facts around to suit his purposes.

'Well we are the medicine men,' said Silas. 'We are the observers, the witch doctors, the sociological sports of our age. We are part of the process of natural selection; for we deprive the stupid and the inefficient of wealth and prestige. Without us the balance of nature would be upset. If the stupid prosper, then our society must lose its dynamism and finally falter. We are part of the life-cycle of the capitalist system.' Quietly and sincerely he added, 'That's a system in which I devotedly believe, and for which I fought in the war.'

'I believe in it too,' said Liz. She collected our empty plates. 'How about you Bob?' she asked. She was just trying to stir things for me.

'Zap, zap, zap. I hate the stinking system,' I said. 'I thought you knew that.'

'What's wrong with the system?' said Silas loudly.

'Blokes like you are running it,' I said.

A lorry driver at the next table shouted, 'Hear, hear, mate. Up the workers.'

Silas put on his glasses and looked around, surprised that his old leather jacket hadn't made him one of the proletariat.

'I suppose you would prefer Babylon?' he said.

I said, 'Babylon, although often described as a bureaucratic monarchical city-state, provides lots of evidence to suggest that the Babylonian citizen could be more directly compared to a communist citizen when we consider burial fees, land dues and taxes.'

Silas nodded but I could tell he was niggled. 'That's good to hear,' he said. 'Very good to hear, but now let's try to have one small segment of the day in which no one is talking about Babylonians.'

'O.K.' I said. 'If that's what you want.'

Chapter 10

SILAS

Napoleon had a maxim about combination of arms. 'Infantry, artillery and cavalry cannot dispense with each other,' he said. I saw the three of us like that. That is not to say that we would *never* be able to dispense with each other, but during an operation it was essential that there was good communication and cooperation between us. I saw Liz as my cavalry; her role was recce and infiltration. Using her feminine skills, a pretty girl can see people and dig out things that would take a man weeks. In this operation she had found this fellow Geegee in the first place, and he had confided in her straight away and been delighted to have her along, to talk to and pump Mr. Ibo Awawa.

Bob was artillery; not very imaginative, not able to think on his feet, but as a way of dropping a bombshell of careless talk right into the enemy camp he was a gem. Bob's clumsiness was his great value. My role was not only the infantry, but also supreme commander. Planning, research and execution were all my responsibility. The trip down to the railway yards at Southampton was a typical example of the care that I was prepared to put into a rehearsal. I had re-stencilled all the boxes personally, and I had put one – carefully marked – case in position. Mr. Awawa or Geegee Grey might want to look inside. These Vigilant anti-tank weapons are nearly four feet long with their launchers so I had put four of them in padded racks as the top layer of the case. They had all been old and damaged when I got hold of them, but repainted and bulled up with instruction stencils they looked as good as new. Of course I wouldn't agree to opening a case at the first suggestion of it. (In fact I would try to prevent them going to Southampton at all.)

The documents for the purchase and shipment of the scrap metal were very impressive; signed, countersigned and cleared for export. I put them into an old War Office folder I had, and then clipped the outside and wrote confidential on it. All that remained was to exchange the papers for the Magazarian War Department's money, and that would be done in the Embassy next day, unless they insisted upon the Southampton trip. This was the way a proper operation was planned.

It was a fine operation. I had been responsible for many jobs but none were more carefully prepared. Some of my operations had been successful, some unsuccessful, but I had never been defeated. To be defeated is to be asked something for which you have not prepared an answer. My first line of fortifications was the Defence Ministry documents, manifests, and consignment notes. The second line was that the cases were at the railway yards if anyone should enquire by phone. The third line of defence was that the cases could be inspected, they were correctly stencilled for transhipment and purchased by me. The final position was four reconditioned Vigilant guided missiles in first class condition inside the most accessible packing case. The troops were on the start line and it was one minute to go. I sang lustily as we drove back from Southampton. I sang an old song called 'We're going to hang out the washing on the Siegfried Line'. It had been hard and cold work stencilling those cases and as it was lunchtime I thought it would be good fun to stop at one of those lorry driver's pull-ups. I parked outside a filthy old hut marked 'Bill's Cafe. Egg and chips all day.' I locked up the Bedford and we went inside for egg and chips. I was somewhat amused to record that there was but one teaspoon which remained chained to the counter like a medieval bible. There was a babel of conversation about dog racing and television, the air was heavy with steam and burned fat, and the plastic tables awash with tea. But I entered into the fun and soon Bob was asking me questions about his new interest – archaeology. As usual Bob was more interested in the trivia of the subject rather than the broad platform of oriental scholarship.

When the conversation had degenerated into a comparison of Ancient Babylon and modern Russia, I felt we were beginning to excite too much attention among the lorry drivers, so I gently but firmly steered the conversation on to more everyday topics.

As a way of maintaining contact with the enemy forces I had decided to have dinner with Geegee Grey that evening. This would enable me to have some idea of what the Magazarians might ask when I attended the Embassy next day for lunch and payment. I had promised to phone Geegee before three p.m. and I used the cramped, graffiti-adorned phone box at the café. A woman's voice answered Geegee's phone. 'Hello,' she said, and then before I could reply, she said, 'Hello. Hello. Hello, who is it?'

'It's a friend of Mr. Grey,' I said authoritatively.

'Oh dear,' she said.

'What's wrong?'

She said, 'He's in an awful state, I can tell you. He's soaking wet, he'll catch his death of pneumonia, you know.'

'Who?' I said.

'Mr. Grey, that's who. He's had a bash on the head and he's black and blue.'

'How did it happen?'

'How should I know. I come in from two to four-thirty on Mondays, Wednesdays and Fridays. I just came in and found him unconscious. Shall I phone the doctor?'

'Luckily Mrs. . . .'

'Sanderson. Mrs. Sanderson.'

'Well luckily Mrs. Sanderson. I am a medical man myself.'

'Is that a doctor?'

'Exactly, Mrs. Sanderson. You've put it rather more neatly than I have. I am, as you have intimated, a doctor. Is he breathing Mrs. Sanderson?' I asked. There was a clatter as she put the phone down. After a long pause she returned, 'Yes, he's breathing. Do you want to know anything else?'

'Breathing is the main thing,' I said.

'Yes,' she agreed philosophically. 'Breathing is the main thing. He's bleeding you know,' she said.

'Not spurting though,' I said.

'No, not spurting,' she agreed reluctantly. 'Just oozing, but I'm worried about him. He's such a nice man; Mr. Grey.'

'Let him ooze until I get there,' I said.

'I'll be waiting,' she said.

'Look Mrs. Sanderson. I've got a young daughter of my own, and I wouldn't ask either you, or her, to get your name dragged through the police courts and mixed up in a nasty case in the newspapers. Goodness only knows what might be behind it. You think of yourself first, Mrs. Sanderson. You let yourself out and forget the whole business. It will take me only a couple of minutes to get there. You leave these unpleasant matters to us, we get paid to sort them out.'

'That's what I'd like to do doctor.'

'Well, you do that Mrs. Sanderson. Be sure to leave the door on the latch and toddle along home.'

'If you say so doctor, but I don't like to leave him alone.'

'I'm only around the corner,' I said. 'He'll be all right for a moment or two.'

I went back to Bob and Liz and mobilised them quickly. I drove back trickling through vast armies of road repair workers who constantly occupy Britain's highways. It was nearly two hours before we reached Bayswater. I parked behind the block of flats in which Geegee lived and hurried inside. I avoided the caretaker and then made sure that there was not a lift man.

Mrs. Sanderson had left the door ajar. Geegee was sprawled across the bed. He was bruised and cut and still bleeding slightly. I put my hand on his shoulder in an attempt to rouse him. He was soaking wet. He opened his eyes.

'Brigadier Lowther,' he said weakly. 'Have to call off dinner I'm afraid.'

'Never mind dinner,' I said. 'What the devil's happened here?'

I looked around the flat. It was like the furniture department of Harrods; silk, gilt and bobbles. 'What are you doing dressed like a Teddy boy?' asked Geegee. I went into the bathroom and came back with a damp cloth to bathe his bruised face. The floor of the bathroom was awash. The soap and sponges and cloths had been thrown in every direction.

'Security, Geegee,' I said. 'A special assignment. Can't talk about it, I'm afraid.' Geegee flinched as I washed the tender abrasions on his cheek and chin.

'I quite understand,' said Geegee. 'Intelligence; I've just been reading a book about it.'

'Good chap, I said, 'well you understand. Now, tell me what all this is about.'

'Gambling,' said Geegee. 'I owe a gambling club three thou. They think I'm being difficult, but I just don't have it.' I nodded.

'You'd better take care who you're opening the door to Geegee.'

'I won't be able to go to work for a few days,' said Geegee. 'I mean, I'll look a sight until the swelling goes down.'

'You will,' I said.

'Get me a mirror,' said Geegee. I unhooked one from the bathroom and took it into him. He studied his face. 'I'd better not come to the Embassy with you tomorrow,' he said.

'Perhaps you'd better phone,' I said. 'Give them your apologies and tell them to expect me.'

'No need for that,' said Geegee. 'They never forget anything. They will be expecting you.' I nodded and walked into the living room. There wasn't much damage except for a broken ash tray and a dented standard lamp. 'Do you want a doctor, Geegee?' I said.

'No,' said Geegee. 'Just let me sleep.'

'Call me if you want anything,' I said.

Geegee just groaned gently, so I closed the curtains, lit the electric fire and let myself out. I hurried around the corner to where Liz and Bob were waiting in the Bedford lorry.

'He's been beaten up,' I said. 'He's bruised and he's bloody.'

'Beaten up, what for?' said Bob.

'He says for gambling, a three thousand pound debt. A debt he can't afford to pay.'

'What's going round in your mind now?' Liz asked me.

'Supposing he asked me to pay his debt for him because he couldn't face the idea of getting beaten up again?'

'Well, what's wrong with that?' said Liz. 'He's the middle-man in the deal.'

'That's just human,' agreed Bob. 'That's just what anyone would do. Especially since we are collecting three hundred grand tomorrow. What's worrying about that? Anyone would ask you.'

'The worrying thing,' I said, 'is that he didn't ask me.'

I was due at the Magazarian Embassy in Belgravia at one o'clock. Bob and I both wore civilian clothes. A flag moved sluggishly in the damp morning air. The brass plate with the words 'Republic of Magazaria Embassy,' was brightly polished and so was the big bell pull under it. I tugged at it and the doors opened instantly.

'Come in sir,' said a thin elegant negro in a black suit and dazzling white shirt. Two other men similarly attired, stood in the hall, just in case there was a sudden onslaught of hats and coats and umbrellas. It was a large entrance hall, the floor was black and white marble, and there were two antique mirrors that reflected a bowl of fresh flowers into an infinity of gilt and blooms. A sign on a wooden pedestal said 'Visa Department', and at the foot of the staircase there was a large hand-coloured photograph of a man in a fez, captioned 'Our President'. The frame was slightly askew. Dark-suited footmen opened a double door leading off the hall and ushered me through. There was a waiting room with leather armchairs, new and unused, placed strategically around a glass topped coffee table. Scattered around there were copies of *Autocar*, *Whats on*, *The Connoisseur* and some journals about engineering. Before I had a chance to sit down, the door at the far end opened and a young man approached me smiling and extending a hand.

'Brigadier Lowther?' he said. And without waiting for a reply said, 'I'm Ali Lin. The War Minister has been unexpectedly tied up, but he urges me to commence lunch without him.' He smiled again. His English was precise and fluent. His suit was Brooks Brothers, and with it he wore a button-down shirt and a college or regimental tie that I did not recognise. He walked through a couple of small connecting rooms and into a rather grand dining room. I followed. Holland blinds at the windows made the light yellow and sunny as it fell across the meal, set out on the floor in Arab style. Six places had been laid. Small bowls of nuts, pickles and sweetmeats were dotted upon a fine damask cloth and soft leather cushions arranged around it. Two negroes were already seated. They wore Arab headdress and dark glasses. On the walls there were antelope and leopard skins. There were carpets too: soft Kirman carpets and silk floral ones from Kashan. Antique Mujur prayer mats and modern ones from the Caucasus. I'd say there was £20,000 worth of carpets in that room, and I'm not a bad judge. We sat down. A waiter in a starched white jacket pushed the drinks trolley to me. I noticed that the two negroes were sipping water.

'I'll have a soft drink,' I said.

'I'm having Scotch,' said Ali.

'Then I will too,' I said. The waiter poured a treble

measure into a heavy tumbler and I took it with plenty of water. Ali took the same. He held the glass up, 'Here's health,' he said.

'Bottoms up,' I said.

'I have taken the liberty,' said Ali, 'of inviting your driver to join us for lunch. I hope you don't mind.'

'Not at all,' I said, although I trust I left him in no doubt that I considered it rather bad form. Bob came in looking awkward and sheepish. He handled it very well. He took a drink, snatched his cap off and then fumbled about, trying to hold cap and drink at the same time. 'Sit down,' said Ali. 'Sit down next to your Brigadier.'

'Hello sir,' said Bob. He didn't sit down.

'Hello Cartwright,' I said frostily.

'I'd just as soon have mine in the kitchen,' said Bob, putting his weight first on one leg, then on the other, and shuffling his feet.

'Not at all,' said Ali. 'I won't hear of it.'

'This foreign food upsets me,' said Bob.

'Nonsense,' said Ali, smiling warmly. 'I shall select what you eat personally. You will enjoy it.'

Bob sat down next to me. Ali clapped his hands. Four waiters entered. They wore red jackets and green aprons. They placed huge silver platters on the damask cloth in front of us. There were four chickens from which came the smell of coriander and honey. There were small balls of ground mutton that Ali called kefta and urged upon Bob. Saffron flavoured rice, olives and large bowls of yoghurt were placed near each guest and so were discs of Arab bread scorched golden in the oven and almost two feet across. Ali reached for some bread and tore it apart greedily. He kept up a conversation all through the meal pronouncing upon everything from the state of the London theatre to the discomforts of jet travel. Ali wrenched choice pieces of chicken from the dish with his hand and offered them to Bob in Arab fashion. When we had eaten enough, servants brought brass bowls and poured warm, scented water upon our greasy hands. Then came soft, sugar-dusty Turkish delight sparkling with rose water. Turkish coffee came too, and tall ornamental hookahs glowing with hot coals. I put the mouthpiece to my lips and inhaled the cool smoke. We smoked silently for a few minutes. Ali offered us liqueurs and brandy, but I declined and Bob took his cue from me.

'You have enjoyed our hospitality,' said Ali. There was the merest hint of a question there. I nodded. Ali swivelled around, clenched his fist and aimed a blow into his soft leather cushion. He leaned back into it, and plucking a segment of Turkish delight from a silver bowl, he said, 'And now you will doubtless be wanting to see the War Minister.' He bit into the sweet.

'He's not joining us for lunch?' I said.

'Alas,' said Ali. 'He has been tied up all this time.'

'Tied up?' I echoed. It seemed rude of Ali to offer no fuller explanation.

'That's it,' said Ali, 'but he will see you now before he leaves for Africa.'

'Is he going to Africa?' I said. 'He didn't mention it.'

'He didn't know himself until today,' said Ali. 'It came as a complete surprise to him.'

'When does he leave?'

'There is a special air freight service that leaves London Airport in ninety minutes time. We have arranged to put him on that.'

'A freight plane,' I said. 'That will be an uncomfortable trip.'

'It will be,' agreed Ali, 'very uncomfortable.'

He got to his feet and led the way to see the War Minister. We went along the corridor and up the main staircase. There were two more black suited negroes upstairs. One of them opened the doors of the room into which Ali showed us. There were no pictures, decorations or carpets hanging in this room. There were partially packed tea-chests surrounded by wood shavings and stacks of antique chinaware and vases. Near the fireplace there was a large packing case marked 'Air freight to Usharu, Magazarian Republic. Handle with care. This way up.'

Ali signalled to the two men who had followed us into the room. 'The War Minister will see you now,' said Ali. He waved them into action. They produced jemmys and levered the front off the packing case. It came away with a loud crack, the bent nails squeaking in the new wood. Inside the crate, Mr. Awawa the War Minister sat, stone still and formal, like Rameses II surveying the Nile. He was clad only in blue striped pyjamas. His wrists and ankles were strapped tight to the throne upon which he sat. A wide cloth band sealed his mouth, and above it his eyes were dilated in terror. One shoulder of his pyjama jacket was spotted with blood.

'Go ahead,' said Ali. 'Conduct your business with the War Minister.' I said nothing. Ali reached for his gold cigarette case and selected a king size filter tip. He closed the case with a loud click. A bead of sweat dribbled down the War Minister's face and his eyes followed Ali as he walked slowly towards the crate. Ali found a loose match in his pocket and after inspecting the match carefully he struck it on that rough edge of the crate nearest to the Minister's face. Without hurrying he lit his cigarette.

'I am delighted to see that you gentlemen display that reticence and modesty for which your countrymen are so renowned,' said Ali. 'Perhaps you will allow me to dwell upon your talents and ambition with less restraint. You told my War Minister that you could supply him with some special type of guns. . . .'

'Anti-tank missiles,' I volunteered.

'Precisely,' said Ali Lin. 'Our tank regiments stayed loyal to us. But now, it is of little consequence what type of weapons,' said Ali with a smile. 'Our War Minister applied to purchase British Army equipment in the usual way that it is sold to friendly countries. Alas I am desolate to admit that he found that we cannot include my own country in that short list. You, however, offered to not only remedy that situation, but to do it at bargain prices. You had him convinced that the consignment (for which you now doubtless hold all the documents) contains guns. By the time my War Minister could have found out that the crates actually contain only scrap metal you will have disappeared. Not a very intelligent swindle, but then our mutual friend is not a very intelligent man.' Ali moved away from the crate and the War Minister's eyes watched him fearfully. 'This fellow you see, had ambitions of his own. He did not want your guns to make his country strong. He wanted them to stage his own revolution and put himself on the throne. Oh yes, the throne, and so we have given him a throne for his journey back to Magazaria.' One of the guards smiled.

'We did the deal for Magazaria,' I protested. 'I've written many articles on the subject of African nationalism. I want to see your nation strong and . . .'

'Close your mouth please,' said Ali. 'You have written nothing. You care for nothing. You are a cheap petty criminal.' There was a sudden flash of anger before he recovered his cold composure. 'Let me explain, Brigadier Lowther. I am here in London as, what they are pleased to call in an age of euphemisms, the Chief of Security. I have a file on you and your pugnacious young colleague and your lady friend too. Any small detail that my men missed was provided by Mr. Guthrie Grey. An unusually incompetent solicitor known to his few friends as Geegee. As kind and co-operative a friend of the Republic of Magazaria as I have ever half-drowned in a bath tub. You see, we have had our ambitious War Minister under observation for several months.' He clapped his hands.

'We'll report you to the Foreign Office if there's any rough stuff,' I said.

'Yes,' said Ali gently, as though speaking to a lunatic. 'Of course you will.' We were seized from behind by several guards and marched from the room. Bob kicked one of them in the ankle. He wriggled free and aiming a glancing blow at another guard, he ran down the corridor.

'Bravo! Get the police Bob,' I called after him. Three guards in the hallway ran up the staircase to stop him, but Bob threw a leg over the banister and slid down it past them. A fourth guard, waiting at the foot of the stairs, took Bob's feet in his chest and was bowled over like a ninepin. Bob and the guard moved across the hall, a blurred ball of flailing arms and legs. They hit the hall table and its great vase of flowers. That in turn toppled a gilt mirror and two oil paintings. There was an awe inspiring crash. The heap of bodies, furnishings, crushed flowers, and torn canvas was quite still for a full minute. I thought they were both dead. Then the heap disinterred itself slowly, the ugly triangles of broken mirror repeating each movement a hundred times. The three guards at the top of the staircase held me very tightly.

'Let the old one go too,' said Ali to the guards. 'Help your stupid friend,' he said to me. 'We were only escorting you to the door.' I hurried down the staircase and began to pull the broken picture frames and smashed pieces of table off the two bodies. The negro guard was unconscious. Bob was holding his head and whimpering with pain. I tried to lift him up. 'He needs a doctor,' I called to Ali. He stared at me. 'We have only witches,' said Ali. 'I am but a poor ignorant native.'

'Get me out of here,' groaned Bob. I put my arm around him and half carried him to the door. Ali and the guards stood at the top of the staircase. Their faces gave no sign of any emotion at all, not even interest. I felt my face flush with shame.

'Get up out of that cot sir,' said Colonel Mason. I stood up and saluted, a difficult feat in the narrow space of the tent. It was the first time I had seen him since the explosion had knocked me unconscious miles away in the desert.

'Don't salute me Lowther,' he said. 'You are not even in the army as far as I'm concerned. You'll go back to Cairo for court martial, until then you can consider yourself under close arrest. You'll take your meals here in this tent, you'll speak with no one. I don't want you contaminating the Regiment. As soon as I can spare an officer as escort I'll send you packing.' Colonel Mason was a plump man of about forty and he stood absurdly at attention while he spoke to me. Each evening he affected breeches and shining boots but in the daytime he wore these tanker's overalls as issued to the other ranks. Th ˋ overalls were grease marked and one sleeve had a cigarette burn in it.

'We'll be going back into action tomorrow,' he said. 'You will not accompany us of course.' The bright sun came through the green canvas and gave a shimmering light like you get when swimming underwater.

'How is my troop sergeant, sir? Sergeant Brian Thetford.'

'He's dead,' said Mason, he watched me carefully.

'I thought it was just his foot burned,' I said. 'I spoke with him after the explosion, he can't be dead.'

'You've a lot to answer for, Lowther.'

'Yes sir,' I said, quietly. Odd, the way a man's face will tan dark brown while his ears remain bright pink.

'Well, that's all,' said Colonel Mason. 'I won't wish you ill Lowther, but my report will do nothing to help you.'

'I don't need help,' I said. 'I don't need help from you, or anyone else.'

We looked at each other for what seemed like a long time. His eyes were grey-blue like Liz's eyes. His face showed no feelings. He turned about rather stiffly. At the tent flap he paused, 'I'll send you a few cigarettes over,' he said, 'and a splash of something.'

'Thank you sir,' I said.

He grunted and as he marched off into the white hot sand, the Embassy door slammed shut behind me.

I helped Bob limp across Belgrave Square. We reached the

ornamental railings and Bob draped himself across them, trying to convince himself that he had no broken bones. I looked at his badly cut knee and at his blood-matted hair and I consoled myself with the wisdom of Sun-Tzu who said, 'The general who advances without coveting fame and retreats without fearing disgrace, whose only thought is to protect his country and do good service for his king. He is the jewel of the kingdom.' We retreated. I helped Bob into the car and I assured him that all would be well.

'Are you crackers?' said Bob. 'They've got your mate Awawa gift-wrapped. Didn't you hear, they are posting him home for Christmas, like a plump turkey.'

'I've other cards up my sleeve,' I said. 'This set-back wasn't entirely unexpected. Wait until I discuss my new plans with you.' I tried to cheer him up. Vegetius, the 4th century Roman commander, had put it better than I ever could. 'Never let your troops imagine that you are retreating in order to avoid an action,' said Vegetius. 'Tell them your retreat is an artifice to draw the enemy into an ambush or put you into a better position.'

In the car I outlined some tentative counter-attacks. Bob said, 'Belt up, Silas, will you, and stop treating me like a five year old kid.'

When the car arrived at the Chester, the doorman – a burly man in a blue coat and shiny top hat – leapt forward to open the door. He shrank back as Bob emerged with his clothing ripped and hard patches of darkened blood across the side of his head.

'My friend has been knocked down in the street,' I explained.

The doorman seemed reluctant to help. 'He's a hotel resident,' I added. The doorman nodded. I said, 'He was knocked down outside Boodles by one of those new Rolls Royce convertibles.'

'Let me help you,' said the doorman, springing into action. He put his beefy hands around Bob and helped him to the lift.

Liz met us at the door of Bob's suite. 'What happened?' she asked.

'Everything went wrong,' I admitted. Then for the porter's sake, I added, 'Bob was knocked down coming out of Boodles,' and winked at her. She nodded, 'You didn't get the money?' she whispered.

'No,' I said angrily. 'I didn't.' She turned away and helped the porter with Bob. He rolled across the bed groaning. The porter wanted to get a doctor, but I told him I was a doctor and gave him ten bob. He went away behind a blur of salutes.

I undressed Bob and tipped him into his bed. A half bottle of whisky would work wonders for him. I poured a whisky, but he demanded coca cola and so I gave him that instead and downed the whisky myself. 'What are we going to do?' he said.

'Speaking for you,' I said. 'Sleep, and that's an order.' I smiled, Bob saluted and toppled lazily back into the sheets.

There was a tap at the door. 'Come in,' I called. It was Bob's waiter friend. 'Yes,' I said. 'What is it?'

'Is Bob all right?' he asked.

'Mr. Appleyard is quite well, thank you,' I said.

'They said he was hurt.' He advanced towards the bed.

'Is that you Spider?' said Bob.

'Yes mate,' said the waiter. 'I heard they had roughed you up a bit.'

'He was knocked down,' I said. 'If you must know.'

'By a brand new Rolls,' said the waiter. 'The doorman told me.'

'I'm all right Spider,' said Bob.

'Shall I get you a drop of soup?'

'I'm going to sleep,' said Bob.

'That's best,' said the waiter. 'I know what it's like.'

'Do you?' I said.

The waiter said, 'But luckily the sort of fellers I cross swords with ride around on bicycles.'

'We'll send for you if we need room service,' I said.

'You can send for me if you need anything sir,' he said. I wasn't sure whether he was trying to be insolent. I nodded and let him go.

'Spider's all right,' said Bob.

'You say that about almost everyone.'

Bob said, 'And I mean it about almost everyone.' I watched him for a minute or so.

'I'll think of something, Bob,' I said. I switched the light out.

'I bet you'll think of something, Silas,' Bob said into his pillow.

I went into Liz's suite. 'Tell me what happened?' she asked. I explained it to her. 'What are we going to do, Silas?' she said.

'It will be all right, caterpillar,' I said. She held me and hung on tight, she was frightened, just like the other one. Sometimes I thought that they would die of starvation if I wasn't along to ring a bell at mealtimes. 'I love you, Silas,' she said.

'And I love you, caterpillar.'

'Could you live without me?' she whispered.

'You know I couldn't, caterpillar,' I said. She held me tight and breathed a sigh of relief.

'How much money have we got left?'

'Five thousand six hundred and sixty-four pounds eighteen shillings and fourpence,' I said.

'And there's the lease on the mews cottage.'

'And there's the three cars and that bloody scrap metal too,' I said. 'But I don't suppose we'll get anything like the price we paid for any of them.'

'Don't you ever get scared, Silas?'

'Sometimes.'

'You never show it.'

'I do,' I said. 'You just don't know the signs.'

'What are the signs?'

'One of the signs,' I said, 'is refusing to answer questions.'

'You're not scared now,' she said. 'Not really scared.'

'You've got to keep a sense of proportion,' I said. 'We are in a luxury suite in the Chester. We have only to press a button to be showered with delicacies to eat, drink and fondle. We have more money in the bank than lots of families save in a lifetime. You have to keep a sense of proportion.'

'Perhaps that's what bravery is, keeping a sense of proportion.'

'You may be on to something there,' I said.

'Don't leave me Silas.'

'Is that what you think of me? We have a slight setback and you think it's a rout. Why should I leave you?' I asked. 'I need you more than you need me, how would I ever replace you? Tell me that and I'll think about leaving you, perhaps.' I gripped her arm and pulled her to me.

'Don't joke,' she said. 'You can find plenty of girls to do the things I do. Plenty of them.'

'There, there, my love,' I said. I knew I must convince her. I held her tight. We stood there in silence for a long time. From Park Lane came the roar of evening traffic. There was fog in the park but the really tall trees didn't have to worry about that, because they could see over it. I said, 'You think I'm some sort of machine. You think I'm unable to have human emotions like love or fear or pain or hunger, just because I try not to show them. But I'm eaten up with fear and pain, and I'm so much in love with you that when I awake in the morning I'm frightened to open my eyes, so convinced am I that you won't be there. When you go shopping I feel I must be with you or you'll be hit by a passing bus. You speak with another man and I'm convinced that I have lost you. And when your looks are reserved solely for me, I fear you are seeing a man old, and wrinkled, and frightened of being left alone.'

'No,' said Liz. 'No,' and she kissed me and hugged me as though she would never let go.

Chapter 11

LIZ

At first Silas had been over-concerned about Bob, and so had I. I was still worried, but after all, Bob had been hurt trying to save his own skin, not performing any act of heroism, so I didn't feel it necessary to hold a sacred vigil at his bedside while he drank coca cola and groaned and felt sorry for himself.

The fiasco at the Embassy had upset Silas to a point where I was worried about him. Not that I encouraged him to feel sorry for himself, on the contrary, I did my best to help him pull himself together. After we had got Bob off to sleep, Silas came tip-toeing into my room.

'You'd better tell me what happened Silas,' I said. He explained how he and Bob had fought their way out of the Embassy, with Bob losing his nerve half way through, and trying to make a bolt for it.

'It will be all right though,' said Silas.

I put my arm around him to comfort him. 'Of course it will,' I said.

'I love you, caterpillar,' said Silas. 'I couldn't live without you.'

'Of course you could,' I said. He hung to me like a survivor on a piece of flotsam. We stood silently for a moment or so. Finally I said, 'How much money do we have left?' Silas said, 'Five thousand six hundred and sixty-four pounds eighteen shillings and fourpence.'

'What about the mews cottage lease and the cars and the scrap metal?' I said. 'You're forgetting about those, aren't you?'

'I'm sorry,' said Silas. 'Yes I'm forgetting those.'

'Don't be scared Silas,' I said.

'Everyone is scared sometimes,' he said.

'Try not to show it,' I said. 'We need to be at our very best. Any time now someone might start asking questions.'

'Well, I just might refuse to answer questions,' said Silas angrily.

'That would be a sure sign,' I said.

'To hell with them,' said Silas. 'I've got to rest up in the hotel for a bit, take it easy, we have enough money left for me to take a rest surely?'

'Depends what you call a rest,' I said. 'We couldn't stop for three months the way you wanted to, when the money seemed ours for certain.'

'Keep a sense of proportion,' said Silas. 'I'll handle the bravery stuff; you keep a sense of proportion.'

'If you say so, caterpillar,' I said.

'Maybe I should leave you,' said Silas. 'Perhaps that would be best for both of us.' He searched my face awaiting my reply.

'Don't think of it, caterpillar,' I said unemotionally. 'We need you.' He gripped my arm spitefully, but I shook myself free.

'I need you,' said Silas. 'I need you more than you need me, how would I ever replace you?'

'There will always be plenty of girls running after you Silas; prettier ones than me, cleverer ones than me. You'd have no trouble replacing me. You are a Svengali with women, so don't pretend you don't know it.'

'There, there my love,' said Silas. He came close to me and held me gently. There was just the last dusty light of day coming into the room. We stood still for a long time. Outside in Park Lane there was the sound of the traffic. A wintry mist was piling up in the park, softly cloaking the trees and exposing only the highest. I kissed Silas briefly. Silas was not as tall as he once was, or was it Bob and I who had grown.

'Don't treat me like a machine Liz,' said Silas. 'I have human emotions like love and hunger, so why shouldn't I show fear once in a while.'

'It's nothing to do with fear Silas, and you know it. Just stop trying to manipulate me.'

'Sometimes I wake up in the morning and I'm frightened to open my eyes, I'm so convinced you won't be there.'

'Stop it Silas,' I said.

'When you go shopping I feel I must be with you, or you'll be hit by a passing bus. You speak with another man, and I'm convinced that I have lost you.'

'No, Silas, no.'

'And when your looks are reserved solely for me, I fear you are seeing a man, old and wrinkled and frightened of being left alone.'

'No Silas,' I said. 'I won't fall for that stuff again. You think you can twist me around your little finger. You don't even bother to vary the sales talk, but it won't work any longer.' I sobbed and kissed him. 'No,' I said, 'No.' I didn't want to cry in front of him but I couldn't prevent myself.

Silas took me for an evening on the town. I put on my silver dress and my mink stole and Silas wore his new evening suit with a tall old-fashioned collar and a gold rimmed monocle that he could hold in his eye, even when he laughed. We hired a chauffeur and used Silas's sleek black Rolls as we purred from a restaurant to a party and from there to a discotheque and gambling club named Ysobels. Silas won fifty-two pounds at the tables, and bought champagne for everyone and tipped the croupier too lavishly. He was twelve pounds up at that stage and feeling reckless, he put a ten pound chip across 10 and 11 and it paid him one hundred and seventy pounds. He put the whole lot on to the odd numbers and thirty-three came up, so he doubled his money, then he put twenty-five pounds each on to 1, 2, 4, 8, 16 and 32. This doubling up of the numbers being, what Silas calls, his system. Thirty-two paid off and he had nearly a thousand pounds. I pulled him away from the tables and we wént downstairs. We had a drink at the bar and then we danced. Silas was happy.

This was a discotheque for short haired, starch linened, middle aged, wealthy swingers, and the music was slow and square, and so were the dancers and no one pushed or spilt drinks on you. For a moment I again saw Silas through the grease lensed haze in which I'd fallen in love with him. I held him and danced close and tried to pretend that it was five years ago.

We were having one last drink before going home when a fat man in a dinner suit and white carnation spoke to Silas.

'Did I see you make that most comfortable little win upstairs, sir?' said the fat man. He fingered his slim moustache.

'That's right,' said Silas finishing his drink. The barman arrived to serve the fat man, who ordered a large brandy and added, 'and the same again of whatever they are drinking for my two friends there.'

Silas hated people speaking to him in bars – perhaps because con men make contact with suckers that way – but I suppose he thought that in our present position a new acquaintance couldn't hurt us.

'I love lucky people,' said the fat man. 'I always hope that a little of their luck will rub off on me. Forgive me for presuming to buy you a drink, but don't let me delay you if you were just about to go.'

'We're not in that much of a hurry,' said Silas.

'Good,' said the fat man. 'Have a cigar.'

Silas nodded. The fat man called to the bar tender. 'Kenny. Bring my Coronas over would you.'

'I feel I should be treating you,' said Silas.

'No, no, no,' said the fat man. 'A win is good for a place. At least every one says it is. Too much good like that, I sometimes say to my partner, and we'll be in Carey Street.'

The fat man laughed gently to conclude his joke.

'Are you the owner?' asked Silas.

'My God, I wish I were,' said the fat man. 'No, I have only twenty-eight per cent. My line is movie making. I'm a rich producer.'

He laughed again in self mockery. A cigarette girl came past and he clicked his fingers at her and asked for matches. On the cigarette tray there were boxes of chocolates and some fluffy toys. The fat man held up one of the fluffy toys – a panda. 'Isn't that cute?' he said. His voice had a faint transatlantic burr. 'I think they are really cuddly,' he said. 'I have one in the car. The kids play with it all the time.'

I tried to muster the appropriate amount of enthusiasm. I said it would look nice on my dressing table.

'On the bed,' he said. 'Put your nightdress under it, ready in case of fire.' He laughed. Then he whispered to the cigarette girl.

'Are you in the entertainment business?' the fat man asked Silas.

'I'm in mining,' said Silas. 'Amalgamated Minerals, that's my line of country. I'm the President of the U.K. subsidiary.'

It was typical of Silas to revert to his previous success. By now guns from Magazaria was ancient history, almost erased from his memory.

'Fascinating,' said the fat man. 'I've often been advised to put all my money into mining.'

'I wouldn't go so far as to say that,' said Silas cautiously. 'No, I certainly wouldn't. A fortune is easily lost if you aren't well advised.'

'Like jade,' said the fat man. 'I bought fourteen thousand pounds worth of jade last September. Half of it was worthless. They say it's the most difficult thing in the world to judge the value of jade.'

'Well, mining is like that,' said Silas. This time Silas ordered drinks. Then the cigarette girl came back staggering under the weight of two of the most ridiculous looking fluffy toys that I've ever seen. One was a panda and the other a rabbit, each was over four feet tall, and I'm telling you they were awful. Since the fat man owned the place, what could I do, but say they were gorgeous.

'Put them on your bed,' said the fat man.

'I couldn't accept them,' I protested.

'I insist.'

'Thank you,' I said finally and deposited them gently on the floor where they stood almost as tall as the bar top, like a couple of children waiting to be taken home.

'It's been nice talking to you,' said the fat man. 'Are you coming in again this week?'

'I might come in tomorrow,' said Silas.

'Eric Friendly is my name. Friendly by name, friendly by nature. My friends call me Lucky Eric.'

'Are you lucky?' I asked him, after all, he had bought me those awful toys.

'My friends say I am,' said the fat man. He tugged on the ends of his bow tie very hard as though trying to choke himself. He released his grip and then smiled with relief. 'My friends say anyone as simple as me is lucky to stay solvent.' He laughed and slapped Silas on the arm with glee. 'Ask for me here at the bar any time. If I'm upstairs in my private office I'll come right down.'

'Right ho,' said Silas.

'Thanks for coming,' said the fat man. 'Don't forget your toys.'

'No, I won't,' I said. I picked them up and gave them to Silas. Silas gave a sickly little smile as we walked out through the bar with everyone looking at him.

When we collected our coats Silas said to the doorman, 'That chap at the bar, Bert, is he a new member?'

'Yes, Colonel, he joined a couple of months ago.'

'Talks like he owned the place.'

'Some new members get like that sir.'

'What do you know about him?' Silas asked.

'Well sir,' said the doorman. 'We've known each other a long time sir, if you don't mind me reminding you.' He paused deciding how to go on. 'And he's not the sort of feller a gentleman like you should play cards with, if you take my meaning, Colonel Lowther.'

Silas pushed a tightly wadded pound note into his hand, and said, 'I do indeed Bert. I do indeed.'

Bert the doorman put the toys into the car alongside the chauffeur, and saluted us. Silas said to me, 'Lucky Eric, eh? Cheap little gas meter bandit.'

'How can you be sure?' I asked Silas.

'I can smell them,' said Silas. 'And do you know something, some people with a sharp nose, detect a similar odour on me? There but for the grace. . . .'

'Oh no, darling,' I said. Silas shrugged and for a moment or two was silent.

'The Chester,' Silas called to the chauffeur and his sleek black Rolls slid gently through the night.

I touched Silas's arm and he leaned over to kiss me on the face. 'Happy?' he asked.

'Wonderfully,' I said. We came past St. James's Palace to turn into Piccadilly. There were no sentries there but some of the tiny windows were lit up. I tried to imagine what it would be like inside the palace rooms. The streets were wet and the rain continued to fall as light as a mist. Two policemen were standing under the portico of the Ritz watching a well-dressed drunk stealing an oil lamp from the road works. He picked it up carefully, so that the draught would not blow out the flame, he carried it high to light his way. The policemen didn't move. They didn't have to, a few more steps and the man would be on top of them. The traffic lights changed and our Rolls moved smoothly forward, I tried to see through the dark blue glass but the story had no end. So many stories have no end.

I'd had too many whisky sours. I leaned back on the seat and saw Silas glamoured up and slightly out of focus. His hair was disarranged and chin was dimpled the way I had noticed it the time I'd first met him when I was not much more than a child.

'I wish we weren't . . . what we are Silas.'

Silas laughed. 'So does everyone,' he said.

'I mean I wish we had never pulled any con trick on anyone ever.'

'Perhaps you do now,' said Silas, 'but what about tomorrow, when you wake up sober and cold and without enough money to pay the rent?'

'Perhaps I still would then,' I said.

'Look, caterpillar,' said Silas. 'I've been around a long, long time, and one thing I'll tell you true; there isn't a man, woman or child in this world who can say they have never conned someone out of something. Babies smile for a hug, girls for a mink, men for an empire. No one, I promise you; no one, caterpillar.' He took my hand. His hand was cold and hard.

'Do you ever feel Silas,' I asked, 'that it would be nice to have a home? Somewhere to go back to. Somewhere other than a hotel room. Somewhere we could leave things that we weren't using?' I tried to make the suggestion sound practical and my enquiry without motive.

'A base you mean?' said Silas.

'Yes a base.'

'No caterpillar. I never do. Never. I'm a wanderer, always have been. I fear I'll never change now.' He kissed me again. 'Why, do you feel that you'd be happier if we had a base?'

'Never,' I said. 'Certainly not. I'm a wanderer too, remember. I'll never settle down in one place. I'd hate it.' Silas patted me affectionately. 'Lucky Eric,' said Silas scornfully.

Chapter 12

BOB

Spider Cohen came back into my room about half an hour after Silas had tipsy-toed out. 'Hello Spider,' I said.

'I've got iced water and surgical spirit. You want to get a cold wet rag on those marks or you'll be looking a right mess of G.B.H.'

I took the bowl of water and ice and wrung the cloth out before plastering it across my face. 'That's the way to do it sir,' he said.

'Cut out the sir, Spider,' I said. 'You remember me from the Scrubs don't you? I was in B Block when you were a red band.'

'I remember all right. Being in nick's not so simple to forget is it? I didn't want to embarrass you, that's all.'

'You mean with Liz and my boss; Silas Lowther? He's a nob, a Brigadier in the tanks. Good bloke.'

'Yeah. Well that's nice Bob.'

'Oh Christ I'm sorry Spider. I wouldn't do it on *you* mate. Really I wouldn't. He's my opposite number . . . you know, we work together. He's the world's oldest juvenile delinquent.' I laughed.

'I know Bob. I had it sussed when you first checked in. You are a really high class con now. Really high class.'

'It's that obvious eh?'

'You get good at spotting the scene working here.'

'Yeah, I suppose so.'

'Has your guvnor got any form?'

'Silas, in the nick? Give over mate. He's a real gent. Harrow, Oxford, Royal Armoured Corps, Alamein, D Day, the lot.'

'How did he get on to this game then?'

'Fiddling in the army. He was in Germany in 1945. Made a bomb of money. When he got demobbed, he couldn't get used to being without the luxuries.'

'Well, looks like he hasn't *had* to get used to doing without them. That bird of his is really a dish.'

'You're right there,' I said.

'You've done well too, Bob. Are you happy with the way it's gone?'

'Right up until this smack in the kisser,' I said. 'But it's a mug's game really. I've enjoyed it up until now but I've known for a long time that it has to come to an end. It's O.K. for Silas, but I want to do something more positive, something a bit more worthwhile. Do you know what I mean Spider?'

'The grass always grows greener on the other side of the fence mate.' Spider said. 'Have a mouthful of this.' He pulled a hipflask out of his pocket and wiped the top before passing it to me. He still hadn't lost the furtive manner of the Scrubs days. I said, 'There's some booze next door.'

'Have mine,' said Spider.

'O.K.,' I said, and drank.

'Good stuff eh? The wine waiter is a mate of mine. I've got good friends Bob.'

I drank some more. I said, 'Did they give you a remission?'

'Three years, all but four days, I did,' he said. 'And I ain't never going back.'

'What's that mean?' I said. 'Villains say that when they are facing half a dozen coppers with a loaded machine gun in their hand.'

'I'm straight. Dead straight. I work hard, I live on my wages and my brother-in-law is a copper.'

'Get away.'

'It's true, as true as I'm standing here. My brother-in-law is practically a copper; he's a screw.'

I laughed. He said, 'Remember my sister Ethel. Nice little kid, blonde; long straight hair, good looker.'

'Everybody remembers her. She came to see you every week. The only good looking bird that ever came into that nick.'

'Right. Well she comes in to see me every chance she gets, doesn't she. She brings me snout and sweets, and sometimes a cake from Mum. Lovely kid, and it's a long way for her to come, Balham. Never misses, and she's all for me, all for me. You know, when Mum is sitting there and saying "take your punishment Sydney. . . .'

'Is that your name, Sydney?' I said.

'Yeah. Well, when she's saying that, little Ethel is saying "don't go on at him", and she went round to Charlie Barrett, who I worked for, made him promise to give me my job back, when I came out of prison. She was a real angel. I'm not kidding Bob, she was great, that kid. Well, anyway she even chats up one of the screws and talks him into giving me messages on the weekends when she hasn't got a visit. Then she gets him to give me some fags that she'd bought for me, so you can guess what happened.'

'No kidding?'

'Yeah. He meets her outside to get the fags and messages, then one day he comes up to me and says, "I'm going around with your sister," I could have sloshed him, nearly did in fact. "Steady Spider," he says, "We're serious," he says, "we love each other." "Get out of it" I said. "I don't want my sister marrying no screw." But you know something; he's all right.'

'I believe you,' I said unenthusiastically.

'It's true. He's a funny geezer, but he's all right. He's crackers about Ethel mind you. If I thought he was playing around with anyone I'd murder him.'

'Fancy that,' I said. I laughed, my bruised face hurt. 'You're a tonic you are Spider,' I said.

'Yeah, you looked a bit down in the mouth. You looked

like things weren't going too well.'

'Well we. . . .'

He raised his hands. 'Sorry. Sorry. Don't get me wrong. I wasn't trying to pump you.'

'Hell Spider. It's all gone wrong, that's all. We spent a bit of money on this one too. It looked good, and the money was right in the palm of our hand. A lot of money, oh well.'

'Here, come up west tonight,' said Spider. 'It's my night off.'

'With this face?'

'Who will worry. Will you worry? No. Will I worry? No. We'll meet ourselves a couple of birds and if they worry, we'll ditch them for another couple.'

'It's an idea,' I said.

'I finish at eight. I'll be changed and ready by eight thirty.'

'Shall we use my Rolls?'

Spider was taking a drink of his brandy at the time, and he nearly choked as the notion hit him. He spluttered and chuckled and cried with the thought of it. 'What a caper,' he kept on saying as he left the room. 'What a right turn-up for the book; us two yobbos and a flash Rolls Royce, that we haven't nicked.' I could hear him coughing in the corridor outside on his way back to the pantry.

I slept until half past seven, when I got up and changed into my suit. I knew Spider would be wearing his best gear. I met him round the corner so as not to let the hotel staff see us together, and then we drove into Soho whistling from the Rolls at every good looking bird we saw on the way.

Once a big bloke in a sports car caught me up and wanted to start an argument because he said I'd insulted his bird at the last lot of traffic lights, but I said, 'Couldn't have been me ducky, I can't whistle, and anyway us two are . . . that way dearie.' I gave a camp wave of the wrist.

He looked at us but then revved up and drove off like a maniac while Spider fell under the dashboard in convulsions. You could easily tell it was going to be a great night.

In Soho we stopped for a chinwag with two of Spider's cronies who were leaning against the wall outside a narrow entrance. There were a dozen or more signs naming enterprises that had failed upon that spot.

'It's a billiards room,' said Spider, 'fancy a game?'

'No thanks,' I said.

Two tourists came past. One of Spider's friends – a man called Newmarket Tony – spoke to them softly and respectfully. 'Like to see a blue film sir? Just about to start.' In his hand he had a book of numbered tickets.

'How much?'

'Five pounds for each of you gentlemen. Just about to start.'

'Make it three pounds each,' said one of the tourists. Newmarket Tony considered the matter but reluctantly declined. 'I'd like to do it,' he explained, 'but there's the projectionist to pay and the fellow that owns the place. I couldn't do it for less than four pounds ten, and that's losing half of my own ten bob.'

The two tourists bought tickets from Tony's friend, a tall boy with spectacles who said very little. The tourists went upstairs, 'Have a cup of coffee first,' called Tony after them. 'He's just sorting out the reels.'

Three football fans had gathered around Newmarket Tony by this time, realising that he was dealing in something illicit and delightful. He sold them each a ticket and within four minutes had disposed of tickets to an elderly man with a briefcase and two Chinese waiters. 'Look son,' said a passerby to Tony. 'I want to see a special blue film. Got me?'

'Sure thing,' said Newmarket Tony. 'What do you want?'

'I saw it before in a hotel room in Miami,' said the man. 'I'm Canadian and I've searched around the world for that film.'

'I've got all kinds,' said Newmarket Tony.

'This is a coloured boy, wrestling in mud with a Chinese girl. It's in the deep south and there's no referee. Got me?

Two Lascar seamen join in at the end of the film. That's the only blue film I'd be interested in seeing.'

Behind the Canadian, an Italian boy with an expensive camera around his neck was asking for a translation of the Canadian's request. Before Newmarket Tony could reply, the Canadian added, 'I remember now, there's one bit where they all dress up in policeman's uniform.'

Newmarket Tony thought for no more than a second or two, 'You almost stumped me there sir,' he said. He smiled, 'That one came in today.'

'It did?' said the Canadian. 'Say that's really something.'

'Pay for this first one,' said Tony, 'and I'll get him to put that on right after.' The Canadian was as pleased as punch. 'Is that so,' he said. 'Well you fellows really do pick them out.' He rubbed his hands gleefully and went upstairs. So did the Italian boy.

'No cameras,' said Newmarket Tony. 'One of our rules. Cameras must be left at the door here.' The Italian reluctantly handed Tony his camera.

Newmarket Tony looked at his watch. 'Will you tell the others, it starts in three minutes. He's putting a new lamp in, the last one's going a bit dim.' The Italian boy didn't understand too well but finally nodded.

'Let's scarper,' said Newmarket Tony's friend.

'Can't we see the blue film?' I asked.

'Is your mate crackers?' Newmarket Tony asked Spider. 'Let's split.'

'It's a billiards place,' said Spider to me. 'I told you, didn't I?'

Newmarket Tony said a brief goodnight and hurried down the road stuffing the camera into his pocket. His friend hurried after him.

'Let's go,' said Spider. 'Sometimes they're really mad when they come out. One night six Irishmen smashed the billiards hall to pieces.'

Not one hundred paces down the road and zap, I am

suckered by a con man. What am I saying hundred, not fifty paces even. A ragged old man in a greasy cap and shoes that don't belong on the same human together, came hurrying out of a pub with a hunted look in his eye, and a torn carrier bag clasped to his chest. He clawed at me as I passed and pulled me to a halt. Then he gives me the old I-just-found-this-ring-and-do-you-know-if-it-might-be-valuable-give-me-ten-bob-and-it's-yours routine. I tried to get away from him, it's the oldest con trick in the world, but he held on to my arm and flashed his eyes like the second chorus of the Ancient Mariner.

I said, 'I fell out of my cradle laughing at that one Dad.'

'Seven and a tanner,' he said. 'I need it son.'

I gave the poor old bugger three half crowns and he put a warm little Asprey's box into my hand. Inside it was a flashy little fake diamond ring, but anyone would have to have been half drunk to take it seriously. He shuffled back into the public bar and I knew the seven and six would be gone inside five minutes. I dropped the ring into my pocket and hurried after Spider.

'What did you give him?' Spider asked.

'Nothing,' I said. 'I told him to clear off before I hung one on him.'

'You liar,' said Spider cheerfully, 'you're the easiest touch in town.'

Spider knew all the places. There were low dives full of clerks trying to look like gangsters. There were restaurants where the tourists looked at each other and thought they recognised film stars, but best of all there was a Palais de Danse. A great big barn of a place full of noise and smoke and people. Inside were Irish labourers who'd put ink on their hands so that they could tell the girls they were clerks. There were hairy little pop groups with smelly clothes, and big flash fellers with diamond rings. There were girls everywhere in all shapes and sizes. We sorted out a couple and bought them fizzy drinks.

'Course we are just looking at this place on behalf of an American TV show,' says Spider in his fake posh voice.

'Go on,' says the tall bird. She's a tall, well-built girl with blue eyes and long straight blonde hair. Her name's Marlene – or so she says – and she's dressed in a sort of open work knitted top and a really tight-fitting pair of hipsters. The other bird – Meg or Peg or something the name was – has a funny little short dress with sparkling stuff sprinkled all over her hair. A right couple they made.

'A TV show,' said Marlene. 'Do me a favour.'

'Straight up,' insisted Spider. 'He's got his Rolls outside, and he's got a suite at the Chester.'

'Get away,' said the shorter girl.

'I'm telling you,' says Spider. Then he turns to me and from behind his hand says, 'Don't let's worry about these two scrubbers,' he says. 'We'll go for something a bit more classy.'

'What do you mean?' says the tall bird, and I could see she was ready to have a go at him.

'No thanks Spider,' I says. 'There's no one here a patch on these two broads if you ask me.'

'No one is asking you,' said the short girl refusing to be mollified.

'Well it makes me mad,' said Spider. 'Here we are with your brand new Rolls, and all they've got to do is step across to the door in order to check the facts, and all they can say is as how we are liars.' Spider would have made quite a con man.

'Have you really got a Rolls?' said the tall girl, the one I fancied.

'Come along and have a ride,' I said.

Of course they came. Spider and the short girl got in the back with the stereo full on – bossa nova – and the drink cabinet open and the tall girl Marlene sat alongside me in the front.

'It's a lovely car,' said Marlene, 'did you nick it?'

'Watch your language,' said Spider. 'We'll start thinking you are a right couple of slags.'

'Yeah,' I said. 'Try and behave like ladies.' Both girls giggled. 'Ladies,' said Marlene. Then the other one said, 'Are you behaving like a lady in the front there, Marlene?' and they started convulsions of giggling again.

I drove them right across London, stereo all the way. Gilbert and Sullivan outside the floodlit Tower of London, Pomp and Circumstance in Trafalgar Square and the Irish Guards in stereo outside Buckingham Palace. But the girls weren't interested in anything but hoping to see, and wave to, someone they knew. I dropped Spider at the back of the hotel and then drove up to the front with the girls. The doorman stepped forward to open the door and I slipped him the car keys wrapped up in a pound note.

'Park it for me,' I said.

'And the keys, sir? You'll want those sent up?'

'The morning will be soon enough,' I said. He touched his top hat. Then he caught sight of the two birds. ''Ere,' he says. 'Hold on,' he says. 'Where do you think you lot is going?'

'They're with me,' I says. 'So lay off.'

We walked past him into the hotel and we're all playing it cool until Marlene – who can't leave well alone – says to the doorman, 'Where did you get that hat, Dad?' which in a 'pool accent sounds like 'Weer deejer ge' thut hut, dard?'

Of course the geezer on the door goes spare. 'Get out of it you lot,' he says. 'We don't allow ladies in here with trousers on sir.'

'You saucy old man,' says Marlene, screaming as loud as she can in her Liverpool accent.

'What?' said Meg or Peg.

'He wants me to take me trousers off,' says Marlene.

'You saucy old Dad,' said Meg or Peg. Marlene by this time had taken her belt off and had got the front of her trousers unzipped and half over her hips.

'You'll get us all run-in,' I said, but by that time the doorman was remembering another appointment at the far end of a line of parked cars. I grabbed the two birds and held their arms as we walked into the entrance.

'You're hurting me,' said Marlene, and the other one said I was hurting her too.

'Good,' I said, 'that's for nothing, now be careful.'

We walked through the hotel foyer. It was two a.m. and it was still and silent. I walked over to the lifts with the two dolly girls. They were shy now, and looked out of place in their Carnaby Street dresses and Woolworth sun glasses.

Waiting for the lift were Liz and Silas. Goodness knows where they had been that evening, they were both dressed to kill, and Silas was carrying a gigantic panda toy and an equally large fluffy rabbit. Each toy must have been more than four feet tall, and Silas had trouble holding them.

'What are you doing out this late?' demanded Silas. 'We were anxious about you.'

'I can see that,' I said. 'All four of you look worried to death,' Silas tried to hold the toys less conspicuously, but that's difficult to do with things that size.

'I have a new plan,' said Silas. 'I'll give you your orders in the morning.' My two girls were looking at Silas in ill-disguised awe and studying Liz's silver dress and shoes, as though trying to commit every stitch to memory. Every few minutes they both had little fits of giggling.

'Who's your friend?' I asked, nodding at the panda. Silas said, 'We'll go back there tomorrow and this time pull it off.' Liz said nothing, but she was clutching Silas anxiously, hoping that he wouldn't cause a scene. I suppose he must have had a lot to drink or he wouldn't have bought those stupid toys in a nightclub. I pretended to examine the panda closely. 'Your friend's ear-hole is coming unstitched,' I said. The girls giggled.

'This time it *will* come off,' repeated Silas.

'Well, you'd better get it stitched on,' I said. The lift arrived and we all got in.

We gentlemen allowed the three ladies to enter before us. 'After you,' said the dolly girls to Liz, remembering my admonition to be ladylike, but spoiled the effect by breaking up with laughter right after saying it. Then I let Silas enter which brought him face to face with me except that we were both looking over the head of the toy panda and fluffy rabbit. The rabbit was cross-eyed and the panda had an inane stare, but I didn't mention this to Silas as he seemed to have adopted a rather paternal attitude to them.

'Are you *all* going into your suite?' asked Liz caustically.

'Yes,' I said, 'Are you all going to yours?' The lift arrived at our floor. The three girls walked ahead. Silas said softly and vehemently. 'Just don't say another word, Bob, because this might just be the wrong moment.'

I looked pointedly at his toys, 'Yeah all right,' I said. 'I'll wait until you are alone,' I walked down the corridor. I opened my door and let the two girls in. I could hear them oohhing and arring but I stayed at the door watching Silas. He put the big toys on the corridor floor while he reached for his key. He stepped inside Liz's suite and waited a moment before reaching around the door for the toys, like a naked housewife getting the milk. I had my head around my door at the same level as his. He glanced around apprehensively, I smiled goodnight.

No sooner had his door closed than I heard the jingle of glass and cutlery. Along the corridor came Spider in a waiter's jacket. He was smiling drunkenly, his bow tie askew and white jacket half tucked into his trousers. Before him he pushed a trolley loaded with champagne in an ice bucket, caviar, pate, and smoked trout. He clattered through the door and closed it with exaggerated care.

As he came level with me I said, 'I think you've over-estimated these two,' I nodded towards the sitting room.

'Not me,' said Spider and whisked the cloth off a tray and

revealed trifle, a cream cake decorated with fairies, two multi-colour jellies, and an ice cream cake with almonds on. 'Our children's diet. Compliments – my mate in the kitchen.' He removed his white jacket to reveal bright red braces and a torn shirt. He began pouring the champagne.

'Oooo,' screamed the dolly birds when they saw it all, which was more than they had said of my red Rolls Royce. 'See Spider,' I said. 'You don't need money to get girls.'

'Whoopee,' yelled Spider and, helped by the two girls, he pushed the trolley at breakneck speed across the carpet, through the bedroom door and on until it hit the far wall of my bedroom with a terrific thud. It tore the wallpaper, and a picture of Chinese wild horses fell to the floor and smashed.

'Careful Spider,' I said.

'Aw shurrup,' said Spider, laughing and kissing the girls. 'It's only a party wall.'

'We don't want everyone to know we're having a party,' I said. I was a bit drunk too.

'What's in here?' asked Marlene. She opened my wardrobe and began smashing back the hangers to inspect my clothes.

'Soldier's uniform,' she yelled. 'Fur flying jacket, motor racing gear, kinky leather overcoat, Nazi uniform.'

'What no drag?' says Meg or Peg. The girls tittered.

'Leave it alone,' I said. 'That's my theatrical gear.'

'It's his theatrical gear,' said Meg or Peg. 'Get him.'

'What's this?' said Marlene. It was my box full of archaeological specimens. I didn't want her looking inside.

'That's my crystal,' I said. 'Put it down.'

'What's a crystal?' said Marlene trying to remove the lid. 'It ain't half heavy, isn't it?'

'It's for looking in, to do my forecasts,' I said. Spider who was a good hand at the powerful dialogue said, 'He does the forecasts, you know, astrology in the papers.'

'Which papers?' said Marlene.

'Nearly all of them,' said Spider. 'Under all kinds of different names. They all come to him; he's famous.'

'Get away,' said Meg or Peg.

'That's it,' I said. 'I do all of them.'

'You weren't much cop in Teenage Sweethearts magazine this month,' said Meg or Peg. 'Not for Pisces anyway.'

'It's funny you should say that,' I said. 'That was deliberate. They owe me my fees going back three months. So this week I messed up their Pisces and the Capricorn, I told them I would.'

'Can you do hands?' said Marlene.

'Can he do hands,' said Spider. 'He did my hand last week and told me all about you two coming back here tonight.' Spider gave a short sardonic laugh. 'Can he do hands,' he said.

'What did he say about us tonight?' Marlene asked.

'Brief moment of happiness,' said Spider sadly. 'Snatched from a life of toil and torment.'

'What else?' Marlene asked me. She held her hand out to me.

I took her hand gently and sat her down on the bed. 'A vibrant spirit,' I read from her palm. 'A passionate will, longing to be free.'

'Free of what?'

'Free of the bourgeoise restrictions of society.'

'I ran away from home,' she said. 'I ran away from Liverpool.' I ran my fingers across the palm of her hand. It was a sad little hand devoid of much character.

'You rejected the conventions and would risk all, to gain one brief moment of bliss.'

'Leave orf,' said Marlene, she laughed but left her hand in mine.

From the sitting room I could hear Spider and the other girl giggling and struggling. 'Do mine,' called Meg or Peg.

'Spider will do yours,' I called back. 'Spider's just as good as me at it.'

'But you'll do me later?' shouted Meg or Peg. I turned my attentions to Marlene's knitted top.

'Yes,' I promised. 'I'll do you later.'

*　　*　　*

I don't remember the two girls leaving. I suppose Spider led them away in the early hours of the morning. I remember them having no eyebrow pencils and being short of hairpins. They were worrying about being late for work and complaining that I didn't have an alarm clock. 'I'm never alarmed.' I said. 'That's why I don't have an alarm clock.' I turned over and went back to sleep.

It was 11 o'clock when I finally staggered out of bed and ordered breakfast. I was sitting there in my dressing gown, working my way through orange juice, cornflakes and egg and bacon, when Liz came in. There was a connecting door between the suite that Silas and Liz were using and my suite. She tapped lightly on the door and came in. She looked very beautiful.

'My God you look awful,' she said.

I didn't answer. She pulled up a chair opposite me and using my clean cup poured herself some coffee. I tipped the sugar from the basin and used that as a coffee cup for myself.

'Who were those terrible girls you were with?'

'Marlene and Meg,' I said. 'Or it may have been Peg.'

'They were pretty tarty.'

'They were,' I agreed.

Liz was wearing a simple woollen dress and she must have spent half the morning fixing her hair. She took a piece of toast, buttered it and dipped it into the yolk of my last fried egg.

I said, 'I was saving that.'

'I could see you were.'

'Haven't you had breakfast?'

'I had breakfast at 7.30 a.m., before Silas went to Winchester.'

'What's he gone to Winchester for?'

161

'He's got a client for the scrap metal. After that he's going to see someone about the lease on the mews cottage. He'll be out all day.'

'Why didn't you go?'

'He wouldn't let me. He might need me as a second string to get rid of the scrap metal. He doesn't want us to be seen together.'

'That's too bad,' I said. 'That's good marmalade, try some.'

She took more toast, and coffee too. 'I didn't want to go with him really,' she said. 'He was in a bad mood.'

'Yeah,' I said. 'I'm getting real fed up with him.'

'It's your fault. Why did you needle him last night in the lift?'

'I don't know,' I said.

'You snap at each other all the time.'

'Yeah, sibling rivalry.'

'Silas has been good to both of us,' said Liz.

'Maybe he has, but how long do we have to go on touching our forelock to him, and not answering back, and letting him have his bad moods? What's more I'm fed up with always being the chauffeur, or the stupid little feller who's just found these old documents in this attic and can't understand them, or Silas's butler or the Security Guard or the officer's batman. Why can't I play the big shot once in a while?'

'You're always saying that,' said Liz. 'Why don't you speak to Silas about it?'

'I'm going to,' I said. 'It's time I made a few decisions around here.'

'What would be the first decision?'

'Stop taking the mickey out of me,' I said. But she persisted in asking the same question again. 'Look,' I said finally. 'I don't even *like* this business. I don't even like *Silas* if you really want to know.'

'Go on,' she said. 'You two adore each other. I've never known two idiots to understand each other so well.'

'He's everything I don't like,' I protested. 'And I don't like the Establishment, old school-tie and the officer's mess type of fiddles he does. He's so old-fashioned. That's nearly disappeared, that sort of world. People like Silas have been running things too long. Now it's for blokes like me to take over. This is the age of the technocrat.'

Liz laughed. 'That's what you are, is it; a technocrat?' She laughed again. 'You are going to be the first of the technocrat con men.'

'I don't want to be a con man. Can't you understand what I keep on telling you? It's for useless, inefficient ponces, this game. I don't need to fiddle to make a living. I'm just as bright as those people out there in the street. I don't need no swindles, or lies, to make my living.' Liz smiled. She could be very snotty when she felt like it. 'Nor do you, Liz,' I said.

She leaned forward. 'Well, perhaps I don't, my love,' she said. 'But I'm not complaining, you are.' She looked so beautiful at that moment, that it was hard not to tell her that I was madly in love with her and ask her to run away with me, but I was frightened she would laugh and say it was another sign of my immaturity. She was determined to talk about Silas.

'Perhaps you are wanting to take over our trio,' she accused me. 'Personally I'm prepared to take orders from him, no matter if he is a bad-tempered old bully sometimes. He's got all the worries on his shoulders, you must remember that.'

'I wouldn't mind having a few of the worries, if he'd give me more money and a say in what we are doing,' I said.

'I'd just as soon things remained as they are,' she said. 'He's quite brilliant in his way, and even if he does throw his weight around he's been very kind to us in the past. I'll admit it, even if you won't.'

'You're just trying to convince yourself,' I said. 'When was Silas ever kind to you?'

'Silas had been a friend of my father for years before I met him. I was a hotel receptionist in a crummy hotel in Frankfurt when one day he came up to the desk and said, "You're Elizabeth Mason, aren't you?"

'I said I was and remained very suspicious, but he just asked me to remember him to my mother next time I wrote home. He was always kind and considerate to me, and I needed some kindness at that time. I was only a kid. You don't know how awful it was working for that German hotel. The managers were like Gestapo men and the visitors weren't any better. Those tourists would treat me like dirt, until one day they lose their camera in a restaurant, or their little boy had been sick in the bedroom, or they must find a dentist at two o'clock in the morning, or, there was this German girl see, and she's making a bit of a row back up in the room and perhaps I could get her out of there, and here was a little cash to smooth things over. Well I hated those bastards and I'll always be very happy to con them like they were happy to con me. What did they care for my troubles, when I was earning five quid per week and eating potatoes and sauerkraut for a week to get enough money to have my shoes mended? They cared nothing. Silas cared.'

'Yes,' I said. 'He cared, I can picture it.'

'Well, you could be wrong. I saw Silas every day, for weeks, before he ever asked me for a date. He was kind and generous. He'd take messages to my mother when he came to London, and once he brought an iced birthday cake all the way back from my mother's, balancing it on his knees in the 'plane so that it wouldn't damage the icing that said, "Happy Returns to Liz from Mummy," He didn't have to do that and he didn't take advantage either.'

I could see all the signs of Liz getting sentimental.

'What was he doing in Frankfurt?' I said.

'He had been there after the war as a civilian with the left-over bits of the Allied Military Government. He has lots of contacts there even now. He was younger at that time and he laughed more than he does now. He was funny and active

164

and reckless and rich.'

'How rich?'

'Oh not rich as we understand it now. But he had half a dozen really good suits and a Bentley. It was a two year old Bentley, but it was still a Bentley, and I adored it. He had accounts with a couple of restaurants, and the idea of eating and signing afterwards was so impressive that I couldn't get over it. One day he said that I could sign the bill on his account if I ever wanted to go there. I was so thrilled that I used to detour to walk past it, so that I could casually mention to my friends that I was authorised to sign the bill there. But I never went there without Silas.'

'Good thing you didn't,' I chuckled. 'It was probably Silas conning you. They would have probably put you out on your ear if you'd tried to sign the bill.'

'Why should he, he was rich. His flat was full of pictures and silk and. . . .'

'Vulgarity,' I supplied.

'Yes,' she said. 'Silk and vulgarity, and I loved it. I was just crazy about him. I was in love more deeply than I thought it was possible to be. Well he never exploited that fact. He could have gone around with a dozen girls and I would have put up with it. But he didn't. He just had me. He always has.'

'What are you talking about?'

'Oh yes, there was Else, and that girl at the agency in Baltimore, but they were just furtive little affairs. Those girls were never any sort of threat to my position and they knew it. Those girls really did love him. I felt sorry for them, they were so miserable, they knew they would be too. Well Silas was powerful then, he had looks and the talent, the brains and the money. But he didn't abuse that power. He loved me, and he looked after me, and tried not to give me a bad time, and that's what I'm doing for him, I always will.

'But you don't love him any more,' I said. 'That's obvious.'

'There has to be something beyond love, something that lasts, something stronger and yet more comforting too.'

'There is,' I said. 'It's called money.'

'Is that all you ever think about?' Liz said.

'I never think about it,' I said. 'It's you and Silas who need money all the time. Who spends money on clothes and cars and diamond rings? Not me, baby. I'm still wearing the sweater and jeans I bought in Macys last year. My only suit came from an East End tailor near my mum's nearly six years ago. It's you and Silas who delight in trying to make me look stupid because I spend a lot of time reading about archaeology and history, and trying to improve my mind, while you two are rolling around trying to look like royalty rubbing shoulders with the serfs. You want to know how much I spent last night? I spent six pounds eighteen shillings and fourpence. Spider spent ten quid. He was keen that he shouldn't ponce on me, so I let him have his way. Right. Now how much did you two – who never think nothing about money – have slide through your hands?'

'Silas gambled and won, so we came back eight hundred pounds up.'

'O.K. you win,' I said. I poured the last of the coffee for us both.

'No, I don't,' said Liz. 'You are right. I shouldn't have said what I said. You don't think about money all the time. There's no one who manages to be so happy with so little of it. But you are wrong about Silas, because whatever you don't like about him; he is clever. Really clever.'

She looked at me for corroboration. 'He's clever,' I agreed. 'When I first introduced him to my mum – she only saw him once – she said, "He's a real box of tricks, that bloke." Every time I've seen her since then she has said, "And how's the box of tricks doing? Is he still winning all the time?" '

'So what's wrong with winning all the time?'

'Not a thing, if you are Silas. But for my mum, winning means that someone is losing, and it's probably someone she knew. My old man was the world's champion loser.'

'Losers winners. It's like hawks and doves, and U people and non-U people. Why was your old man a loser?'

'He was a loser,' I said. 'He left school when he was twelve. He was still working on the day he died.'

'Doing what?' Liz said.

'He worked in a tatty fountain pen factory. The boss made him promise not to join the union, before he would employ him. So he didn't join the union. One night in the pub half a dozen union blokes picked a fight with him and knocked him half silly. He didn't go in to any pub for two years after that. Then he joined the union and they went on strike, so that he lived on ten shillings a week, strike pay, for five months. The week they returned to work he broke his leg.

'He went to fight in the Spanish Civil War. Naturally he fought on the losing side. He didn't do anything glamorous. He got a bug from the drinking water. He came back to England hardly able to walk and couldn't get a job anywhere. My mum went out cleaning to keep us. That's the story of my old man. Do you know I can sometimes tell that story and have people in fits of laughter.'

'I'm sure you can,' Liz said. 'It's awful.'

'You're right,' I said, and I was grateful that she understood how awful it was. 'When I was a kid, I often told that story and I'd make everyone laugh. I'd tell it when they met my old man for the first time. One day the old man came in the room. He didn't overhear much, just the last few words but he guessed the theme.'

'What did he do?' asked Liz.

'He laughed too,' I told her. 'After that he'd relate his story for laughs.'

'You worry too much, love,' Liz said.

'At the last stage of each of these capers I suddenly see the mark as my old man. I think "It's someone's old man we're making a sucker out of", and it gives me a pain in the gut.'

'We all have that sort of feeling,' Liz said. 'That's an

occupational hazard. All jobs have dangers; leather workers get anthrax, steeplejacks fall off a roof, pilots break up in mid air. . . .'

'That's right,' I said. 'Well I prefer breaking up in mid air.' I walked across the room and switched on the radio. The music was low and schmaltzy. I took Liz's hand. The tune was an oldie and we danced close until, at the end of the music, there was tumultuous applause. We both took a curtain towards the radio. I grabbed the window curtains as though it was the end of our routine and I turned to Liz saying, 'They loved you baby. Do you hear that applause?' I grabbed the fresh flowers from my breakfast tray and presented them to her. 'They are going crazy out front tonight. You're a star baby, a big, big Broadway star just like I said you'd be when we were kids sitting beside the tracks in Schnooksville.' Liz fluttered her eyelids. 'Oh Mr. Hardcastle, I'm so happy. So deliriously, foolishly happy.'

'Don't call me Mr. Hardcastle, Linda baby, my name is Jimmy and this seems the moment to ask you if you couldn't reach down, and let me ride up there on the stars along with you.' I touched her arm and came close to her.

Liz buried her head in the hotel flowers and said demurely, 'Why Mr. Har . . . Jimmy I mean. Whatever could you be talking about?'

'Just this Linda baby,' I said, and from my pocket I brought the Asprey jewellery box.

'A jewel for little me?' Liz said, holding the box at arm's length. 'But Jimmy you know that my heart is promised to another.'

'Promised, but not given, Linda baby. Reach to the stars now and let us snatch this brief moment of happiness together.' I said, smiling nervously.

Liz held the box close to her face, for by now the soft focus would be doing the big, big C.U. and the jewel box had to be in frame or Cyrus P. Biggelhofer would never wear his cap back-to-front again. She opened the box –

tipped slightly to cheat into the camera – and there, sparkling away merrily, was the fake diamond ring I had bought from the poor old con man in Soho. 'What a marvellous ring Bob,' she said. Her voice reverting back to normal with a jolt.

'Try it on,' I said. I was afraid she would be angry with me, really angry.

'It won't fit.'

'Of course it will fit,' I said. 'It was made for you.' She stared at me until I felt myself blushing and she looked away. She said nothing for a long time. Then she fitted the ring on to her finger, looked at it, and then suddenly snatched it off. When she spoke again it was in her Linda voice. 'Oh Mr. Hardcastle,' she breathed passionately. 'If only my heart was not given to another.'

I kissed her. She was in no hurry to break it up, but eventually she said, 'It will never work Mr. Hardcastle, these things never do.' But she kissed me again unhurriedly before running out of the room.

'Slow dissolve,' I shouted after her, but I didn't follow. I called room service for more coffee, and sat down with my archaeology books.

I was listening to the schools broadcasting, 'Willi in der Krankenhaus,' that afternoon, when Silas came storming into the sitting room of my suite. He said, 'I want a word with you.'

'Die Schule ist zu Ende,' I repeated with the radio.

'Switch that thing off,' Silas said.

'Wieviel Uhr ist es?' asked the man on the radio.

'Es ist ein halb vier,' I said.

'Es ist halb vier,' said Silas fluently. 'Have you been upsetting Liz?'

'Wo steht der. . . .' said the radio, but Silas switched the volume down. 'What have you been saying to upset Liz?'

'Nothing,' I said.

'It's not nothing according to her,' said Silas.

'Well what is it according to her?' I asked. I picked up my

electric razor – I hadn't shaved that day – 'I've got this good idea I told you about,' I said.

'I want to hear it from you,' said Silas.

'Well you shave a bald place on the top of your head, then, when the hair starts to grow there again, you go around selling hair restorer. Living proof I thought of calling it.'

'I meant I want to hear from you what upset Liz.'

'If you are in a funny mood,' I said. 'I'm not going to talk to you.'

'Liz says you were teasing Santa Claus,' said Silas. 'Liz says you were crawling around meowing and finally ate Santa Claus's tin of Kit-e-Kat. Liz says you wouldn't stop teasing the cat and now she's upset about it.'

'I like cats,' I said. 'I might have played with it, but I never tease it.'

But Silas wouldn't be mollified. As I walked past him into the bathroom to shave I began to go over the German lesson again. 'Ich bin ein Kind, wir sind Kinde and sie is ein kleine Kinde . . .' When I got as far as that Silas pushed me roughly so that I jarred against the door frame.

'What are you doing?' I yelled. 'You gone off your trolley or something? What's the matter with you, do you want a clip on the earhole?'

'One of these days you'll go too far,' said Silas, whereupon he pushed me again. He makes me laugh when he gets into one of his tempers, because he's like a little kid who can't have his train. Silas pushed me again and then a third time.

'I've had you mate,' I said and went to grab him, to push him back into Liz's suite. Why should I put up with him? He was so keyed up that when I rushed to grab at him he stepped aside and gave me a bit of his 1943 style unarmed combat, lesson four. Well, he taught me all that stuff years ago. I know every throw Silas ever learned and about five hundred better ones. What's more, I'm half his age and twice as fast on my toes. As luck would have it, however, I went tripping over the carpet, and what with my cut leg from the Magazarian Embassy fiasco still aching and sore, I fell over and hit a small writing table. It collapsed under me. I landed on the floor with splinters of antique woodwork around me. 'I've always hated that table,' I said. I blinked with surprise and got slowly to my feet. You should have seen Silas. He was convinced that he had dealt me a real Tokyo Olympics boy-wonder karate championship haymaker. He was dancing around the room, shadow boxing with flat hands. I laughed aloud to see him. 'Come on sonny,' said Silas. He kept saying it very quickly and dancing up and down. I didn't even raise my hands to him. 'Act your age,' I said. 'Try and be a bit more dignified.' I said, but I couldn't help giggling to see the old fool acting up like that.

Silas grinned too, 'I told you to be careful, didn't I?' he said.

'You are an old fool,' I said. 'If I whack you one you'll know all about it.'

'I told you there's life in an old one yet,' said Silas. 'I told you, you spend too much time with those books,' said Silas. 'Yah. Eee. Bap. Yah.' He was making noises as he dealt blows to imaginary opponents on every side of him. He looked at me and shook his head in pity. 'You poor pathetic character,' he said. 'Look at yourself; unshaven, in that filthy dressing gown, too lazy to get dressed. Get your fists up. What a mess you are, out of condition. Can't even look after yourself. Pull your pyjama trousers up for God's sake.'

I don't know if I looked funny or not, but I felt a clown sparring around the hotel room with Silas shouting idiotic things and going, 'Whoop.' 'Zap.' and 'Yap.' all the time.

'You're a silly old man Silas,' I said and I laughed.

'And you are going to get a good hiding one of these days,' he said.

I lunged at the standard lamp and said, 'You yellow devil you,' and with a 'Yap. Ee. Bap.' I gave it a karate cut across the side of its shade.

Silas squared up to my only suit that was hanging in the

open wardrobe, 'Take that you swine,' he said and with a feint to the shoulder he landed a terrific right in his hanger. Down went that one like a bundle of laundry into the bottom of the wardrobe. Silas came back-to-back with me now. I could feel his firm shoulder blades against mine, as we both prepared to sell our lives dearly.

I grabbed one of the fire irons and shouting 'To the Palace,' I climbed up on to the mantelpiece and fought off the chandelier. Silas leapt across the silk sofa and tried to run along the back of it and jump to the sideboard before the sofa toppled from his weight. He nearly made it. I tried to save the standard lamp and leaned slightly too far. A lot of my cuts and bruises were ones I got in the Embassy, but all Silas's ones were new.

Liz brought hot water and a tin of dressings. She always carries them.

Chapter 13

LIZ

I put some sticking plaster over a cut on Silas's ankle and wiped some blood off Bob's arm. They made me very angry. Just at a time when it was necessary that they should be mature and objective they must start playing children's games. They said that Silas had got a bad electrical shock while helping Bob mend the electric plug. They said that the shock had precipitated Silas across the room and Bob had fallen trying to save him. But I knew it was all lies. There was nothing wrong with the electrical plug.

When I had got their cuts cleaned and dressed and was relaxing with a glass of whisky there came a tap at the door of Bob's sitting room.

'Shhh,' said Silas. 'It may be those African fellows from the Embassy.'

There was a loud knocking again. 'Room service,' said a masculine voice.

'I didn't order anything,' Bob said.

I said, 'You two wait here. I'll go through my suite and look back along the corridor.'

'Cavalry for a quick recce,' said Silas.

'Excellent scheme, but for God's sake be careful.'

I patted him on the shoulder and the two of them sat there like a couple of wounded war veterans, while I went off to recce. It was Spider, 'I must see Bob,' he said.

'What about?' I asked.

'Its business,' said the waiter.

'Yours or his?'

'Very funny,' said the waiter and nodded his head without enthusiasm.

'I'll see if he's well enough to see you.'

I walked through the little lobby. Bob and Silas were sitting there like statues. The waiter followed me.

'Spider,' said Bob.

'Hello sir,' said Spider.

'Yes, what is it?' said Silas.

'Sit down and have a drink Spider,' said Bob.

'No thanks,' said Spider.

'Ignore that bastard,' said Bob, indicating Silas. 'This is my apartment. Sit down and have a drink, or I'll kick you up the arse.' Spider sat down, but didn't take a drink. He was nervous in front of Silas and it was some time before he spoke at all.

Finally he said, 'Do you know Gerry Spencer? Tall good looking bloke with a white Porsche convertible. Always in the bar with great looking birds, very posh accent, fair hair, you must have seen him.'

'Never seen him,' said Bob.

'Honourable Gerald Spencer,' Silas supplied. 'His father is said to be some distant relation to the royal family. Yes I know; Chartervacs and an ice cream company, an investment company (name of which escapes me), and Greengrass which he's just bought into.'

'You know more about him than I do,' said Spider.

'I know of him,' said Silas. 'Good looking young boy, always has his pictures in the glossies. St. Moritz and all that sort of thing. Tried to become a professional racing driver but never got anywhere. Then there was a newspaper story about him taking up fashion photography and then last year his father bought him large slices of some prosperous companies. What about him?'

'Well I . . .' said Spider.

'You what?' said Silas.

'I set him up for Bob,' said Spider. 'I told him that Bob

was one of the richest men in London. I told him that Bob made more money in a day than anyone else could earn on a month of Sundays. I said that Bob was handling a dozen different large deals at a time and that on various days over the last month he has had lunches and dinners here with every really big financier in London as well as a couple of Swiss ones. I told him Bob had had lunch with the Foreign Secretary and the Governor of the Bank of England. I said he was a great pal of the Governor of the BBC, and the commercial TV companies had all offered him directorships just to get his name on their letterheads, but Bob had declined because he doesn't like his name bandied around on letterheads.'

'But wasn't Spencer surprised that he had never heard of Bob?' said Silas.

'Of course not. All these tycoons know there is some bigger tycoon who thinks that they are tiny peanuts. They never need much persuading about that. I said that Bob was the secret power in the financial circles of Europe.'

'And he believed it?' said Silas. 'What I can't understand is how you came to be chatting to him on such intimate terms.'

'That's simple,' said Spider. 'He gives me ten quid a week to listen to business conversation for him. What I was doing was reporting. He was so pleased he gave me an extra fiver.'

'That's good,' said Silas. 'What do we owe you?'

'You owe me nothing,' said Spider.

'Come now,' said Silas. 'I'm sure you can always use a fiver.'

'I don't want it.'

'A tenner then?'

'Can't you understand Silas?' I said. 'He's a friend of Bob's.'

'There is no occasion for you to flare up,' said Silas, he turned to Spider. 'Does being a friend of Bob enable you to live without money?'

'No,' said Spider. 'It just enables me to live without Bob's money.'

Silas smiled at Spider. 'Let's have some champers and a little caviar.' He rang the service bell.

'Had this fellow Spencer seen me with Bob?' said Silas.

'Oh yes,' said Spider. 'He asked who you were.'

'And you said?'

'I said you were his private secretary,' said Spider.

'Oh did you?' It wasn't an idea that pleased Silas, but he continued to ring for caviar and champagne.

'He wants to get an introduction to you,' Spider said to Bob. 'He'd just love to do a deal. You'll have no trouble with him. Not like the African blokes. He'll cough up as easy as a baby. You mark my words.'

'We'll do Amalga Min again,' said Silas.

'No we won't,' said Bob. 'This is my caper and I'll plan it.'

'Don't be a fool, Bob,' Silas said. 'You need technical knowledge for a game like this.'

'If I need it,' said Bob. 'Then you can supply it. You're my private secretary.'

Silas smiled grimly and vented his anger on the service button.

'I'll have dinner in the restaurant tomorrow night,' said Bob.

'Ahh,' shouted Silas to Spider. 'If Bob's been eating all these important lunches here, why hasn't Spencer seen him? Why hasn't everyone seen him?'

'Private rooms,' said Spider crushingly.

Silas picked up the phone and asked for room service.

Bob said, 'Can you get me a really discreet table, and then make sure Spencer knows I'm in?'

On the telephone Silas was saying, 'I've been trying to get a bottle of champagne and some caviar for about twenty minutes. Just what am I supposed to do, to get a little refreshment for the four of us up here in Mr. Appleyard's suite? Lean out of the window and shout?'

Spider looked very pained. To Bob he said, 'Tell your Guvnor to cut it out will you. I'm the room service waiter on this floor. He'll get me the push if he doesn't stop complaining.'

'My dear boy. I'm so sorry,' said Silas. 'That's you I'm ringing for of course. Cut along and get two bottles of champagne and some caviar, there's a good chap.'

'Three glasses and portions of caviar?' asked Spider.

'Four,' said Silas. 'Why don't you join us in a glass.'

The Spencer operation began that evening. We had dinner in the hotel restaurant. Spider had been fussing around the table setting, hours before, making sure that the wines were at the right temperature, and the cutlery gleaming. No sooner had we begun the meal when the manager of the hotel came over and asked if everything was all right. Spider had told the manager that Bob was doing a survey of European hotels for *Playboy*.

We were eating petit fours and sipping brandy when Mr. Spencer sent Bob a note. When it arrived Bob didn't pick it up from the table.

'You read it to me,' said Bob.

Silas read, 'I have heard a lot about you Mr. Appleyard. Perhaps you could join me for a drink.' It was signed Spencer. Bob ran his chair back with a loud scraping noise and, leaning back until he could catch sight of a similarly craning necked Spencer, Bob beckoned him. Spencer smiled and nodded. He was dining with two debby girls and another young man. He said something to them and one of the girls raised her glass to him in a mocking toast. Spencer jumped to his feet and walked over to our table. In tow he had a bright-eyed girl. She was dark, short and in her early twenties. She was wearing a medium priced black dress and some plastic beads, and she was urgently in need of a good hairdresser. She was carrying a short mink cape. She saw me looking at it and threw it across one shoulder in a haughty gesture. Stupid bitch. If she saw my full length she'd die of jealousy on the spot. I smiled at her. Spencer was a very tall, very handsome man in his late twenties. He had long fair hair and was dressed in a dark Savile Row suit with a gold watch chain across his waistcoat. Bob looked him over insolently which perturbed Spencer, who held the front of his jacket closed like a young girl surprised in the bathroom. In spite of his conservative suit Spencer wore a tie of bright green Carnaby Street style, calculated perhaps to prove he was trendy.

'Spencer,' read Bob from the card without looking up at him. 'That's you is it?'

'That's right,' said Spencer. He smiled again but the smile froze as Bob still studied his card with exaggerated care.

'No Christian name,' said Bob. 'No initial. What are you, a lord or a bishop?'

'No,' said Spencer, with a polite laugh. 'I'm a property man.'

'Well, that's what I mean,' said Bob turning to look at him. 'I thought you must be something like that.' He waved a hand to me, 'This is Miss Grimdyke. One of the Hampshire Grimdykes,' he added behind his hand. 'My fiancée. And this old fellow is Simon Longbottom, my private secretary.'

'Pleased to meet you,' said Spencer.

'That's right,' said Bob. 'Waiter, give him some champers. And make sure the glass is iced.' The waiter rushed away.

'I think I saw you the other night in Ysobels Club, playing dice,' the girl said to Silas.

'Not me,' said Silas quickly.

'Looked just like you,' said Spencer's girl, eyeing him carefully.

'Never,' said Silas. 'I wouldn't know how.'

'You're a secret gambler are you Longbottom?' said Bob, and laughed derisively. 'Can you imagine it?' he hooted, 'Ha, ha, ha.' Silas smiled grimly.

'Sit down,' Bob commanded and the waiter inserted two extra chairs at the table, although Bob made no attempt to make room for them, so Silas and I were cramped together with Spencer and his friend.

'This is Rita Marsh,' said Spencer.

'Yeah,' said Bob. 'What 'yer Rita.'

'I'm cramped,' said Rita. 'Why don't you move up a bit?' She had a shrill London accent, and her voice carried right across the room.

'Because I have to have room to breathe,' said Bob. 'The doctor told me. Do you want me to disobey him?'

'Yes,' said Rita, refusing to be taken in by Bob's nonsense.

'O.K.' said Bob, moving his chair. 'Move over double oh seven,' he shouted to Silas. 'I'm blood group O if anything happens.'

'If anything happens,' said Rita. 'I can't imagine *you* losing blood.'

'Now then Rita,' said Spencer.

'Now then Rita,' said Bob sarcastically, but he grinned at Rita and she grinned back. She grinned at me too but I didn't respond. She saw me looking at her and pulled up her shoulders and put her red inelegant hands below the level of the table. Spencer glared at her but she pulled a face back at him.

Bob poured some champagne for all of us. When he got to Silas's glass he said, 'Shaken or stirred, Longbottom?' and laughed again, as the waiter took the bottle.

'I've long admired your financial operations, Mr. Appleyard,' said Spencer to Bob. 'You've been called the secret power in the finance politics of Europe.' His voice was cultured and his tone almost imperceptibly mocking.

'That's an exaggeration,' said Bob. 'As I told the PM just last night.' Bob raised his glass. 'To our nuptials.'

'And may all your troubles be little ones,' said Spencer. 'Is it going to be a big reception.'

'Five days on the *Queen Elizabeth* to New York. One day there, five days return.'

'That's a lovely honeymoon,' said Spencer. He flashed me a boyish smile. 'I'm sure you'll enjoy that.'

'You asked me about the reception,' said Bob. 'And I answered about the reception. One thousand people for a two way trip on the briny. For our honeymoon we are going to a quiet little fishing village I know, and have a week or so of sun and rest.'

Spencer nodded, 'You can't beat the Mediterranean.'

'Well, it might suit you,' agreed Bob. 'But this village I'm talking about is on the Japanese Inland Sea. That beats the Med for me any day.'

'Yeah,' said Rita in a shrill posh voice, 'such a change from fish and chips and a quick grapple in the tunnel of love, at Southend-on-Sea.'

'Well you should know luv,' acknowledged Bob. The waiter came immediately when Bob snapped his fingers. It was Spider. He brought half a dozen boxes of cigars. 'The usual,' said Bob. Spider selected carefully from among the most expensive, inspecting the colouring of the leaf and sniffing each until he finally approved one. He warmed it, cut it and lit it for Bob. Then he brought a tiny glass of brandy. Bob dipped the unlit end into the brandy and Spider took the glass away again.

'I know all about you Spencer,' said Bob, leaning back expansively. 'And I like your little operation. We've got a complete dossier on your business dealings and I like them. You've made a few mistakes of course.'

'I have,' agreed Spencer.

'A few occasions where you needn't have spent so much money.'

'You're right.'

'One place at least where you let your heart rule your head.'

'Quite so Mr. Appleyard,' said Spencer. 'And I'd never

do it again.'

'And at one time – I noticed in the dossier – you put your trust in the wrong people, eh Spencer?' said Bob, ad libbing away quite recklessly.

'My goodness but you are so right Mr. Appleyard,' said Spencer.

'Here, stop touching my leg,' Rita shouted across to Bob.

'I didn't touch your nothing,' said Bob.

'Rita's great fun,' said Spencer in acute embarrassment.

'I'm not great fun,' said Rita. 'Why don't you do something, when someone is touching my leg?'

'It might be the cat,' said Bob.

'Cat? There's no cat in the Chester Hotel Restaurant,' said Rita.

'There *is* a cat in here madam,' corrected Spider. 'It's the chef's. It's something of a pet.' Rita stared at Spider suspiciously.

I leaned to the girl and said, 'That's a nice hairpiece you're wearing Rita.'

Bob waved an encouraging hand to Rita, 'Want to make it three cats?' he asked her.

'I knitted it myself,' said Rita to me. She was furious.

'You should have used finer needles dear,' I said.

'Like yours?' said Rita. Spencer giggled nervously.

'Knock it off, you two,' said Bob.

'Go and sit with Rodney and Fay,' said Spencer.

Rita glared at me and left the table.

Bob swilled his brandy around watching the spirit film the glass. He sniffed. 'Any interests in Lebanon, Spencer?'

'No,' said Spencer. 'I've the usual in Switzerland, just between the two of us.'

'Switzerland's finished,' said Bob. 'I'd get rid of your Swiss holdings as fast as you can. I'll tell you that for nothing. What you say to that Longbottom?'

Silas prepared to speak at length on the subject, 'Well I don't know. A lot of people think Switzerland is still the safest. In a way I agree with them.'

'And that's why you are still a crummy secretary,' said Bob. 'Listen to me Spencer. I need someone to handle a deal for me in Beirut. Can't use Longbottom or any of my regular people because they are too well known. It could just be, that you could handle it.'

'I'd love that Mr. Appleyard,' said Spencer. 'I'm a fast learner and my connections are first class.'

'There'd be no kudos for you Spencer. You know my policy; no press mentions, paper-work through nominees, everything handled with the maximum security precautions.'

'The eminence grise,' nodded Spencer, he ran a hand through his long hair. 'That's my style in future too.'

'Discretion and dignity,' said Bob. 'That's my policy.'

'What is this operation?' asked Spencer.

Spider came hurrying to the table. 'There's a phone call,' said Spider. 'They say it's the Treasury.'

'They say that do they?' Bob said.

'What I mean sir,' said Spider, 'is that it is the Treasury.'

'How do you know?' asked Bob. 'How do you know it's not some little con man?' He turned back to Spencer. 'We have a lot of con men after us,' he explained.

Spider said, 'They said you were to ring back.'

Bob laughed. 'Oh well that sounds genuine,' he laughed again. 'See to it Longbottom. It will be in connection with the loan to the Government of Spain. Tell the Treasury people that the terms are agreed. You can handle it Longbottom, it's only routine.'

Silas got to his feet angrily and as he walked away Bob said to Spencer, 'Never take your staff to dinner with you. Once you start that they get the idea you owe it to them.' He turned away and called after Silas. 'Don't be too long on the phone Longbottom. I might want you to take notes.'

Spencer nodded. Bob leaned across to me and gave me an affectionate kiss. He said, 'Old Longbottom's getting a bit too old for this sort of thing isn't he darling? We'll have to think about giving him the push I'm afraid. Poor old bugger, goodness knows who will employ him after me.' Spencer sat back in his chair, anxious to prove that his good manners prevented him from overhearing us.

I don't know whether Silas heard him or not, but Bob hadn't lowered his voice. Silas turned around to stare back but Bob made an impatient movement of his hand and Silas hurried on to take the fictitious phone call.

'I'm not going to mince words,' said Bob to Spencer. 'What I want you to do is one of the biggest fiddles I've ever heard about. And believe me, I've heard of a few fiddles in my time.'

'My goodness,' said Spencer. 'You are a straight talker old chap.'

Bob said, 'I'm going to clear ten million pounds on an initial investment of about a quarter million quid. Like it?'

'It's fantastic,' said Spencer. 'How could you do it?'

'I have got working arrangements with ten Beirut banks. I can have credit of a little over one million pounds at each bank. My collateral is in the form of bonds which pass over the counter whenever I want to go into the red.'

'But how does the . . fiddle work?' asked Spencer.

'At a certain hour on a certain day a man identifying himself as me – and I shall supply the identity document – will pass the usual bonds across the ten counters and, by previous arrangement, will receive about a million pounds in U.S. currency from each bank.' Bob paused. 'The man will not be me, and the bonds will not be my bonds.'

'Forgeries?' said Spencer.

'Forgeries like you've never seen them before,' said Bob.

'Suppose the banks have doubts?'

'They won't have doubts. We have been putting lots of bonds in and out of all those banks, and so far they have all been genuine.'

'But this is a lot of money.'

'It isn't actually. We have been putting far more valuable

bonds across those counters, and these sheiks spend a million on a week's holiday.'

'Suppose a bank cashier smells a rat?' said Spencer.

'He'll smell nothing. They have all been told that I'm doing a currency fiddle and I make a point of keeping on the right side of the chief cashier of each bank because I like them to handle my transactions fast, just in case I'm with one of my important clients when I go in to the bank.' Bob smiled. 'It wouldn't do to have them going off and looking to see the state of my account before cashing a cheque for a few thousand quid.'

'No,' said Spencer and he laughed. 'But why do you need me?'

'People are going to think that I have something to do with it when someone with my identity papers walks off with ten million pounds. I'm very keen to prove that I had nothing whatever to do with it. You will handle it Spencer, and you will have ten per cent of the profit.'

'One million pounds,' said Spencer.

'A bit less,' corrected Bob. 'I said profit, not gross. You'll have to find a quarter of a million to bribe the bank cashiers. So you'll get ten per cent of nine and three quarter million, plus your own quarter million back of course.

'You want me to shell out a quarter million pounds?' said Spencer.

'If there had been no initial investment I wouldn't have offered it to you,' said Bob. 'If I'd just needed a works manager I would have gone around the labour exchange. I'm paying nearly a million pounds for this errand boy job, if you haven't noticed.'

'You don't want to put the money into this yourself?' said Spencer.

'It would look nice wouldn't it?' Bob said scornfully. 'One of my companies paying you the money. Do you think these bank insurance investigators are dopey or something? I heard you had a bit of spending money available Spencer.'

'Well I can get it all right.'

'Look Spencer,' said Bob, leaning close to him. 'These forged bonds aren't going to be a bit of winkle bag printing. They are going to be the van Meegerens of bond forgeries and they will cost three quarters of a million pounds which will come out of my share. Got it? I'm the only man in the world who could get these things like this. It will take the banks months, maybe years to discover which are the real ones and which are the forgeries. Just on the spur of the moment, acting on a generous impulse, of a sort that I seldom allow myself, I thought I'd swing a million quid your way. Maybe I picked on the wrong geezer. Let me tell you this Spencer boy. I don't usually let strangers anywhere near my territory. Until I have them in the salt mines . . .'

'The salt mines?'

'My investment company. I use it as a training ground. But this is a unique situation. This is the first time I've needed someone from outside my organisations for a top level assignment, but I can see it's not so easy. Let's just forget it Spencer. If you can turn down one million oncers, good luck.'

'Hold it Mr. Appleyard, I didn't say no. Give me a little time. When shall I come to your office?'

'Are you crackers Spencer? You're not coming within miles of it until you arrive to hand over the 9,750,000 quid, less your 10 per cent. You'll liaise with old Longbottom and you won't see him more than once or twice. You don't understand my system Spencer.'

'I do,' said Spencer. 'And I admire it.'

'Well you'll soon find out what you don't know,' said Bob. 'Isn't that right Longbottom?'

Silas had returned and was sitting listening to Bob with wide-eyed disbelief. 'What?' said Silas.

'He's getting past it,' said Bob. Then in a loud clear voice he said, 'I was just saying, Spencer will soon understand our system won't he?'

Silas nodded and said, 'Yes sir,' but under his breath I heard him say, 'and if he does he'll be ahead of me.' Spencer shot him a quick glance.

Bob said, 'You know anything about archaeology, Spencer?'

'No,' said Spencer.

'Well, I think I'll have an early night,' said Bob. He got to his feet, grabbed me, kissed me long and lovingly, and taking my hand he said, 'Good night Spencer. Call me in the morning if you are interested, I'll be in my suite – meanwhile keep your mouth shut, or I'll tear your ears off.'

'Yes,' said Spencer going white.

'Just a joke,' said Bob, and punched him hard between the shoulder blades as we walked past him.

As we reached the hotel foyer, Bob grabbed me by the waist and swung me around madly. 'See you in the morning Longbottom,' he shouted. 'And let's see if you can't be early for a change.' Suddenly Bob had lost his physical awkwardness. From being a stumble-footed youth, he'd become a man; poised and confident. His success with Spencer had done it. This new Bob was a little bit overwhelming. I'm not sure if I liked it; but I thought I did. At any rate it was worth hanging around, if only to see what happened to the little monster. He ran along, propelling me faster than I could run in my white dress. Everyone stared as we raced past the reception until I nearly fell, and we both collapsed on the stairs, breathless, giggling and silly.

There was no one on the stairs. Bob kissed me again. I said, 'Did you have to touch that awful girl on the leg?'

'Are you out of your mind? I didn't go near her.'

'Well I'm sure I didn't,' I said huffily, 'and the only other person within arm's length was . . .'

'Ha, ha, ha, ha,' yelled Bob. 'Woody Woodpecker strikes again.'

'That bloody Silas,' I said, and I kissed Bob without fastening my safety belt.

Chapter 14

SILAS

That evening was a nightmare. Bob seemed to have taken leave of his senses and was bothering Liz with little squeezes and more than one kiss, as well as overplaying his role to a ludicrous degree. He openly declared to Spencer (a young man of good family, with excellent connections in the city, should he decide to disobey Bob's warning to keep quiet), that we were about to perpetrate a fraud. I gave Bob several warning glances but every time I did so, he would make some insulting remark to which I was powerless to reply, without stepping outside my unasked-for role, of Bob's private secretary and dogsbody.

I said good night curtly. He had behaved with criminal recklessness but I knew that this time it was my responsibility to preserve discipline. I prayed that his foolish over-confidence would not lead us into adversity, penury or penal servitude, although to tell you the truth, I feared it might well do so.

The following morning we all took breakfast together as was our usual custom. And, as was his usual custom, Bob had not bothered to dress himself properly, and was wearing the same dressing gown that I remembered from many years back. I remembered the garment because I had in fact given it to him when I had no further use for it. Since that time I had discarded three more dressing gowns. I never wore them at breakfast. I held *The Times* in front of my face but I didn't read it.

The sun was high. I don't know how long I had been unconscious. I sat up. There was no movement anywhere.

The desert road stretched away to hazy infinity. Nearby there were three tanks parked in a line. They were all burned out. One had got hot enough to ignite the paint, and now it was white, like the ghost of a tank. Toddy and Wheeler were laid out side by side alongside the nearest tank. It didn't need a second glance to decide that they were dead. Wheeler's body was badly burned. I looked around for Brian, my troop sergeant. He was half conscious, his eyes wide open and his uniform in tatters. He waved to me, 'Tanks ahead,' he called softly. 'Tanks ahead, captain.' He seemed to get annoyed, that this didn't provoke me into action. 'Tanks ahead,' he shouted very loudly.

'O.K. Sergeant,' I shouted just as loudly. 'I see them.' He smiled, and laid back in the hard white sunlight. There was no movement anywhere from horizon to horizon, just wreckage and fragments of petrol tins.

'Are you burned Brian?' I said.

'Just my foot, sir,' he said. 'How about you?'

'I must have been thrown clear,' I said. I was on the extreme edge of the black area of the explosion. The effort of talking was very tiring. 'I'll come over there in a moment, Sergeant,' I said. 'But first I must have a little snooze.' I put my head down in the shade of the blackened tank and felt the hot sand in my ears and pressing my cheek. I closed my eyes but the red light drilled through my eyelids into my brain until I lost consciousness. Brian must have died soon after that.

Bob was wolfing down huge amounts of everything in sight and talking as fast as he could go. As I turned the page I heard him saying, 'And then there's the old bank manager's office trick. You go into the bank with a box full of paper money. You tell the manager that you work for some stupid firm in the sticks. You've got to hand this money over to one of your firm's most important clients. Can you use the bank manager's office, because you've read about all these terrible bank raids. The bank manager looks at you, sees you are a country yokel and so he says yes. Don't you want your cornflakes, Liz? I'll have them then. So he lets you use his office. You sit down behind the desk and your mate brings in the mark. You straighten up, say you're the manager, and take the mark's money. He thinks he's paying it into a bank. Good, eh?' I turned my *Times* to the stock market news. I said, 'Bank manager's office. It's a very old trick. Done a lot during the war, except that you said your office was bombed and can you therefore use the bank's office. Quite good for small time operators, but a waste of our talent.' I went back to my paper.

Bob said, 'O.K. then; another trick. You find a company that deals in any kind of metal; copper, tin, or even . . .' Liz said, 'Can't you shut up even at breakfast?'

'What have I done? I was just talking about work. You're always saying I don't take enough interest in my work. You're always saying that if . . .'

'Please be quiet,' Liz said to Bob.

'What's wrong darling,' I said to her.

'It's this town,' said Liz. 'Ever since the Magazarian business went wrong I feel cooped up.'

'Of course you do love, but just for the time being we should stay here in the hotel as much as possible.'

'But why here, in this hotel? I feel depressed and lonely cooped up here.' She hadn't mentioned our prospects with friend Spencer and neither did I.

Bob jumped to his feet, making a film frame with his hands, and yelling, 'I think I got me an idea S. L. It's New Year's Eve. Get it? Maybe it's her birthday too. I don't know yet, but I think I see it. She's poor, S. L. She's poor and lonely and she's looking back to her days of fame and fortune. . . .'

'When she was a famous star singing in a speakeasy,' I prompted. 'Old Mr. Moneybags from her speakeasy days comes knocking at the door.'

'You've got it S. L.,' said Bob. 'You've still got the old magic. "Hello old Mr. Moneybags from my speakeasy days," she says.'

I nudged Liz and she began reluctantly, 'Hello old Mr. Moneybags from my speakeasy days.'

Bob said, ' "It's your birthday Dolly" (it *is* her birthday, it's all falling into place now . . .).'

I said, 'Yes, it's her birthday. He leads her along to a hall, full of people in claw-hammer coats waiting to have dinner. On the tables there is caviar, champagne and fresh flowers. . . .'

Bob said, 'And up on the wall; a banner – "Little Dolly Daydream of Idaho," it says.'

' "Happy New Year," they all shout, and start clapping.'

In an old frail Mr. Moneybags voice I said, 'You don't have to spend your days sad and lonely and cooped up in this little garrett. Your friends are welcoming you back to Broadway. And now, Dolly sweetheart, to make your old friends happy, sing like in the old days.'

'Lean in,' shouted Bob, who was moving the camera around and framing each new shot with shouts of joy and creative genius. 'Cheat a little to camera. Heads close.'

I said, 'The audience shout, "Please Dolly a song".'

Bob tried to be a couple of hundred people shouting for a song.

'Just like in the old days Dolly,' said I.

'I can't,' said Liz. She was playing now. Bob and I hummed Little Dolly Daydream intro four bars. Liz began falteringly, 'Little Dolly Daydream, pride . . . no, no. I can't go on.' Liz brought out a handkerchief and wiped away a tear. Bob dollyed in for a big C. U. Her voice was a hoarse whisper, 'I think I've forgotten the words.'

'In that case,' I said in my Moneybags voice, 'Your old friends will help you remember them. Little Dolly Daydream, pride of Idaho.' Liz joined in with us.

'Who's standing in the wings,' said Bob. 'I'll tell you who; her old boyhood sweetheart, that's who.'

I said, 'Rock Hudson could play it.'

Liz said, 'Cary Grant could play it.'

Bob said, 'Let's face it fans, even Donald Duck could play it.'

I pulled the curtains, 'The light's dim,' I said. 'And there's just one spotlight on Dolly.' I lit her.

'Now the band plays, The Man I Love,' said Liz. Bob and I gave her the first few bars. She was cheering up. Liz sang, Bob said, 'She looks at him from the stage. He's in the wings in shadow and then he steps into the light.'

'Rock Hudson wipes away a tear,' I said.

'Cary Grant wipes away a tear,' amended Liz.

'Quack, quack,' said Bob. 'Quack . . .'

The phone rang. We all froze. We looked at each other until Bob said, 'That might be Spencer.'

'It might be,' I said. 'But personally I doubt it.' I walked to the phone and paused a moment before answering it. Perhaps the distaste in my voice was too evident as I told Bob that it was his friend Spider. He wished to know if he could borrow the Rolls for half an hour.

'That's all right,' Bob said. 'The doorman's got the keys. Tell him not to leave the back seat full of hairpins, will you?'

I relayed that intelligence to Spider who grunted a laconic thanks and rang off.

'It wasn't your friend Spencer,' I reminded Bob.

'It will be,' he said.

'You seem very sure of yourself,' I told him. 'My personal feelings are that although last night he might have been carried away by your assumed *savoir faire* he will, upon reflection this morning, review your performance as what the critics call "a bit over the top".'

'Never on your nelly,' said Bob without looking up from his breakfast. 'I just behaved the way that upper class nit Spencer thinks a working class yob would behave if he had two million a year coming in. The more he thinks about it the more he'll believe. You'll see, you'll see. I'll murder him.'

'You really hate Spencer,' I said. 'You're a terrorist guerilla of the class war.'

'You watch the blood and snot and feathers fly, and you'll see how much I hate him.'

I tried to make the boy see some sense. I said, 'What have you suddenly become Bob, some sort of mechanical man, operated by dynamos, servo mechanisms and electrical cut-outs? Last night you pounced upon Spencer like a newly promoted pest exterminator, not because he was a mark, but because he was a wealthy young man with a public school accent.'

'Dead right,' said Bob.

'We're not pest exterminators my boy, we're anglers. Let your float drift and bob and drift some more. Take your pleasure from the light on the water and the slight threat of rain. Tie up each pretty fly with care, and never hurry. Above all my boy, learn to love the fishes.' I glanced across at Liz and caught her eye, she smiled.

'You hypocrite,' said Bob.

'Perhaps I am, but I never despise my marks; never. You keep telling me that Spencer is stupid, but he has all the sophistication and shrewdness that good schools and good family give a man of his breeding. You're over-confident, my boy, slow down a little, give the Spencers of the world their moments of success and power and glory. Give all and each, what their little egos crave. Entertain them, just as any clever man entertains a woman he wants. Entertain them, entrance them and soothe them, and never, never hurry.'

'I *am* in a hurry,' shouted Bob.

I pushed the breadknife across the table to him, 'Then take this, and go for some drunken tourist in Soho tonight.

You'll never master my game.'

'I'll have Spencer," said Bob. 'If it's the last thing I do.'

'It might just be that,' I said, looking at Liz.

It took a few moments for Bob to detect the uncomfortable silence. He looked up at us sharply. 'Wait a minute. Don't say both of you think that Spencer won't come through?'

Liz said, 'Well Bob, you were laying it on with a trowel.'

'You'll see,' said Bob. 'Don't you want any more of that toast, Silas?'

'No,' I said. 'I've had enough.'

It distressed Bob to see us so lacking in confidence in him. He went across to the telephone and said to the operator, 'Phone Mr. Spencer at Chartervac. Just say you have a call, don't announce me. Got it? Right, ta.'

When he was connected Bob said, 'Listen Spencer, you know who this is don't you. Well, let's keep it to ourselves shall we? Do you want to do this little job for me or don't you? Right, well that shows you've got a bit of sense anyway. I've got the chief cashier of one of the biggest banks in Beirut over here now. I'm too busy to see him, and even if I wasn't I wouldn't see him, because that's just why I'm giving you such a fat screw. Right? Well I told him to be in the George – that's a boozer in Southwark – at 1.30 tomorrow lunchtime. I want you to see him there. He's an Arab gentleman and he won't drink no strong drink, so it'll only cost you a couple of tonic waters. Yeah, well, sort him over then. After that tell me about it at New Zealand House. I bought it last week. I'll meet you in the foyer at three tomorrow afternoon. Yeah, well, of course it's a long way across London. I told you, didn't I? I don't want to be too near this deal, that's what I'm paying you so much money for. I'm beginning to think I'm paying you too flippin' much Spencer to tell the truth, so don't start complaining or you'll be out with a capital ow. Yeah, yeah, yeah. Amusing; that's what it will be all right. Yeah, the same to you Spencer mate. See yer.' He hung up.

'He's doing it?' I said incredulously.

'Course he is,' said Bob contemptuously. 'He's a right mug. I don't know what you are making all the fuss about. I've told you Silas, you are getting too old for this caper.' He smiled spitefully.

'What's this Arab gentleman bit?' asked Liz.

'That's Silas dressed up as an Arab,' said Bob.

'Never,' I said.

'I'm running this show Silas, matey,' said Bob. 'From now on you are my dogsbody and don't you forget it. Get yourself some wog clothes a bit smartish. Stain your face a bit, tinted specs . . .'

'Don't be a fool,' I said. 'He's seen me at close quarters. He'll recognise me immediately.'

'You do as I say,' said Bob. 'You'll be in proper Arab gear – head dress and robes. Those fellers at the Embassy gave me the idea. You could hardly see their faces behind that stuff.'

'And what sort of accent am I supposed to acquire?' I asked, hoping, to tell you the truth, that that would end the matter.

'Your posh accent,' said Bob. 'English public school Arab. That's just right for a senior staff member of the biggest bank in Beirut. . . .'

I said, 'I don't even know what *is* the biggest bank in Beirut.'

'That's all right,' said Bob. 'Nor does Spencer.'

'He might look it up.'

'And so might you then,' said Bob. 'Research, Silas. If you've told me once, you've told me a thousand times: research.'

It was no use arguing with him so I agreed.

'I don't like it,' I said. 'Can't we use Liz for the third party as we usually do?'

'No we can't,' said Bob. 'This is an Arab caper. They wouldn't let a woman do the household accounts, let alone become the chief cashier in a bank. We can't use her.'

'Why didn't you tell him she was your secretary?' I asked.

'I had my reasons,' said Bob.

'No doubt,' I said. 'So that you could nibble her ear and be damn rude to me at the same time.'

'Yeah, that's it,' Bob said. 'Well now you know how I've felt, being the low-life for the last few years, while you two have been living it up. You've always told me that command is vital. What was that military axiom; only a commander can comprehend the importance of all aspects of the battle?'

'Yes; Napoleon,' I was strangely pleased he had remembered my words. 'The risk of any job means nothing to me. It's just the inconvenience. . . .'

' "The first duty of a soldier is to put up with hardship, fatigue and privation. Courage comes second," Napoleon I think.'

'That's right,' I said. I didn't know whether to be displeased at being defeated in argument, or delighted to find that at last my words had borne fruit.

The George Inn at Southwark is an old galleried inn. In the summer it is packed from morning to night by coachloads of tourists. In the winter it belongs to the local inhabitants, men from the vegetable market across the road, and staff from Guys Hospital. I approached the place by taxi in order to reserve the moment of public appearance until the last possible instant. I alighted from the cab in my long Arab robes with my headgear in place and peering myopically through small gold-rimmed, pink-tinted spectacles. While I was still staring around me,

Spencer came striding across to me to make himself known. With him was his bright-eyed little girl friend Rita.

'My name's Spencer,' he said softly but full of self-importance. I nodded.

He said, 'I'm Mr. Appleyard's second-in-command and this is Miss Rita Marsh.' I simulated great respect and admiration.

'Mr. Appleyard is a most respected man in our part of the world,' I said.

'Is he?'

'Don't you know?' I asked suspiciously.

'Of course I know. Of course I know,' said Spencer. 'He's a man respected all around the world. What are you drinking old chap?'

'They don't have yoghurt?'

'No,' said Spencer, he laughed. 'Little chance of that. What about a glass of beer?'

'Alas,' I said, copying Ali's form of address. 'I fear my religion forbids strong drink. Perhaps a coca-cola.'

'Coca-cola coming up,' said Spencer. When he had got the drinks and found us seats in the far corner, he said, 'Well to business.'

'You Englishmen, get to the point rather earlier than we Lebanese, Mr. Spencer.'

'Well, that's our way. Businesslike and straightforward, that's what we try to be.'

I nodded but said nothing.

'What's wrong?' asked Spencer.

'Your companion,' I explained.

'Good grief,' said Spencer, 'don't worry your head about Rita. She won't understand a word of it.'

Rita fixed me with a cold stare until I had to avert my eyes from hers.

'Go ahead,' said Spencer.

I nodded. 'I have examined the forged bonds Mr.

196

Spencer and I want you to tell Mr. Appleyard that they are the most remarkable works. . . . I might almost say of art; works of art, Mr. Spencer.'

'Yes. Good,' said Spencer nonchalantly, anxious to prove that he was *au fait* with every last detail.

'There will be no question of difficulty. Who will be presenting them to the cashier?'

'I will,' said Spencer greedily. 'I'll be handling that job.' I looked at him. He added, 'On Mr. Appleyard's behalf naturally.'

'Naturally. Well, I will be available if you wish me to accompany you to the other banks. You will collect from the ten banks within one and a half hours?'

'That's it.'

'I have made a note here, of when the managers take their midday refreshment. As you see there is a period between 11 a.m. and 1.30 when only one manager will be at work. This ensures that the men we have. . . .' I looked around anxiously, to be sure we were not overheard, and whispered it behind my upraised hand. '. . . sweetened, will be the men in charge of the bank. Even if the cashier did query it, our man will say it's O.K. In the case of my bank, I will do the same. It is understood?' Rita continued to stare at me and I started to feel that she might have penetrated my disguise.

'It is,' said Spencer. 'But aren't these assistant managers taking a risk?'

'On the contrary,' I said. 'As I have told you, the bonds are so exquisite that there is little or no chance that they will be called upon to express an opinion about them. Therefore when eventually the . . .' I threw up my hands in mock horror, '. . . tragedy, is discovered the responsibility will be entirely that of the manager. If any action is taken. If, for instance, the managers are dismissed. . . .'

'Then your johnnies will be promoted to managers. Bloody marvellous. So that's the game? You'll be promoted to manager.'

I nodded graciously.

Spencer said, 'So they are that good, these forged bonds?'

'They are masterpieces, Mr. Spencer. Quite magnificent.'

'Do we have a date for the job?'

'The fourteenth of next month.'

'That soon.'

'All is prepared. Delay is but a temptation to providence, Mr. Spencer.'

'Righto, the fourteenth of the month.'

'You will phone me at the Credit Central du Liban at 11 a.m. on the thirteenth. Ask for me by name. My name is Hamid. Ask for Mr. Hamid, do not give your name.'

'Would you give me the phone number?'

'It is better that it is not written. You can get the number from the International operator. Book the call in advance so that you will not be late. Do not call me at any other time whatever the emergency. It is understood?'

'It is. That's the way Mr. Appleyard and I both like to do business.'

'You are wise. Both of you.'

Spencer smiled complacently but he was no fool, and it seemed only too possible that he would see through Bob's scheme before he paid the money over.

I said, 'On the phone, I will say merely that I have nothing to tell you. You will then take the Olympic Airways aeroplane at 22.45 on the evening of the thirteenth from London to Beirut arriving at 08.25 on the fourteenth. You will go to the Hotel Phoenicia where a suite will be booked in the name of Smith. We are used to incognito travellers in Beirut. At 10.45 precisely you will phone me at the bank and if I say, "Come over to the bank right away," you will bring the black leather bag containing eight hundred thousand dollars that Mr. Appleyard is supplying. . . .'

'That *I'm* supplying personally, said Spencer. I allowed myself a gesture of respect and amazement. 'You will wait in my office at the bank while I bring you the one million pounds in exchange for the first packet of bearer bonds. If there is any query – and I guarantee there will not be – I will be there to handle it. I will then, if you wish, accompany you to each of the other banks. I will use my own bank messengers to distribute the . . . gratuities. For it is vital that those tokens arrive before we do. For I fear my friends at the other banks will not otherwise cooperate.' I made a gesture of the hand, 'This then is all.' At this Spencer touched his girl friend on the arm, got to his feet and terminated the meeting.

'I have a conference with Mr. Appleyard at three,' said Spencer. 'If you are sure that's all. . . .'

'That is all,' I said. 'Now everything depends upon you and your,' briefest of hesitation, 'partner, sticking to the schedule.'

'You needn't worry about that, Mr. Hamid,' said Spencer.

'I'm sure,' I said.

'Can I drop you anywhere?' he said. 'I've got my Porsche outside.'

I searched his face as though he might be trying to find out something he was not entitled to know. 'The Savoy Hotel,' I said.

'Wherever you say,' said Spencer.

I looked at Rita. She had hardly ceased to stare at me since I arrived. Now she allowed herself the merest trace of a smile before closing one eye in a slow wink. I looked away from her. Spencer went striding across to his open sports car. All three of us fitted into it, but only if Rita all but disappeared in a back-breaking crouch behind me. He was not a good driver and we were very nearly in a number of slight collisions, even before reaching the far side of London Bridge. Several times he was engaged in raucous argument with lorry drivers, one of whom shouted, 'You'd think he'd drive a bit more careful 'aving his mother in the car.' That being a reference to my head-dress. I said nothing, and we drove in silence for fifteen minutes or so, apart from Spencer's occasional verbal clash with other road users. Finally I said, 'I hope I have made everything quite clear, Mr. Spencer.'

'You've made it all very clear Hamid old bean,' said Spencer flippantly. 'This must be very exciting for you. It's a brilliant idea eh? He's a bright young chap that Appleyard, and entirely self taught. I mean, I wouldn't imagine he's been to any sort of university. He's a rare character, perhaps even a genius.'

'As much as I respect Mr. Appleyard's talent, I humbly suggest that there are even greater forces at work, using him merely as an instrument.'

'What the devil do you mean?'

'Perhaps I have said too much. I did not mean to dis-parage the brilliance of your employer. Everyone knows that he is a most powerful financial figure in his own right.'

'Get this Hamid. My partner. My *partner*, not my employer, and you'd better explain exactly what you mean.'

'There is little to be gained from discussion, Mr. Spencer,' I said. 'And even less from argument. But I think we both know where this idea was born, and even more to the point, where the forged bonds themselves originated.'

'What the devil do you mean?' said Spencer.

'You are not as naïve as you pretend,' I said with a smile.

'What makes you think that?'

'Because no one could be,' I said. 'Your partner, Mr. Appleyard, has been given these forged bonds by people who can spend unlimited time and money on them. Men who have unlimited resources of print, paper, ink and engraver's skill to get them exactly right. And, believe me, they *are* exactly right. There is only one set of people who would gain if the free banking area of Beirut was dealt a blow that would discourage speculation in, and manipulation of, bonds and currency. Most particularly speculation in the pound sterling.'

It took a few moments for Spencer to get the message. 'You don't mean?' he gave a low whistle, 'you don't mean, that it's the British Government who have backed Appleyard in this swindle?'

'I perceive you are not party to all of your partner's dealings,' I said sardonically.

'You mean they would give him the bonds. . . .' Spencer ended the sentence in a whistle. 'It all fits. Dinner with cabinet minister. That's why he's not charging the cost of the bonds. He was paying three-quarters of a million, he told me. The lying swine. I see it all now.'

I let Spencer review my theory in the panorama of his mind and then I said, 'You see why I am confident that it will go as planned?'

'You bet I do,' said Spencer. 'To think of the British Government giving Appleyard ten million pounds on a plate. It's almost beyond belief.'

'You have mis-stated it, Mr. Spencer. They are giving him engravings. It's our Beirut banks that are giving him the money.'

'Yes,' said Spencer. 'Yes, you are right.'

'I am right,' I said. Spencer turned sharply into the narrow street that forms the Savoy Hotel forecourt. He stopped the car under the hotel front that so resembles a Rolls radiator. 'I look forward to your phone call on the thirteenth,' I said. He revved the motor until it was deafening.

'Don't worry about that,' said Spencer. 'You'll be hearing from me. Meanwhile keep your mouth shut, or Appleyard will tear your ears off.'

'Will he?' I said coolly.

'But only in fun,' said Spencer. He smiled a magnificent smile. He was like a model that advertisers use when they sell things that are too expensive.

I nodded. Already Spencer was weighing his chances of picking up a bagful of money and not sharing it with the 'secret power in the finance politics of Europe.' Not a bad idea.

Rita waved a perfunctory farewell and they drove away with a loud roar. I stepped across to where my chauffeur was waiting in my Rolls. Even before I had closed the electric blinds the car was turning onto the Strand and heading towards Trafalgar Square. I opened the hand-made dressing table, and switched on the lights behind the long mirror. I poured a little warm water into the sink and stripped to the waist before cleaning off the skin colouring with soap and water, followed by generous applications of cold cream. I had taken off my false moustache with one jerk and now I removed the last traces of the adhesive with spirit. From the wardrobe I got a clean shirt and suit, and by the time we were through the heavy traffic jam on Trafalgar Square I was nearly ready. I took off the elevator shoes that my long robes had concealed and put on the virtually heelless ones. With the slight stoop that years of back breaking office work could produce I would make Longbottom at least three inches shorter than Hamid the Arab. I was pleased with the result and poured myself a tiny glass of whisky.

I used the side entrance of New Zealand House going in via the covered arcade past the bookshop and the florist.

Bob had no jacket in spite of it being a rather cool day. He was attired in dark trousers and a white short sleeve open-necked shirt. In his hand he had a clip board with a stop watch attached to it. Now and again he scribbled notes.

Bob was standing with Spencer near the notice board which tells visitors from New Zealand what time the ballet starts, and warns them about confidence tricksters. I think Bob must have been reading the notice about confidence men aloud to Spencer as I arrived. I heard him say that he wished he could meet a con man, he'd sort him over something rotten.

'Yes,' said Spencer solemnly.

'Come on Longbottom,' Bob shouted as he caught sight of me. 'How long does it take to go up to the eighth floor and back?'

'I was as quick as I could be sir,' I said.

'You're telling me,' said Bob. 'You're getting past it Longbottom. What I need working for me is Fastbottom.' Spencer laughed, for which I will not be in a hurry to forgive him. He was an aristocratic lout. Thinking as I was about Spencer's gratuitous rudeness, I was a little slow to answer. Since I was crouching forward a little to suggest less than my actual height, Bob (affecting to believe that I was attempting to listen more closely), said, speaking well above normal volume, 'I said you're getting past it Longbottom,' then without bothering to lower his voice added, 'the old fool's as deaf as a post.'

'I am not deaf,' I said.

'Lip reads,' Bob mouthed silently to Spencer.

'I don't lip read,' I said angrily, before I realised the trap he had set for me, Spencer and Bob laughed together. Rita was there hanging on to Spencer's arm and watching me like a stoat. She didn't laugh.

'Leave that one here,' said Bob, jabbing a pencil in the direction of Rita. Spencer whispered something to her and without a word she went and sat down in the waiting room.

'Where are the papers then?' said Bob. 'Where is the telex stuff from New York, and the minutes of this afternoon's meeting?'

'She's still typing that,' I said. 'It will be ready in a few minutes though.'

'Buy a dog and bark yourself,' said Bob disgustedly.

'Come on, I'll get it.' He stamped off into the lift as the door pinged open, dragging Spencer with him. I only just got into the lift as the doors closed.

'You were nearly a shortbottom then, Longbottom,' said Bob. Spencer laughed again. At the fifth floor Bob got out of the lift and went striding down the corridor as though he owned the place, which was exactly what he had told Spencer he did do. He pushed open doors of offices at random and shouted, 'Have you see Charlie Robinson today?'

The office staff looked at him blankly and Bob shouted, 'Forget it.' and, slamming the door loudly, said, 'Get that bloody chief clerk fired, Longbottom, he's bloody useless.'

After a lightning foray into one office Bob came back into the corridor brandishing a telex slip. It said, 'Go ahead. Paperwork complete and ready for despatch.' Bob gave this to Spencer but when after reading it, Spencer put it in his pocket, Bob said, 'Give over Spencer, mate. That's got to be destroyed. With that answerback code? You'll get me hung.'

That's all it needed for Spencer to make sure he saw the code as he handed the message slip back. The code was that of a company that has a world-wide reputation as the printer of Government bonds, money and postage stamps. The telex slip was a fake of course, we had typed it in the public telex office that morning, spelling out a false answerback. Bob fastened the telex slip to his clipboard. It's hard to say whether Spencer was more impressed by the telex slip, or by Bob's proprietory tour of the new office block. The more Spencer registered respect, the more reckless Bob became. One door he pushed open was a typing pool. I could see that Bob was surprised, but he nevertheless recovered himself quickly enough to shout, 'Everyone change ribbons.' They looked at him in amazement. 'There's going to be some heads roll around here,' he yelled. 'And we'll start with clearer typing.' At the end of the corridor a fat old lady was arranging cups on a tea trolley.

'You're Gladys, aren't you?' asked Bob.

'I'm Alice, sir,' said the woman.

'That's right,' said Bob. 'Gladys was the woman you replaced.'

The woman looked worried. Bob threw sugar into three cups of tea and gave them to Spencer and myself. 'And I'll have a doughnut too,' said Bob. 'Then I won't have any more tea today,' he sipped it. 'Better than last week's tea,' he said and patted her on the back encouragingly.

'Yes sir,' said the woman who, never having seen Bob before in her life, was beginning to wonder if she was suffering from amnesia. A door opened down the corridor and a typist came out. 'I must see Miss Schmidt,' muttered Bob. He hurried down the corridor and held a conversation with the girl. Goodness knows what he said, but when he came back he told us that he had another meeting in five minutes. We both hustled Spencer back to the lifts and I stepped in with him. An important looking man got out as we entered. Just before the doors closed, I heard Bob say, 'Up in the directors' conference room by four o'clock. They need to have visas for Argentina, and foreign currency. . . .' The lift moved before Bob had to extricate himself from that conversational gambit, which I understand he did by pretending he was from a travel agency and had brought the required items to deliver them.

Spencer was impressed, but as I tucked him into his car he said, 'Have you met this fellow Hamid?' Rita had seated herself next to Spencer and she watched me as I replied.

'Yes,' I said, 'I have met him.'

'He's a bit like you,' said Spencer.

'I hadn't noticed any resemblance,' I said. 'You mean I look Arabian?'

'A bit,' smiled Spencer. 'A bit like an Arab.'

'Goodbye Mr. Spencer,' I said.

'Goodbye Longbottom,' said Spencer. He patted me on

the head. Then he took the lobe of my ear, and twisted my head, so that he could look at my face. 'A bit like an Arab,' said Spencer. He laughed, Rita didn't.

I pulled away from him rubbing my ear, as his white sports car roared off in a cloud of smoke. I could hardly see for tears of rage. It was as though everyone in the world was intent upon humiliating me. Bob could never let up for even a moment, and this Spencer was only too quick to follow his lead. Liz had kept away from me, she had convenient headaches, and appointments at the hairdressers whenever I needed her. I walked north not knowing where I was going. I blundered into pedestrians and near Piccadilly a taxi nearly killed me. I found myself sobbing, and once I had started found it difficult to stop. I realised how the last couple of weeks had affected me. If only Bob had failed, then I wouldn't have felt so badly, but he was doing all right. They all were doing all right, and how I hated every last one of them.

I could make sure Bob failed. His humiliation would delight me, as well as putting me back into the driver's seat. Oh my God, what had happened to me that I could contemplate betraying a comrade. My father would have killed me for such thoughts. It had been a long time since I had walked with no thought of arriving anywhere.

It was a long walk and I was tired. It was autumn and I'd been kicking the dead leaves furiously. Now I sat down and asked my father to carry me. He said it would be better if we both rested for a moment. He said that if we sat down on the old tree for five minutes, I would feel more than fresh enough to walk home. It was less than two miles. We both sat down under a huge silver birch. It was a distinctive tree, large in girth, and its silver patches reminded me of the silver in my father's hair. We sat very quiet, very, very quiet. Soon there were the noises of the birds moving around. Probably they were getting ready to go to bed, for it was beginning to get dark, even though it was only tea time.

My mother had been making seed cake when I left. I can remember the smell of it now. I never drink schnapps. I got up from the old trunk and said I was ready. There were pieces of bracken sticking to my father's trousers, and there were the stains of toadstools. He hadn't noticed them when when we sat down. I complained of the marks on my coat. The big birch tree was whining softly in the evening wind and I leaned against it. 'I'll push it over,' I told my father. He nodded. I pushed it again. The birch tree moved, creaked, and with a terrible groan began to fall. It ripped a passage through the forest snapping a hundred twigs and tearing loose their fine green leaves. Crump. The crash echoed through the dark trees. I ran to my father crying. I was afraid that the tree would fall and crush us. My father didn't move. Around us, the last tiny pieces of debris and leaf settled quietly to the forest floor. 'I pushed the tree over,' I said to my father. I was both proud, and yet in awe of what I had done. I prodded at the fallen tree. The wood fell away like powder. Inside it there were hundreds of beetle grubs and moths.

'It's been dead a long time,' he said. The fungus and the grubs had eaten its heart away. I looked at the yellow razor strop fungus, it looked friendly and pleasant. 'It was six times as big as me,' I said.

'More than that,' said my father.

'I didn't know it was dead,' I said. 'It looked strong and important. It looked as though it would never fall down, never ever.'

'Yes,' said my father, 'no one knew.'

* * *

Beirut, Lebanon; I took the mid-week aeroplane there, leaving Liz and Bob to close down things in London. I stepped off the aeroplane into a hot dry day. The glare seared my eyeballs and the air smelled of my youth, and well it might, for this is where the young man that once was me, died one day in nineteen forty-one, or did I survive till forty-two, a grizzled veteran skilled at ducking death and duties. Was this to be the place where I would die again. Or would I begin once more to really live.

The streets were just as I remembered them; trays of sweet cakes and the yelps of unwanted dogs. Shiny American cars sliding along the waterfront under dusty palm trees. Men in baggy trousers arguing in shrill Arabic. Crew-cut kids full of energy and know-how, streaming from the American University, and into the soda fountains for strawberry milkshakes. Smells of spices, excrement and the desert, were a catalyst to my memories. I went out to Pigeons Rock, and walked along the cliffs, watching the sea batter itself to death against the sharp black rocks. It was all flashy villas now, where the old depot had been, and the night clubs that once had served stolen army rations and home-made scotch, were now plush and painted, and garlanded with neon tubes.

The hotel was the same though. A creaking old slum near the port, with Papa Kimon to laugh until the wormy floor boards shuddered. From my window I saw the grey rusty ships. They grunted and groaned as the cranes and hooks probed deep into their bowels and laid their entrails along the waterfront for sages to study and butchers to bargain for.

There was recce work to do, and now that I had been relegated to the role of supernumerary under Bob's command it became my duty to attend to detail.

I purchased a Land-Rover vehicle for seven hundred pounds sterling. It wasn't cheap, but I wanted one in excellent running order. Positioned on the vehicle were jerricans for water and fuel, spades, rifle rack, perforated steel channels for extricating wheels in soft-going, a heavy winch, a crude metal sun compass welded to the mudguard, and an extra fuel tank with changeover switch, to warn when fuel was down to the last five gallons. I installed a long range radio and four small walkie-talkies for local communication. I had the vehicle painted bright colours because the people in the depot in Beirut told me that nowadays this was considered an aid for location by air in case of a breakdown. I also got the usual equipment; sleeping bags, blankets, fly sprays, maps of the region, a tent that forms a lean-to against the vehicle and a tiny Japanese generator that would provide light and power for a drill and pump. Unfortunately a misunderstanding arose. Some preliminary work was done on an unsuitable short wheelbase model, and there was a certain amount of argument before I could persuade the vendors to change it. Eventually however they agreed and by the time Bob and Liz arrived it was quite ready. Bob loved it. He went around patting it and admiring every square inch. On Sunday we drove up over the mountains through Sofar and Bar Elias. The weather was superb and we drove very fast across the Syrian border to Damascus. We took lunch there and drove back to Beirut in the afternoon. Halfway between the two mountain ranges we turned off the main road.

I told Bob to drive down the disused parallel road, and when we came to a bend hidden from the road above by two small trees, I told him that this was Rendezvous Two. 'If anything goes wrong we'll all meet here,' I said. We sat there for a few minutes just smelling the hot land.

'The men say this is bad place Bwana,' Bob said, 'Men say they can no go on.'

'Your ancient tribal superstitions Uruanda,' I laughed scornfully. 'We are going to find the lost treasure of the ancient kings.'

Bob said, 'Men say this is bad place Bwana. Men say they can no go on.'

'Doesn't the lost kingdom stir your blood, Uruanda?

God knows you may be only a savage, but surely the legends of the lost city hold a magic attraction for you.'

Bob said, 'Men say this is bad place Bwana. Men say they can no go on.' Bob clapped his hands twice. He looked around us at the empty landscape. 'See master, the bearers have fled. They believe the legends of the seven headed python that rules this forbidden land.'

'But that's just an old wives' tale Uruanda.'

Bob said, 'Men say this is a bad place. . . .'

'Do you know of the ancient treasure of the Kings of the land of Fire? There are rubies, diamonds, gold, lying there just for the taking. Scores of them, mountains of them. You'll be rich, rich. Richer than you've ever dreamed of being, Uruanda. You will have cattle, wives, perhaps even a Raleigh bicycle of your own.'

'I go with you master.'

'That's the spirit,' I said. I got out of the Land-Rover. Bob stretched his arms lazily. We were all wearing our expedition clothes; khaki shorts and bush shirts. The sun was hot, and I let it trickle over me like a warm shower, seeking out the winter and drying my joints. There was no traffic along this road. Many years before a landslide had clipped it for the last time. The local engineer, tired of replacing this road across the hills, had built a new one high above us, along which I watched the brightly coloured cars and smoky lorries moving between Beirut and Damascus. Liz threw a blanket on the ground. She had a swim suit under her clothes and now she reclined in the methodical postures that women adopt in the sun. It was a glorious day.

'This is better than the airport?' Bob asked.

'Anything is better than the airport,' I said. 'They haven't forgotten the Intra bank disaster yet. When the Intra bank failed the vibrations were felt in every corner of the financial world. The Government was damned unpopular, what with half the population not paying their debts because they had lost their savings, and the other half not paying their debts because they said they had lost their savings.' I paused. 'The chances are that Spencer won't say a word,' I said.

'Of course he won't,' said Bob. 'That's why I specified dollars, so that he would transfer them out of some private hoard he's got in Switzerland, or the Bahamas or something. He won't be able to complain to anyone about losing them.'

'All the same,' I said, 'if there is the merest whisper of a fraud anywhere near a bank, the police will close this country off at once. The first place they will clamp down on will be the airport. That's the logical way to exit. We, on the other hand, will be an expedition on our way to an old city in the desert. . . .'

'Babylon,' said Bob.

'Exactly. You can keep them convinced with all your archaeology jaw-jaw, and then when we get to Damascus – and you can see how short a journey that is after today's run – we abandon the Land-Rover and take a plane, I've checked the schedules. There will be a plane for Calcutta, which gives us plenty of leeway.'

'Show me the jerricans again,' said Bob.

They were special jerricans designed to hold the dollar bills.

'The jerricans will be ready late tomorrow evening,' I said.

'This is supposed to be a rehearsal,' said Bob. 'Or have I got it wrong?'

'It's a dress rehearsal,' I agreed.

'Well you know the standing orders,' said Bob. 'You ought to, you old fool, you wrote them.'

'I wrote them,' I said, 'so I can break them.'

'Oh no you can't, Longbottom,' said Bob. 'I say Longbottom, because that's what you are. The reason you do that clerk role so convincingly is because that's what you've become, and not such a good one at that. Do you think I haven't noticed you glugg glugging on that hip flask of whisky as though you can't go for ten minutes without giving yourself a bit of courage. Do you think no one notices your hands shaking like a leaf, and your miscalculations. The short wheelbase Land-Rover, and now the jerricans. Can't you do anything right?'

'I'm sorry, Bob,' I said. I had my own reasons for avoiding any sort of trouble.

'It's all right,' said Bob. He rubbed his face. 'You're just a bit tired. Keep going till next week and then we can all take it easy.'

I said, 'You're the boss.'

'No bosses,' said Bob.

'I'll drive going back,' I said. We came over the mountains at dusk. Beirut was a galaxy of lights far below us, and beyond the town, the whole sea was afire with the last light of the sun. What a sight it made.

I was driving the Bedford. Brian was beside me and Private Wheeler and Todd were on the back with the fuel drums. It was dark, and hard to see the blacked-out convoys moving toward the front, let alone the Arabs who walked along the centre of the road oblivious of the danger from the traffic. The fuel drums clanked and clattered behind me, and Brian was forever turning around and staring back into the night. 'Relax Sergeant,' I said.

'It's a court martial offence,' said Brian.

'Relax,' I said.

'You're a bit drunk,' said Brian. 'Shall I drive?'

'Relax for God's sake,' I said. I pulled over to avoid a couple of Matildas parked at the roadside.

'Ten years,' said Brian. 'And not in a civvy prison. Ten years in that military prison outside Alex. Double marching with full pack in the sun, and those gun-shy MP bastards trying to kill you. The buzz is that the New Zealanders shot one of their corporals who was found selling Army petrol.'

'This isn't Army petrol,' I said. 'It's Eyetie petrol. We

captured it. You and I captured it, with Wheeler and Toddy. It's our petrol.'

Brian smiled grimly, 'I wouldn't bank on that as an excuse,' he said. He leaned out of the cab and shouted, 'All right, Toddy?' The soldier on the back waved an affirmation. I put my foot down. There was another thirty or forty miles of desert road to cover before we could hand over the petrol to Kimon, the black market man.

'Tanks ahead sir,' screamed Toddy from the back of the lorry. He beat frantically upon the roof of the cab, 'Parked tanks,' he called, but it was too late. There were no lights on them. We hit the rearmost of the parked Shermans at about fifty. I don't know what ignited all the petrol.

Bob stopped the Land-Rover. We got out, and stood looking at the flaming sunset until the sun disappeared. When it was quite dark we drove on to Beirut. We dressed up that night, and ate and drank more than was good for us. The next three days were a holiday. We swam and skied and sunbathed, and drove to Byblos and Tyre, and we all got along better than we seemed to have done for an age.

Chapter 15

BOB

Silas went off to Beirut and it was left to me and Liz to get rid of the flat and cut ourselves back to hand baggage, so that we would be free to go anywhere we pleased after the con trick was complete. London would be too hot for us. Pow, that nit Spencer would go spare when he realised he'd been taken. I'd spent a bit of time on Spencer. His old man had bought him a piece of the various companies of which he was a partner; property companies that knocked down old streets so that they could put up a flash hotel. Progress, Silas called that, well that's not the word the people that had been kicked out had used. Coppers and people from the town hall came to help kick them out, and offer them an iron bed in a sleezy dormitory. I'd screw Spencer while smiling. I'd screw him without even making money out of it. I'd take him for his quarter of a million quid if it was the last thing I did. Even if I had to climb through the kitchen window of his flat in Eaton Square I'd take him; that's how I felt about this job. Of course I played it dead cool. Liz and Silas thought I was careless and indifferent and I let them think so. I played them up at times, watching them out of the corner of my eye when they thought I was overdoing it.

Me and Liz got along very nicely nowadays. She had dropped a lot of her snootiness and even her accent was more human than it once had been. Of course I was crazy about her; you've guessed that. I'd always been crazy about her. Tall, big boned broads have always been my style and Liz was the best ever. She always used to let me know that she was not for me, but lately she'd been a different person. It was all over between her and Silas, you didn't have to be Philip Marlowe to figure that out, but she was letting him down as lightly as possible. I told her that, and she got mad at me. She said she was still crazy about Silas, and always would be, but you can tell about people even before they know themselves.

We had a load of stuff to get rid of. Why should I throw away my Encyclopaedia Britannica. And why should I sell it cheap either. Finally she said her mother would look after some of our stuff for us. I borrowed a Dormobile from a fellow I know in Islington and he helped us load up our gear and things to take down to Liz's mother in Dorset.

It was a lovely day for our trip. Talk about a picture calendar. Little thatched cottage wasn't in it. Her mum had this place that was so English that I thought I was on the lot at Paramount; Hollyhocks and a spaniel dog, the runner beans are doing nicely and I'll ask the gardener to cut a few for you. The gardener!

Liz knocked on the door as I marched up the path between two ranks of stone men shouting, 'Gnomes of the world unite.'

Her mother opened the door to us. 'You've nothing to lose but your pedestals,' I finished lamely. She gave me only a brief glance.

'Elizabeth darling, how nice.' She was a white-haired old lady of about sixty-five. She was wearing a severe tweedy suit with woollen stockings and brogue shoes. A black and white dog was playing some game in which my shoes were rabbits and he was trying to chase them away.

'Nice doggy,' I said, getting a grip on the back of its neck.

'Don't tease the dog,' said Mrs. Mason, 'or he'll bite you.'

'This is Bob, mother,' said Liz.

'Bring it all through the side gate,' said her mother studying my clothes. 'I can't have you treading all through the house.'

'O.K. Missus,' I said.

'This is Bob, mother,' said Elizabeth. 'He works for Silas.

Works with me.'

'He can't leave that van there,' she said. 'The vicar won't be able to get his car out.'

'It's just while I'm unloading,' I said.

'The lane is very narrow,' said Mrs. Mason, determined not to abandon the discussion. I began unloading the bundles of books and Liz's clothes, and stacking them in the garage. That was a spooky place too; full of cobwebs and dust, with an old bull-nosed Morris tourer asleep under a dust sheet.

'It belongs to the colonel,' said Mrs. Mason. 'It hasn't been on the road since petrol rationing began.'

'When was that?' I asked.

'The beginning of the war,' said Liz.

'The colonel had his official car of course, so we could do without this one.' Mrs. Mason marched off into the house. I breathed on the brass radiator and polished a little place with my sleeve. My reflection had a big yellow nose.

'Come and have tea,' said Liz.

'It's a smashing place,' I said. 'Prettiest house I ever saw.'

'Do you really like it?' Liz asked as if she was worried about my reply.

'Of course I do,' I said.

'I'm glad you like it,' she said. 'I've lived here most of my life. I can't bear being away too long.'

'Come along,' called Mrs. Mason. 'Vera has the tea ready.'

'Who is Vera, your sister?'

Liz giggled. When we got into the house the table was set with cakes and sandwiches. 'Would you like to have a wash?' said Mrs. M.

'I'm all right,' I said. 'I went when we stopped in the village.'

'Don't play up,' Liz whispered, she knew when I was geeing people up. 'All right,' I said and went for a wash. The house was separated into dark little cubicles by lots of lace curtains and potted plants. There were old photos everywhere and copies of *Country Life* in the bathroom.

'Could we have tea in the garden, mummy?' Liz asked.

'The colonel would never have tea in the garden, everything blows about so much. Tea inside is best.' The maid came in dressed in a black and white uniform and an old-fashioned starched white cap. 'More hot water, Vera,' said Mrs. Mason. 'And cut the honey loaf.' Mrs. Mason wielded the silver teapot and dispensed nourishment and advice.

'I'm eating all your honey loaf and cream sponge,' I said apologetically.

'It's of no account,' said Mrs. Mason, 'The colonel could eat one of my honey loaves at one sitting.'

'That colonel sounds quite a character, whoever he was.'

'My father,' said Liz. 'We always call him the colonel. He was killed in the war.'

'I'm sorry,' I said.

'He was with Silas,' explained Liz.

'My husband was leading a column of tanks,' said Mrs. Mason. 'They ran into heavy artillery fire. The colonel got out of his tank and was killed while attending to his wounded driver. He won the Victoria Cross.'

'Was Silas with him?' I asked.

'Yes,' said Liz. 'Silas was a captain in daddy's regiment. He was less than half a mile away. There were heavy casualties among the tank men that day. No one will ever know quite what happened, there were no survivors from my father's troop. Silas survived and became the senior officer. It was Silas who sent in the report that gained daddy his posthumous V.C.'

'I didn't know that. I mean about Silas being with your father.'

'That's how I got to know him,' said Liz. 'He visits my mother whenever he's in London.'

'A dear sweet boy,' said Mrs. Mason. 'I remember him in 1939. He was young and terribly shy. The colonel often brought his young officers back here for lunch, so that he could talk with them informally away from the depot. He said it was good for morale.'

'I wasn't even born the first time Silas came here,' said Liz.

'He's a dear sweet boy,' said Mrs. Mason.

'So you couldn't have known your father?' I said.

'No. I was just a baby when he died. I never knew him.'

'He was a wonderful man,' said Mrs. Mason. 'You don't find men like him nowadays.' she added, looking at me.

'Things change,' I said. 'Men reflect the age. Each generation has to come to terms with the world as it finds it.'

'Well you can have the world as I find it,' said Mrs. Mason, and she gave a squeaky little laugh. 'Beatniks beating up policemen. That's the younger generation. I don't know where it will all end.'

'It's better than having a war that beats up millions,' I said. 'That's what your generation had.'

'Beatniks,' said Mrs. Mason again, as though that was some kind of code word.

'I'd sooner have beatniks than Hitler Youth,' said Liz.

'You're all alike,' said Mrs. Mason. 'You have no respect for religion or family. I'm glad your poor dear father never lived to see it.'

'See what?' I said.

'Elizabeth,' explained Mrs. Mason. 'Young Captain Lowther; running about all over the world, instead of settling down to a nice steady job in the city. He had a good job in the city, why couldn't he go back to that?'

'That was nearly thirty years ago mother,' said Liz. 'He gave that job up to go into the army.'

'He's a very gentlemanly boy,' said Mrs. Mason.

'He's not a boy at all,' said Liz. 'He's middle-aged.'

'He's old, if you ask me,' I said.

'Why must you defy me Elizabeth? Captain Lowther asked you to marry him four years ago, and I wish you had accepted him. After all, he was a fine officer and decorated

218

twice in the field.'

'You don't marry people because they are heroes,' said Liz.

'Not even in a field,' I muttered.

'Well the colonel was a hero,' said Mrs. Mason. 'And that's why I married him. One of the reasons anyway. He was a fine man.'

'Oh please mother, can't you leave me alone? I don't want to marry Silas.'

'You must think about marrying someone,' said her mother. 'You're not getting any younger. Another few years and no one will want to marry you.'

'I'll always want to marry her,' I said. 'I always have wanted to, and I always will.' Liz kicked me under the table.

'Well that confirms my opinion,' said Mrs. Mason. 'You are exactly what I mean by no one.'

Chapter 16

LIZ

I loved Bob. I realised that one morning sitting under the dryer and listening to the stylist talking about her boyfriend. And suddenly I began to dream the things I'd never dare let myself think about before. I've no idea how long I had loved him, but at that moment everything seemed clear to me. And right. I purred with pleasure thinking of him. I had known him for nearly five years, and for a woman the years between twenty-five and thirty are very long years. There were so many decisions to make and all of them vitally important, at least they seem so at the time. Emotional changes occur almost imperceptibly (even though they become apparent like a lightning flash), and I suppose my feeling for Bob had been creeping up over me for many months, until now I was quite certain.

I loved Bob. He was quite infantile at times and Silas had more everything; more experience, more sophistication, more knowledge of how a woman wants to be treated. Silas may be a bad tempered martinet but he had the power and presence to go with it. When I was with Silas, I had the feeling that nothing would go very wrong, whether it was the doorman complaining about my trouser suit or some mark threatening to go to the police.

Bob, however, had an innocence and ignorance that attracted trouble like a magnet, and yet it was his very ignorance that protected him too. Bob was like a water skier, dependent upon his forward speed for his buoyancy. At any moment, one suspected, he would stop, realise how impossible the whole process was, and sink like a stone.

Bob kept going though, faster and more gracefully if anything. The changeover of roles with Silas had provided all sorts of problems which Bob had surmounted by not understanding that they existed. It was nerve-racking to watch, and yet graceful too. The tasks that tightened Silas's face muscles, gave him fidgeting hands and a bad temper, had exactly the opposite effect on Bob. With each new development he relaxed more and more. Whenever Silas or I suggested that Spencer might not have the money, or might not part up with it, if he had it, Bob looked at us as if we were imbeciles, and so sincere was the look of dismay, that both Silas and I had given up offering him words of caution or even modifying his confident predictions. So far in any case he had been one hundred per cent right. If this annoyed Silas, he gave little sign of it. His earlier show of irritation and supercilious mockery had gone. Silas applied himself to the project with all his skill, and carried out Bob's instructions to the letter.

The prospect of choosing between them numbed me. Why could we not go on as we were. I needed both of them: Silas although I no longer loved him, was easy and reassuring to be with, while Bob, whom I loved, annoyed and exasperated me with his restless and ingenuous personality.

I remembered Bob reading aloud from one of his self-improving history books. It was a passage about primitive tribes eating the heart of their enemies and thus becoming brave. It had captured Bob's imagination and he'd mentioned it several times since. Well these days since Bob had taken command, he had been making a meal from Silas's heart, for just as each day saw Bob a little braver and confident so did Silas lose confidence.

Of course I should have been able to put the steel back into Silas. Well I tried, I tried hard, but somehow it had no effect. It was as though Silas didn't want to be the leader any more, and as though I was the symbol of the leadership that he no longer needed. Well, Bob needed me, really needed me, and that is really all any woman wants of a man.

In Beirut Silas seemed to have to spend every minute checking out details of the job. He had bought a Land-Rover and he was at the depot every day, watching them modify it, and equip it for an expedition, so that we could disappear into the vast deserts of Arabia and surface again with new histories and names. The detail work that Bob usually did had now become Silas's responsibility and, as would be expected, he did it with his full fanatical attention, instead of in the rather casual way that Bob had done things in the past.

It was almost as if Silas wanted me and Bob to leave him alone. Silas was a loner of course. I had always known that. He had to have his hour alone every day. That's why Silas and I always had our own rooms when we were in hotels. I had accepted that by now, although at one time it had affected me deeply, and I had cried that he should want to be away from me at all. Bob was just the opposite. He didn't need any time alone; he didn't give a damn for anyone, whether he was alone or in a crowd.

In Beirut Bob and I had lots of time for swimming and sunbathing and water skiing. At first Bob had not been able to do it, but I taught him, and as with so many things he did, he soon excelled his teacher, until he was moving across the water with a smooth skill to which I'll never aspire. Mind you, I let him ski better than I did. I wanted him to hold me, and tell me how to improve my balance. 'I'll catch you,' he said. 'I'll catch you if you fall.'

'I'm caught already,' I told him and he tightened his grip on me.

It's funny stuff water. It washes away your memories and gives you a chance to start afresh. That's why all those religions are so keen to dip you into it. That's what that water in the Bay of St. George did for me. Or for us I suppose. I let go of the rope from the speedboat. So did Bob. The water was a warm, and silky-green world, and we entered it through a lace curtain of spray. Immersed in it we embraced, and I did not attempt to swim clear of his arms and legs and lips.

We broke the surface, 'I love you,' I said.

'There's a clever girl,' said Bob grinning. He splashed water in my face just as I was gasping.

'No. I'm serious,' I yelled. 'I really love you.' He wouldn't stop grinning. 'Lucky me,' he said. I was furious that he wouldn't take me seriously, and I dragged him underwater. I punched him as we sank slowly down, and he held my arms captive until I was frightened I would have to gulp in water. Then, in submarine slow motion we revolved and slid upwards. Fifty yards away our motor boatman saw us surface and revved up and turned around.

I held Bob around the neck, 'I love you. Really love you,' I shouted. 'Listen to me will you? Be serious for just one minute.'

'Cool it,' said Bob.

I hit him, really hard this time, but as we both sank, scrambling and fighting under the warm water, he held me tight, and I knew he too was serious. Above us, I saw the hull of the motor boat. It stopped and there was a sudden flurry of bubbles around the propeller blades.

We dragged ourselves up on to the speedboat and collapsed into the bottom laughing and exhausted. I stretched my hands languidly toward the sky, as though I might be able to pull it over my head like a blue silk coverlet, but instead I wound my fingers around Bob's neck and pulled his wet dripping head down to my lips and we kissed in an urgent way that we had never kissed before.

'I love you,' Bob said. His lips tasted salty and his wet hair was absurdly misplaced and formed two demoniacal tufts. I smoothed his hair. I loved him and I was wonderfully and foolishly happy, and yet it meant that I must be sad. Not for the Silas that I no longer loved, but for the Silas that once I had. Sad for the Liz and Silas that could have been, if both of us had worked harder at it. Poor Silas, poor Silas.

'I love you, Bob,' I said. I pulled his head down toward me again, and the speedboat driver, like a discreet cabby, looked ahead. He started the motor with a roar, and we sped across the water scarring its glassy surface and transforming the still, blue liquid into a frenetic boiling spray that would never be the same again.

Chapter 17

SILAS

Stage five; crucial stage of any operation. Wednesday began stage five. I awoke at 8.30 a.m. and, without disturbing either Liz or Bob who occupied rooms on either side of mine, I put on my dressing gown and rang for coffee. I applied a trace of skin dye to my face and arms. Not too much, just enough to be an Englishman who sits in the sun, or an Arab who stays out of it. A trace; no more. I patted the false moustache into place and held it while the gum dried. Then I twisted my face about to test it. Good. I opened the shutters and half-stepped onto the tiny wrought-iron balcony, for the structure was ancient and crumbling, and one felt disinclined to trust it with one's entire weight. There was a faint haze over the sea, and Mount Sannin was almost obscured in mist. Below me in the courtyard the proprietor – Kimon – hurried into the kitchen to get my coffee. I knew every room of this hotel. Number ten; small double on the first floor. I'd once ordered breakfast there, and then made love to the waitress, while every guest in the place was screaming for breakfast. Eight; cramped single, ground floor back, lost 25 pounds sterling in an all night whist game Christmas 1945. Sixteen; . . . but what was the use of remembering: it saddened me. I had known this hotel since the war. I knew each chugging pipe, creaking stair, malfunctioning lock. I knew the uncertainty of its mattresses and hot water, and the rooms, curiously shaped where bathrooms had been inserted between them. It had not seen a new coat of paint since the eight gallons of whitewash that I had given

Papa Kimon from the mess stores. Papa, the old villain, had owned the place for only one month then, and I was the first guest in it after the repainting. Some Vichyite collaborateur had previously owned the hotel and had let Kimon have it for fifty-three gallons of petrol and an ancient Berliot lorry upon which he had loaded all his movable possessions and headed north. Kimon lived on the ground floor. For the greater part of the day he sat on a tiny chair outside, drinking grappa or arak and grumbling endlessly about the heat and flies. On the few days of the year when the weather was too cold to sit outside, he played draughts with the old men in the café next door, or walked along the harbour watching the big ships unloading.

He tapped lightly upon my door and rattled the china handle which had been broken since '46 or '47. 'Good morning Papa,' I said. He had brought thimble sized cups of coffee for himself and for me. He sat down heavily on the battered easy chair before replying.

'Welcome back *mon colonel*,' said Papa. He poured two glasses of grappa.

'Not for me,' I said, but he held the glass out to me and I took it, and raised it to my dry lips. It was raw stuff; acrid like smoke and as hot as fire. Two flares ignited by accident burned bright green crackled loudly and suddenly went out.

The sun was hot, very hot. The tank snorted and writhed like an old rhino dying in a poacher's trap. Another shot tore into its carcass breaking a track. The driving w'ls screeched and slowly threw the broken track away. With the third shot the motor died, and there was just the sound of the draught, roaring through the vents to feed the air-hungry flames.

Poor bloody Italians, I thought, what chance did they stand in those inflammable sardine cans. Across the floor they packed sandbags as a pathetic attempt to give the crew a little added protection. I could smell the rubber and cordite now. On the skyline were two Matildas – 11th Hussars perhaps, or New Zealand people. They turned and moved slowly away to the north.

'More Eyetie tanks coming over the horizon four o'clock now sir,' shouted Wheeler my driver. The gunner was turning the range drum and pumping the manual traverse, sweating with the effort.

'Traverse right, tank, five zero zero yards,' I called. I kept my voice calm. I wiped the periscope glass with my neck scarf. There was little more than a few inches of them in view and they had stopped moving. There were two or three explosions above the sound of our motor. The tank shuddered and our motor coughed but kept going. Something had hit us or fallen close.

'Fire,' I said. I switched the radio over and called for the rest of my troop. The gun fired. It seemed very loud and I banged my face against the periscope eyepiece.

'They are going,' said Brian and the three brown Italian turrets sank out of sight behind a dune. The gunner put another shell into the hot breech and dragged an oily rag across the flat base of it.

Brian edged us forward, and we climbed straight on over the dunes risking that the Italian tanks might be waiting to hit us as we came hull-up over the skyline.

Below us was the place shown as Musso Dump on the going maps. There wasn't a movement. It covered nearly fifty acres. Most of it was stacked with fuel drums, but there were all kinds of supplies; pasta, wine and prosciutto, some damaged transport. There was a mobile brothel; a huge lorry divided into cells, each one with a fold-down bed, a sink and bright red wallpaper.

Bertie's tank was the next one over the skyline. I closed down for a moment in case it was the Italians returning. Bertie's hatch opened, and he shouted 'Avanti,' and climbed out and stood on the turret top to look around the horizon with his binoculars. 'All gone, old son,' Bertie shouted.

Bertie's driver switched off the engine so did mine. It was a silent war; sun and blue sky. Bertie and I jumped down onto the hot sand, and began to walk around the dump.

'Santa Maria old boy,' said Bertie. 'Quite a collection.' He pushed his sandgoggles down around his neck. 'Must be over 300,000 gallons of acqua and even more than that of petrol. Get that lot back to Alex, amigo, and you'd never have to work again.'

We walked through the golden light inside the tents. A meal was laid in one of them. Goodness knows where they thought they were. We had been living on strong tea and bully beef for weeks, and then suddenly there was this tent and gleaming oak table, places set with fine china and linen napkins. 'Look at that mess table amigo,' said Bertie. 'Like a scene from a Garbo film, what?'

'We'll take some of the ham and salami for now, and the grappa and Chianti for the mess,' I said.

'Can you fit it in down there Brian?' I called to my driver.

'Always room for ham and booze,' he said and we loaded three boxes of the stores down among the machine gun ammo. Bertie and his driver took some too.

'Don't forget the corkscrew,' said my driver and I went back into the Italian mess tent, and came out holding a corkscrew triumphantly.

I heard the radio calling, One Able, that was Bertie. He waved to me as his motor started. I had just started to grow a thin moustache, and now, like a French chef in some corny advert, I kissed my finger tips to Bertie, 'Avanti,' he shouted. He waved a bottle of booze and took a mouthful of it before lowering himself into the hatch and closing down. No one was calling us, so our tank sat there quietly. Brian, Toddy and Wheeler cut thick chunks of salami and munched it without speaking.

'Pass me a bottle of grappa,' I said. A wave of hot oily

air came wafting up through the turret and I took a mouthful of grappa to clear the dust from my mouth. It was powerful stuff, especially this early in the morning.

Papa Kimon nodded and sipped his grappa too. He was fat. Gross, one could have said, with no fear of contradiction except from him. The belt of his old black trousers was drawn uncomfortably tight, and above it his gleaming white shirt was twisted out of his trousers, as his soft body settled into the far corners of the easy-chair. Even as a young man he had never been slim. His head was uncommonly large too, and his ears and chin were those of a giant. His nose was straight and perfect, like a Greek god, but that too was oversize, and hanging sadly under it, like a furry coat hanger, was a large black moustache. His hair was black, combed carefully in a vain attempt to conceal his baldness, not from others, but from his own sight of it in a mirror. His skin was white and shone silkily in the clear morning light. He rubbed a coloured handkerchief across his forehead and then into his open shirt front, and across his hairy chest. It was a reflex action, a necessary prelude to conversation in spite of the coolness of the morning.

'Today is the day Colonel,' he said. He didn't know what I was doing, but somehow the natural tenseness that all humans are subject to, displayed itself enough for him to guess that the climax of my work was near.

'It begins today,' I acknowledged. 'Tomorrow it will be completed.'

'Your hands,' he explained. 'They no longer act as you bid.'

I smiled, and reached for the coffee to show him that it was not so, but he was right. The little coffee cup chattered on the saucer and as I got it to my lips I felt the thick warm edge vibrate against my dry lips. Papa Kimon looked away guiltily.

'Your young man, colonel,' said Kimon. 'Is it well that

he enjoys himself each day, while you work too hard?'

'It is the way that it is arranged Kimon,' I said. I knew that I owed him no explanation, but I knew too that it was not vulgar curiosity that prompted the remark. 'We each have our allotted tasks and each unit is responsible for itself.'

'As in the army?' said Kimon. I nodded. Kimon produced some small black cigars. He offered me one, and although I would have enjoyed it, I knew for certain that my stomach would not be able to endure its powerful sour smoke.

'It is not political?' said Kimon.

'No, not political,' I said.

'Men strive for love and money,' said Kimon. 'But political acts are sometimes designed solely for mischief.'

'It is not political,' I said again. I finished my coffee.

Papa Kimon grasped the bed end. It groaned as he pulled himself to his feet. He tucked his shirt in around his fat belly and leaning toward the window shouted down into the courtyard. A voice replied. Kimon called for more coffee. I would have preferred a whisky and soda, but I muttered words of appreciation.

'The police come,' said Kimon turning back to me. 'They ask who is here.'

'Asking after us?'

'Asking who was here,' said Kimon. 'Perhaps it was for the taxes. Perhaps it is just routine. I tell them that there are two Egyptian gentlemen, and an Egyptian lady here. But it is good that soon you go, for I think they do not believe me.'

'Will they come back?'

'Policemen always come back,' said Kimon.

There was a knock at the door and his son brought two more cups of strong black coffee and two fresh figs. I drank some coffee and ate the soft dark fig. Papa poured two more measures of grappa.

'When it starts you will feel better,' said Kimon.

'Yes,' I said. I touched my false moustache self-consciously.

'Is there much risk?'

'A little.'

'Could the boy not do it?'

'No. It is the way it is arranged. We must do it this way.'

'If it is political, still I would not mind.'

'It is not political . . .' I assured him. We had known each other for many years and now we looked at each other, hoping to catch a brief glimpse of the young man each of us knew. . . . 'It is criminal,' I admitted. It was just as well that he should know, in case there were complications with the police. Together in the past we had done such things.

I got my case down from the wardrobe and from it took clean linen and put it on. I dressed in my lightweight suit and paused a moment before selecting the plain black tie. Into my top pocket I pushed the neat handkerchief I always wore. The small S.L. monogram was just in sight but for this operation I was no longer S.L. I resented that, but Bob had made me Archibald Hammett so there was nothing to do but make the best of it. I tucked the monogram out of sight. Now I looked just right. Old Papa Kimon sat looking out toward the sea, his vast body eclipsing the small chair.

'The girl. You have been with her a long time,' he said.

'A long time,' I said. Papa never referred to Liz by name, just as he had never referred to any of the others by name.

'Is it good that she and the boy are so close?'

'It is the way it is arranged,' I said.

'You do not have to shout at me Colonel,' said Kimon sadly. 'I think only of you.'

'I'm sorry,' I said, 'but it is all part of my plan.'

Already the streets were full. Taxi drivers soliciting custom, children selling chewing gum, buyers buying, sellers selling. Cars hooting, tramcars clattering and everywhere people carrying things.

Beirut would always remind me of the war. I remembered it not without affection. Things were simple in the war; a toy appeared in one's sights, one's mind effected a series of calculations. The calculations were of exactly the right complexity. They were not so simple that one felt oneself a labourer, nor so complex that the physical excitement abated. Pressure on a button. The toy disappeared in a puff of smoke, or sometimes it did not disappear. Tomorrow there would be more models; tanks, aeroplanes, houses; perhaps men. It made no difference. The simulator had prepared you for the game, until it was hard to mark the moment when simulation ended and combat began. Perhaps it never did, was life just a simulator, the targets popping up and, if your calculations were correct, disappearing in a puff of smoke. The simulator did not cheat, the simulator had no bias, the simulator would exist long after I was gone.

Students of the textbook war, calculating deflection, wind and gravity. Pushing buttons, that scarcely-seen dots might transform into puffs of smoke, and pinpoint cremations upon the skyline. Other men in other wars will stare, as flecks of light dance across dark glass screens, and antipodean cities melt, with not an audible sound to mark their going. Target up, three seconds, puff. Target up, three seconds; target down. I pushed open the heavy doors. Target up. The chief clerk came across to me. I had lunched with him the previous week and asked his advice about investment, after which I had sent him a crate of champagne. Under one of the bottles I had left a letter typed on the notepaper of a large London fruit wholesale house. From the letter it was possible to deduce that

    a. The champagne had been sent me as a gift and

    b. That I was Mr. Archibald Hammett, a most influential and prosperous director of the firm.

The chief clerk never mentioned the letter he had found,

but I could tell by the change of attitude in him that he had bitten. It wasn't my intention to look like a very wealthy man – or I would never have stayed at old Kimon's flea-bitten hotel – but to be seen as a sound businessman. Bank clerks you see, are inclined to be suspicious of men who claim to be wealthy, for they are subjected to the snubs and reprimands of such men almost every day.

The chief clerk smiled and said he hoped everything was all right.

'I'm afraid I've done rather an awful thing Mr. Soleiman,' I told him.

'I'm sure you haven't sir,' he said.

'It's my office in London,' I said. 'They are phoning me in just a few minutes,' I stopped.

'Yes Mr. Hammett,' said Mr. Soleiman encouragingly.

'They think I'm staying at the Phoenicia,' I said, in acute embarrassment. 'While actually I'm staying at a tiny hotel near the port. I told them to phone me here.' I finished in a gabble of acute embarrassment. 'Here at the bank.'

'I quite understand,' said Mr. Soleiman. 'We will be glad to let you use the phone.'

'They will phone at ten,' I said. It was five minutes to the hour.

'Welcome Mr. Hammett,' said Mr. Soleiman. 'Why don't you sit down for a moment? As soon as your call from London comes through, I'll let you know.'

'Frightfully good of you,' I said.

The call came through at ten precisely. Spencer asked for Mr. Hamid and with Spencer's kind of voice no one doubted for an instant that the call was for me; Hammett. Mr. Soleiman took me to the phone in his room. I said, 'Hello, yes this is the Central Bank and this is Mr. Hammett speaking.' The operator had already announced that it was the Central Bank and he heard enough incidental goings-on to be in no doubt that it was to the bank that he was connected.

'Everything's all right there then Hamid?' said Spencer.

'It could not possibly be better Mr. Spencer,' I said.

'I'll be coming down on the plane tonight then. I'll be arriving at Beirut tomorrow morning. Is everything ready for me?'

'It is, if you bring the necessary papers and money,' I said. 'Have you collected them from Mr. Appleyard?'

'Can't you get it into your head Hamid that *I'm* putting up this money? I'm putting it up, and I'll be handling things.'

'Just as you say Mr. Spencer,' I said.

'Well that's what I do say,' said Spencer. 'See you tomorrow Hamid.' He rang off. I stared sadly at the telephone.

'Is everything well?' asked Mr. Soleiman.

'It isn't actually, Soleiman old chap,' I said meekly. 'You see, my senior partner, Mr. Spencer,' I pointed at the phone, 'that was he. Is coming to Beirut tomorrow.'

'And all is not well?'

'It's that lady that we lunched with last week,' I said.

'Miss Liz?'

'Yes,' I said. 'You see Soleiman old chap. I mean you're a man of the world and all that. . . .'

'I see,' said Soleiman, getting the point, and giving me a one thousand and one nights' smile.

'Spencer knows my wife. . . . Look,' I said suddenly. 'Do you think it would look funny if I didn't take him back to my hotel? Do you think it would look funny if I did the few minutes of business with him over lunch? No.' I replied to myself. 'It *would* look funny. He'll be carrying a lot of money and documents. He'd not like to discuss them in a restaurant. He'd consider that rather risky.'

'And he would be right Mr. Hammett,' said Soleiman. I nodded dolefully. 'It's not just my wife,' I said. 'Liz has a husband. An awful fellow, a scoundrel really, although I suppose I shouldn't say so. A huge fellow too and a simply uncontrollable temper.'

Soleiman suddenly noticed the Arab newspaper in my pocket.

'Do you read Arabic?' he asked.

'No,' I said. 'It's for my son, a souvenir.'

Soleiman nodded and neither of us spoke again for a few moments. It was essential at this stage that Soleiman should see me as respectable and pathetic, for from such a person no danger can come. Soleiman was still making sympathetic noises when I said, 'Look Soleiman, you could save me old chap. Why not let me use your room here at the bank for thirty minutes tomorrow.' I gabbled on so that Soleiman had no chance to reply. 'After all, my firm will be using your bank quite a bit from now on, if my partner comes here and sees how nice you all are, he'll see the wisdom of that too. We'd be glad to have you sit in on the meeting. Will you sit in on it?'

'Perhaps,' said Soleiman. My God, I thought, that could snooker me. I felt myself blush. I said, 'A banker's advice is always welcome.'

Soleiman decided to bow to the almost inevitable. He opened his extended hands like a man playing a concertina. It was a gesture of Arab hospitality. I let my face light up and I grabbed his shoulders and gave him the briefest of hugs. Mr. Soleiman's face reflected the radiance of my happiness. He smiled. On the next day I could have the use of Mr. Soleiman's office. Perhaps he would sit in with us. If it would make me happy – and it would make me happy – then in front of my partner I would be treated like a lord. At lunch that day we cemented Anglo-Arab relations. Target up, three seconds, puff.

Wednesday morning was a nightmare. The aeroplane bringing Spencer to Beirut was the first problem. I rang the airport at eight a.m. and they told me there had been a delay at Athens. It would be at least an hour late. I knew what that would mean. I didn't take coffee with Kimon.

I awoke Bob and then I went to Liz's room. I told them both what the score was, and suggested that we go to readiness positions, just as if there was no delay, and sweat out the waiting time there. Bob and Liz agreed. I told Bob that I would call him on the walkie-talkie in a few minutes when I collected the Land-Rover. Then I went off to give the garage people the final payment. I checked through the documents. There were tax and insurance documents to cover the vehicle when it went from Lebanon to Syria. I drove out of the garage and called Bob and Liz back in the hotel.

'This is Sugar Sugar calling Baker Love. Over,' I said.

Immediately Bob answered. 'Go ahead Sugar. I am receiving you loud and clear from the hotel balcony. I will pay the hotel bill and bring our bags down now. How do you read? Baker Love. Over.'

'Baker Love from Sugar Sugar. Receiving you strength five. That is roger. See you in a couple of minutes. Sugar, Over.'

'Sugar from Baker Love. O.K. Be right down. Over and Out.' The radio worked well.

We loaded the suitcases in the Land-Rover. It was a long wheelbase model, so there was plenty of room. I said, 'I will call you on the hour, to tell you when to meet me outside the bank.'

'Yes. You've told me that half a dozen times,' Bob said.

'Very well,' I said. 'Wish me luck.'

'Good luck, Silas,' said Liz. She leaned over and kissed me in a way she hadn't done for many long months. Bob waved his hand languidly and let in the clutch. 'See you around midday.'

The Land-Rover leaped forward, and there was an excited clanging of bells as he narrowly missed side-swiping a tramcar. I watched them go and suddenly felt rather lonely. Now I had only Spencer to deal with, and I would need all my skill. I went back up to my room and poured myself a small Scotch. When I called Bob on the walkie-talkie they were already at Rendezvous A, a mile or so along the coast, where they were to wait until meeting me outside the bank.

When I phoned the airport they said the London plane was just arriving. From the window I saw the huge Olympic Airways plane coming in low over the sea. I went into the bathroom. I had been using a little skin darkening ever since we got to Beirut, a tricky task. I was not going to be a Brooks Brothers Arab, I was too old. I was a minor English public school Arab. I looked at myself in the mirror and adjusted my neck and my shoulders and my hands to their new role. It was the devil of a deception I was taking on, and don't imagine Bob didn't know exactly what he was letting me in for. I'd been Longbottom and Hamid and deceived that nasty young Spencer with my play acting. Now I was to appear before him in Western clothes, and yet be not Longbottom, but Hamid. Simultaneously my friends, simultaneously mark you, I must be the Englishman Hammett for Soleiman's benefit. My God, it was a task to baffle an Irving or a Guinness, but I'd do it; I had confidence and training behind me.

Longbottom had been a dozy hesitant stoop-shouldered clerk, a suburban man, a man beaten by the world who could not understand why. This man Hamid however was a courteous, noble fellow; tall, haughty and graceful in speech, walk, manner and gesture. His skin was darkened a shade, and upon his fingers and wrists were jewellery. His moustache was the same as Mr. Archibald Hammett's of course, but today did it have the keen edge of Bedouin pride. My suit was a cream-coloured light-weight one and upon my head I wore a new straw hat. My gold rimmed sun glasses were slightly old-fashioned and in my pocket I carried an Arab newspaper. I put the prayer beads in my pocket. They were a good prop to impress Spencer, but Soleiman must not see them. I looked at myself in the spotty bathroom mirror.

'I can lead you through the minefields General Rommel,' I said. 'My people know the stars and the desert sands, as you know the streets and alleys of your beloved Berlin.' I nodded. 'It is nothing General. We are both men of honour. We are both men who know the loneliness of command.' I smiled. Then I whipped off my tinted glasses, 'My God, Colonel Lawrence; it's you,' I said. 'No wonder the men call you the white phantom of the desert.' I looked at my watch, it was time to go to the bank.

'Mr. Hammett, and all is well?' asked Soleiman as I entered the front door.

I let him see that I had recovered a little of my poise today. 'I'm fit and raring to go Mr. Soleiman,' I said. 'I spoke to London on the phone last night. The directors bonus this year is expected to be in the region of two and a half thousand pounds. We've had a damn good year.' Soleiman nodded.

'Mr. Spencer is due in any time,' I said. 'I left a message telling him to phone me here.' I brought my elegant leather case up onto the table where we were standing. 'It makes me nervous carrying this Soleiman old chap. It's full of share certificates. We – that is my company – are doing a merger with one of your local companies. I'm afraid I can't tell you the name.' I watched Soleiman's eyes as he tried to guess which local company it was. 'And since there will be a share exchange I had to have these close to me. There's certificates there to the value of two million pounds. I can tell you Soleiman it makes me nervous just handling them.'

'You'd like them put into the vault?'

'Yes, please,' I said. 'And give me a receipt for a locked case.'

'Certainly sir,' said Soleiman. Soon after that Spencer rang from the hotel. I told him to come over right away. He arrived with much huffing and puffing at 11.30 a.m.

'Good morning Mr. Spencer,' I greeted him in the foyer.

'This is Mr. Soleiman, chief clerk of the Central Bank.'

'Pleased to meet you,' said Spencer. He was surprised to see me in western garb.

'Hardly recognised you in those clothes Hamid old chap,' Spencer said to me. I took the Arab newspaper from one pocket and put it into another. Spencer looked at it.

'I like to keep up appearances for the firm Mr. Spencer,' I said. 'It's only in the evening that I wear my more casual things.'

'Of course,' said Spencer, man of the world.

'We are using Mr. Soleiman's office,' I told Spencer. 'My place is a little too . . . public.'

'Good, good,' said Spencer. He winked at me knowingly.

I winked back formally in the way I thought an Arab might. Soleiman showed us into his office and I took the seat behind the desk and waved Spencer into a soft leather one. 'The documents have all been examined most carefully. Everyone is perfectly satisfied with them.' I smiled in gratitude to Soleiman. He smiled back, and Spencer turned to him and Spencer smiled too. 'They are locked in the vault at present Mr. Spencer,' I said. 'Mr. Soleiman will get them for you and he will expect this receipt.' I passed him the large printed receipt that Soleiman had given me.

'Businesslike,' pronounced Spencer. 'That's the way I like it.'

Spencer turned to look me full in the face. 'I'll tell you the truth Hamid,' he said. He brought his case up onto the table. It was evidently very light. He slipped the catches and opened it. It had a light blue lining. It was empty.

'I brought no money,' said Spencer. 'Not a bean.'

I stared into the bright new interior of the unused case and I looked up at Spencer. I gripped the edge of the chair in which I was sitting to stop my hands shaking. Spencer went out of focus and inside me there was a tremendous heat, as though my body temperature had risen several degrees. I felt the heat rising into my face. I thought I was going to tumble forward across the desk, and just for a moment there was no noise at all except the physical noises from within my own body – my thumping heart and aching lungs. I could never do this again. I knew it beyond doubt. Bob and Liz had seen what I had been concealing from myself. I was burned out, finished. This operation could never have got as far as this had Bob not taken over the leading part and the command. Spencer and Soleiman were staring at me. I pulled my lips into the smiling position and I leaned well back in my chair while I counted five slowly. Then I gave it to them, 'You will read your newspapers next week Mr. Spencer,' I said. 'And you will blush with shame and agony. The people here in Beirut are good people to deal with. Every single person with whom I've dealt is ready to cooperate with us. It could be said they want our money,' I smiled again. 'And of course they do, but this is not just another coup. This is not a gamble or a risky venture. This is a solid business proposition.' I rapped the desk. 'As solid as this bank, Spencer. Of course the decision must be yours, but I think it's a mistake. In fact I have confided to Mr. Soleiman here my hopes and ambitions for this scheme.' Soleiman smiled and bowed.

'Wait a minute, wait a minute,' said Spencer. 'I didn't say I wasn't going ahead. But I'm a man of caution. Even your famous Mr. Appleyard wouldn't be above pulling a fast one in certain circumstances. So I was careful. I had the money wired through to another bank here from one of my accounts in Zurich. If I can make a phone call I'll have them send a man across here with it.' I pushed the phone across to him. 'Get me the Western Order Bank,' said Spencer.

'Tell them to give it to the cashier,' I told Spencer, 'for Mr. Hamid. It wouldn't be wise to have your name on the delivery slip and receipt.'

Spencer spoke into the phone. 'It's O.K. about that case with the money in it. Bring it across to the Central Bank now. Give it to the cashier. Tell them it's for the attention of Mr. Hamid,' he hung up.

I turned to Soleiman. 'Could you ask your cashier to count the money and give the messenger a receipt for the amount it contains Mr. Soleiman,' I said. 'and after that we will be needing that case of documents from the vault.' Soleiman left the office.

I said to Spencer. 'We'll be going at a fast rate to cover all the banks this afternoon.'

'But we'll do it?'

'I've arranged the list and the last two banks will open the door if we are late.'

'Won't they think it's odd, you accompanying me to the banks?'

'I have a few business interests in town Mr. Spencer. It would be nothing extraordinary.' I looked at my watch. 'About this time I walk through the bank to be sure that they are all working hard. You can come with me if you wish.' Spencer got to his feet. 'You are a brave and reckless devil of a man, Mr. Spencer,' I said.

'Am I?' said Spencer. 'Why?'

'Well, walking around a bank just before you swindle it, showing each and every employee your face in close up.' Spencer nodded. 'Giving them a chance to estimate your height and weight, and remember every detail of your clothing.'

'I don't think I will come with you,' said Spencer.

'I know how you feel,' I said. 'You Englishmen all remind me of the famous story of Winston Churchill in the desert. Struck by so many spears he was as prickly as, as . . .'

'A porcupine.'

'A porcupine, exactly, and his friends asked him if these spears in him were hurting him. "Only when I laugh," he said. Isn't that a wonderful story of Winston Churchill?'

'I'll just sit here,' said Spencer. 'You do your rounds

and I'll just sit here.' I closed the door of Soleiman's office. I saw Soleiman with the cashier and went across to him. They were counting Spencer's money which had just arrived.

'Is anything wrong?' said Soleiman.

'Mr. Spencer is having one of his attacks,' I said. 'He often has them.'

'But we should get a doctor.'

'No, no, no,' I said. 'They are very mild, but his tongue hangs out and he gets into a state of hysterical excitement.'

'But how awful.'

'I just leave him alone for a few minutes. It's all you can do. Is that the money for Mr. Hammett?' I asked.

The cashier had just finished counting it. He twisted the label on the case, 'To be delivered to the Cashier, Central Bank, for Mr. Hamid,' he read out, 'Mr. *Hamid*,' he repeated.

I laughed and so did Mr. Soleiman. 'I'm afraid that's the Arab world for you,' I said. 'My ancestors have been Hammetts ever since 1066, but a few days in Lebanon and I am already a Hamid.' Soleiman laughed. He nodded to the cashier. She repacked the money into the case agonisingly slowly and at one point decided it wouldn't all go in. She brought the bundles out again and repacked them in a different way.

'I'm taking the money now,' I said.

'So much money,' said Soleiman. 'It's dangerous.'

'So is dynamite,' I said. 'Unless you know how to handle it.'

'But why not let me give you a cheque? A certified cheque.'

I said, 'I'm afraid your fellow countrymen are not yet completely confident of the banking system, with all it's trust in small pieces of signed paper.'

'I regret that it is true,' said Soleiman.

'I'm lucky that they will agree to take dollar bills,' I said.

'At one time they were demanding gold.' Soleiman nodded sympathetically. From somewhere across the town came a sad call to Moslem prayer. It was midday. I picked up the caseful of money. 'If you need your office before I return, be gentle with Mr. Spencer. He's very excitable when he has one of his attacks.'

'I understand,' said Soleiman. I was anxious to leave but as I turned to go, Soleiman spoke again, 'You told me a joke yesterday Mr. Hammett. A joke about a sailor who is attacked by the spears of Indian warriors. "Are you in pain?" he was asked, and the reply was "just when I am laughing," but this I do not understand. Where is the joke?'

'Ah,' I said. 'He died right after he said that. That was the joke.' Mr. Soleiman saw it then. He started to laugh. He laughed until the tears ran down his face. He didn't make much noise about it, but he simply throbbed with laughter. The cashier, without understanding, began to laugh too, and that I confess, made me laugh. It was just like the old days. Just like them; target up, one two three and puff. I let the weight of the case handle slide down to the very tips of my fingers and bounced its weight lightly in my hand. It was a good feeling, the weight of all that money.

I was still laughing as I turned away from the cashier's office and stared into the face of Rita Marsh. She was sitting in the bank foyer. She looked very attractive in a silk suit and a new hair cut. She was making more room in a big leather travelling bag. She looked up again and beckoned to me. I walked across to her. She stood up and grabbed my arm, 'There's no hurry, loverman,' she said. 'Your friends will wait while I rearrange my baggage won't they?'

'I suppose they will,' I said.

*　　　*　　　*

Bob was the first one to get angry after Rita insisted upon climbing into the back seat of the Land-Rover alongside me.

'What's the hell's she doing here?'

'I'm here to cut myself in,' said Rita. 'That's what.'

'Get out of the car,' said Bob.

'Take it easy, Bob,' I said. I looked at the bank doors with some apprehension. Spencer might have emerged any moment.

'She thinks we are walking off with Spencer's money,' I explained. I held the case close to my chest.

'Think?' said Rita, 'I know it.'

'Drive on,' said Liz.

'Get her out of the car,' said Bob. 'Then I will.'

'You are assuming a lot Rita,' I said. 'You could get into trouble for accusations of that sort.'

She wrenched the case from my arms. I grappled with her but she managed to open it an inch or so and peer in. She closed the case immediately and looked around at us, her eyes popping with pleasure.

'There must be millions there,' she said. 'Plenty for all of us.'

'Chuck her out of the car,' said Bob.

'Very well,' I said, having regained possession of the case and locked it. 'Come round here and help me.'

'Sit still both of you,' said Liz. 'The first thing to do is get clear of the bank.'

'Yes I agree,' I said.

'Twenty-five per cent,' said Rita. 'And I'll come with you. He'd kill me otherwise.'

'Perhaps I'll kill you,' I said viciously.

'Now, now old Longbottom,' said Rita.

'Let's get on our way,' I said. 'We'll settle this *en route*.'

'Fair enough,' said Bob, exchanging a meaningful glance with me.

'Don't try any tricks,' said Rita. 'We stay here till we agree or I'll scream blue murder.'

'We agree darling,' said Liz without bothering to make it sound sincere.

'First to the Phoenicia Hotel,' said Rita, 'for my mink stole.'

'We can't bother with that,' I protested.

'That rat pelt is hardly worth the petrol, darling,' said Liz. Bob was glad to have an excuse for driving away from the bank though, and so was I. Outside the Phoenicia another argument developed.

'Someone had better go in with her to make sure she doesn't phone Spencer or anyone.'

'I'm not phoning nowhere, I'll only be a minute getting my stole.'

'Go on your own then,' I offered.

'Not so likely, I want one of you three with me,' she smiled.

'One of us will have to go with the silly little bitch,' said Bob.

'You go, Bob,' I said.

'I'm driving,' said Bob. 'You go.'

'Very well,' I said.

'But leave the leather case with me,' said Liz, suddenly suspicious.

'Just as you like,' I said. I passed it to her.

'I'm in a hurry,' said Rita. She reached into her big leather travelling bag, found a compact and studied her face for a moment before snapping it closed.

'So are we,' I said angrily and I grabbed her arm and her bag.

'Ow,' she said. 'Don't be so rough, we've got a long way to go yet.'

'Don't be too sure,' I said softly as I pushed her before me, out onto the pavement.

'Don't be long,' said Bob.

'You don't have to use that tone,' I said. 'It's not my fault.'

Bob merely grimaced, but Liz touched my arm sympathetically. I held Rita's arm and carried her leather bag as we crossed the wide pavement. At the door I paused. Bob put an arm around Liz's shoulder and kissed her.

'That's your girl friend, is it?' said Rita sarcastically.

'She was once,' I said angrily.

So Bob was the young generation, what did he say he did; represented them. Well I think he did. He represented the whole bloody dim eyed, slack shouldered shower of them. National Health spectacles and state aided education, smoking their drugged cigarettes and banning the bomb. Endlessly complaining and running down their country, but never trying to do anything patriotic. My God, one hated to use the very word patriot because people like Bob thought it was some kind of joke. And what did Liz represent then? She was the 'don't knows' in a land where don't knows were in the vast majority. She was waiting to judge my generation versus Bob's generation with godlike and superior impartiality. Did she think it wasn't obvious that they had some secret understanding. I knew that from the way she was always protecting him from my anger, or covering up for him when he'd made some stupid blunder. That's why I had kept away from them; let them be closer still, let them discover each other and find out what each of them are truly like. I knew what they were both like; my God I knew. Two undisciplined, disorganised young fools who would never understand me, or people like me. They thought they didn't need leaders, did they? They thought that they just needed each other. They were moonstruck, moonstruck over each other. I would give them ten days together. Ten days and that was too long. Without me to keep some discipline and respect for regulations they would be at each other's throat within a couple of days. Three days I'd give them. Three days. A camel was walking past the hotel. It was years since I had seen camels in the street. At one time the streets were full of them. This was a mangy beast, with bad teeth. They were vicious creatures. I remember them in the desert after Alamein.

Vicious teeth and foul smelling breath. No one could love a camel. Never, however much you needed a camel, could you love it. I'd give them three days, Bob and Liz, especially if they were broke. Without money I'd give them more like two days. God, that was a vicious camel. I pushed through the glass doors and stepped to one side.

'Hold everything Rita, my little darling,' I said. Once inside the hotel foyer I put her bag down and reached into my pocket for the walkie-talkie.

'Sugar, calling Baker Love,' I said.

'Baker Love, loud and clear. Go ahead, over,' Bob answered immediately, as I hoped he would.

I said, 'Sugar. Take cash and proceed immediately to Rendezvous figures two. Is that Roger? Sugar over.'

'Roger Wilco,' said Bob and I heard him start the motor before he switched off.

'Rendezvous two . . . Roger Wilco. You are like a lot of kids,' said Rita scornfully.

Chapter 18

BOB

The magical land of Phoenicia joins the Aegean to Egypt.
The ancient kings of Mesopotamia and Egypt coveted this
lush, fertile strip, with the sea on one side and two mountain
barriers along the other. The southern part of the inland
range is dominated by the snow cap of Mount Hermon,
at the foot of which the River Jordan begins, and travels
due south through Galilee and flows into the huge Dead Sea.
At that moment the river fish die.

Rendezvous Two was half way between the twin mountain ranges, and as the sun dropped through the sky the
shadow of the westerly heights crept up the foothills ahead
of us until almost the whole mountain was dark.

Liz moved closer to me. She picked up the walkie-talkie
and shook it. Then she took the back off the set, and pressed
each battery tight against its contacts.

'It works O.K.' I told her.

'You mean Silas hasn't tried to call us?'

'That's it.'

'Silas isn't coming?'

'That's it.'

For a moment I thought she would start screaming or
sobbing, but she didn't do either of those things, she just
looked closely into my eyes. I took Silas's black cash case
from the seat and broke the locks with a screwdriver.
Inside the case there were two flat metal slabs that I am sure
weighed exactly the same as eight hundred thousand
dollars.

'It's empty,' I pronounced, although Liz could see that

as well as I could.

'You don't seem surprised.'

'I'm not surprised. In a way we sent him away. He knew we couldn't go on as we were any longer.'

'Did we say we couldn't go on any longer?'

'We hinted,' I said. 'We told him our arm ached.'

'Yes,' said Liz. 'I suppose we did.' She took a little time to think about it. 'Give him another half hour,' she said.

'O.K.' I said, but Silas had gone; for ever. Tucked into a corner of the case there was a calling card. On one side it said "Sir Stephen Latimer. President. Amalgamated Minerals Inc." On the back of it was scribbled, "ha, ha." I folded it up and threw it away.

'He's gone with that Rita,' said Liz.

'That's it,' I said. 'I suppose they had the money in that red travelling bag of hers.'

The air was clear. Cleaner than any air I had tasted. This air had come a thousand miles across the desert, passing not one factory, house, slag heap or pie shop.

'Taste the air,' I told Liz.

She breathed in deeply, looked at me and shrugged.

'Isn't that the cleanest air you ever tasted?'

'It's O.K.' she said. 'Air is air, isn't it?'

'I suppose so,' I said, but to me that air tasted as though I had spent all my life inside a coal mine. Like this was my first chance at a luxury that all the world had known and got used to. Well, I'd never get used to it, I was determined upon that.

I sniffed the air, I hadn't slept a wink all night. Then all of a sudden there's the cell door being unlocked. In came the duty screw with a handkerchief clamped across his boat. That's how you can tell a new warder; they just can't stand the smell of slopping-out each morning. After a few weeks they get used to it though. He was a tall thin screw with glasses.

'Where's Charlie?' I said.

'Gone,' said the screw, 'went on the train last night. Is it always as bad as this?'

'What?'

'The stink.'

'I don't smell a thing,' I said.

He clamped his handkerchief across his face. 'I'll never be able to stand this,' he said, his voice muffled by the cloth.

'No,' I said. 'I'm thinking of resigning myself.'

The screw laughed. He didn't seem a bad sort of bloke for a screw. Fancy complaining about the smell. I laughed and breathed in so hard that my lungs ached with the effort of it. Man I tasted the scent of desert flowers and on deep draughts got drunk.

It's like some crazy kid's toy, the way those shapes and colours change even as you watch them. A slight wind stirred along the valley trying to get home before nightfall, and along the rim of the second mountain range – the anti-Lebanon – the last sun drilled the rocky molars and gave them gold fillings.

'How far away is your river Euphrates?' Liz asked.

'Three hundred miles.'

'As the crow flies?'

'Well, you wouldn't have to detour around the large cities,' I said.

'And there are many ancient civilisations?'

'All along the Euphrates,' I said, 'but Babylon is the place I'd like to see. Hammurabi ruled there in two thousand years BC. What a character he was, running the biggest, toughest empire the world had ever seen, from Beirut back there, all the way across to the Persian Gulf.'

'He was looking out just for himself all the time,' said Liz.

'He brought law. He brought taxes and contracts and promissory notes and wills.'

'What a bastard,' said Liz, 'but that Rita looked in the cash box. She said "Look at all the money." '

'But really it was empty. That was gee-up. They conned us.'

'What's the time?'

'Five-thirty,' I said. She shook the walkie-talkie again.

'Before Hammurabi it was chaos,' I said.

'He planned everything.'

'He was a fanatic but that's what I like about him.'

'The hell with him,' said Liz, 'sometimes I think everyone in the world is a con man. Do we have tents aboard?'

'I'm not,' I said. 'Yes, we have tents.'

'And food and water? There's just a chance you're not.'

'Sure. And spades and petrol and oil and lamps and blankets. Maps, reference books, camera, typewriter, waterproof clothing and even string and pegs to mark out the site. You remember the plan. We equipped like an expedition.' Liz buttoned her coat and tied a scarf around her neck. She leaned across and kissed me. 'I love you,' she said.

'I love you,' I said. I smiled. I liked saying it. Liz ran a finger across my face like she was deciding whether to melt it down and try again.

'Then don't just sit there Hammurabi. Drive me to Babylon.'

THE
OUTCAST
Philip Cornford

The first sign of a cover-up at Tindal air base comes by accident. But that's all Mackinnon needs. A top-notch investigative journalist with a zeal matched only by his recklessness, he digs with the tenacity of a man possessed. For he has a very special reason for uncovering the truth. And his mole on the mysterious Monday Committee, as well as the notorious KGB hawk Yakov and the killer Maguire have their own sinister reasons for drawing him into their lethal web of subterfuge and violence. This time Mackinnon's deadline means exactly that . . .

0 7474 0138 1   THRILLER   £3.50

THE SAMURAI STRATEGY

THOMAS HOOVER

IT BEGINS WITH THE MYSTERIOUS THEFT OF A PRICELESS SAMURAI SWORD. BEFORE IT IS OVER, ONE NATION WILL STAND ON THE BRINK OF RUIN . . .

Powerful Japanese industrialist Matsuo Noda has set in motion a chilling plan, an ingenious strategy that involves hiring Wall Street wizard Matthew Walton to head up a secret investment project. But Walton soon realizes he is a pawn in a takeover plot of astonishing proportions. With time running out and death at his heels, Walton desperately tries to scupper the high-tech coup and prevent the ultimate goal of Noda's frightening scheme: to destroy US financial markets and break the back of the country's economy. For when America stands naked before the world, Noda will emerge as a powerful modern-day Shogun – ready for his next explosive move . . .

Also by Thomas Hoover in Sphere Books:
The Moghul
Caribbee

0 7474 0068 7   GENERAL FICTION   £3.99

BAD MONEY

A. M. KABAL

'Midsummer's Eve, the hard men moved . . .'

01.01 hours GMT: in London, Rome, Panama and Gdansk four men are savagely murdered. No one sees the connection. It's a quiet, efficient start to the international crime of the century . . .

But one victim, reporter Tom Wellbeck, leaves behind his ex-wife, fellow-journalist Caro Kilkenny, who is determined to find the truth about his death. And then there's Tom's friend, John Standing – burned-out, alcoholic, but still the one man with the skill and experience to see the case through . . .

They unravel a thread of intrigue that stretches from Warsaw to Washington, from the silent corridors of the Vatican to the murderous jungles of Central America, a vicious thread of bad blood and bad money. And when Standing detects the hand of his old enemy David Medina, he knows their troubles are just beginning . . .

Financial devilry of a high order . . . knowledgeable and sinister
OBSERVER

Also by A M Kabal in Sphere Books:
THE ADVERSARY

0 7221 5232 9   CRIME/THRILLER   £3.99

All Sphere Books are available at your bookshop or newsagent, or can be ordered from the following address: Sphere Books, Cash Sales Department, P.O. Box 11, Falmouth, Cornwall TR10 9EN.

Please send cheque or postal order (no currency), and allow 60p for postage and packing for the first book plus 25p for the second book and 15p for each additional book ordered up to a maximum charge of £1.90 in U.K.

B.F.P.O. customers please allow 60p for the first book, 25p for the second book plus 15p per copy for the next 7 books, thereafter 9p per book.

Overseas customers, including Eire, please allow £1.25 for postage and packing for the first book, 75p for the second book and 28p for each subsequent title ordered.